SEASHELLS, SPELLS AND CARAMELS

BOOK 1 OF THE SPELLS & CARAMELS COZY WITCH MYSTERY SERIES

ERIN JOHNSON

*For my mom and my sister,
my best readers. I love you two.*

Sign up for the Erin Johnson Writes newsletter
at
www.ErinJohnsonWrites.com

As a thank you for signing up, you'll receive
Imogen's Spellbook
a free book of illustrated recipes featured in
Seashells, Spells & Caramels.

1
LIVING THE DREAM

I quietly slid the wide drawer below my keyboard open and pulled out the folded piece of paper hidden below the pencil tray. I held it in my lap, scanning the rows of low, beige cubicle walls to make sure no one watched me. My officemates shuffled papers, printers spooled and chugged, phones rang, and the low murmur of chatter grew louder.

I unfolded the paper. I'd done this so many times, it had begun to tear along the creases. I smoothed it open on my lap—the real estate listing for my bakery.

Well, not my bakery yet, but the corner spot where I planned to open it. The old brick building crumbled in places, but that just gave it character. Four windows wrapped around the corner, perfect for displays of scones, cakes, and loaves of bread. I could picture Imogen's Patisserie painted on the door. Every day I'd buy fresh flowers for the counter, and I'd wake up at 3:00 a.m. to start baking, while the world still snuggled in their beds.

BEEP BEEP BEEP BEEP BEEP! I jumped and hid the flyer under the desk as the loud, electronic phone ring startled me out of my daydreams. Coworkers filed past my desk to the elevators, coats in hand. I glanced at the clock. 4:59. *Urg.*

It rang again. I groaned and tipped my head to the side as I debated answering it. Friday night. So close to leaving. With a sigh, I picked up the receiver.

"Imogen Banks, Medical Billing. How can I help you?"

Twenty-five minutes later I'd helped the little old lady caller get an extension and coordinated with collections to reduce her bill by half. After she asked if I was single and tried to set me up with her twenty-year-old grandson (I'm okay with being a bit of a cradle robber, but nine years was pushing it for me), we said our good nights.

I slipped off my black work heels, the only dress shoes I owned, and laced up my black leather combat boots. They didn't look particularly professional with my red pencil skirt, which matched my hair, and white tie-neck blouse, but they gave me an edge that made me grin. *Imogen Banks, punk rock medical billing specialist.*

I padded to the elevators, hoping the superglue would keep the sole in place. I didn't need wet feet in the Seattle weather on my walk from work to the train and from the stop to home.

I punched the button for the elevator and rocked on my heels as I waited, itching to escape the sickly florescent lights and step into the cool grey mist outside.

A high-pitched whine made me pause and listen.

"Eeeeeee!"

2
THE GIG

The elevator dinged and the metal doors slid open. I stepped toward it, but froze midstep when I heard another agonized wail. *Get in, you dummy.* But what if a cat had gotten stuck in the walls or something? I headed back into the office, following the noise.

I rounded a corner. A light shone from Victoria's office. *Urg.* I did not feel like dealing with my supervisor. Another wail issued from her open door. *Geez.*

I imagined coming back to work on Monday and hearing that she'd been attacked by a rat, contracted rabies, and died in the office. If only someone had heard her cries for help. I sighed heavily and dragged my feet to her door.

"Hey, Victoria."

The wailing stopped immediately. My boss sat at her desk with her face buried in her arms. Her normally flawless blond hair stuck out at all angles. She'd collapsed on top of a desk piled with wedding magazines, menus, seating charts, and vision boards.

Oh right. She was getting married on Sunday. I didn't know how I could have forgotten. I, and the rest of my team, had been picking up her slack for the last nine months as she wedding planned during office hours.

I cleared my throat. "I, uh—I thought I heard something, but seems like you've got this under control, so I'll just—"

I halted my retreat when Victoria snapped her head up and glared at me, black mascara pooling under her eyes and streaking down her cheeks. "Thought you'd come and have a laugh, huh?" She spread her arms wide. "Let's all have a good laugh at Victoria!"

I blinked. "No, I just—"

"You just what?" Her shoulders hunched like a wounded animal's.

"I just thought I might be able to help." My voice came out just above a whisper.

Victoria pouted and blinked. "Oh, wittle Imogen just wanted to help, huh?" She grinned, a wild smile that didn't reach her crazed eyes. "Okay, how 'bout you help by finding me a new rehearsal dinner coordinator by tomorrow night, along with a two-tiered cake with eighty matching cupcakes."

I stood still, afraid that if I moved or spoke she might lunge across the desk and attack me. She groaned, buried her face in her arms, and sobbed loudly. I took a deep breath, leaned back out the door, and looked toward the elevator with longing.

I could leave. She'd practically told me to leave. I looked back at Victoria. She was a blond monster, but I didn't like to see anyone suffer. Even monsters.

I dragged myself into her office and stood beside her desk. When she continued to sob, I cleared my throat. Then cleared it again. She snapped her head up and rolled her eyes.

"You're still here?"

"Yes. To the utter surprise and disbelief of both of us, I am still here. Listen, Victoria, I know weddings are complicated."

"Oh, do you? Has anyone ever asked you to marry him?"

"Ha ha." I shook my head and closed my eyes. *Oh, give me strength to not strangle her.* "No. But just look at all this amazing work you've done." I gestured at the complicated schedules, charts, and fabric swatches on her desk. "If your wedding planner's quit, I'm sure you're still going to pull off an amazing wedding, and with the help of your friends and—"

She held up a hand. "Let me just stop you right there. My *rehearsal dinner* planner quit. If my *wedding* planner had quit, someone would be dead right now." The way she stared me down, I had a feeling she meant someone in particular.

"Your rehearsal dinner planner?" That was a thing?

"Do you have a hearing problem, Imogen?" She sneered at me.

That was the final straw. I wasn't anybody's punching bag. "Okay, see you Monday." I turned to go.

"Yes, okay, tomorrow night is the rehearsal dinner, and I'm meeting Ben's grandpa for the first time, and apparently when his grandpa met his brother's former fiancée he vetoed the marriage and it was off. Just like that."

"Why's his grandpa so influential?" I shifted on my feet and glanced toward the elevator again. So close...

"He claims to be psychic, and the family believes him." She rolled her eyes. "So when he says this girl is going to lead to disaster, poof, the wedding's off."

"Psychic, huh?"

"The real reason is he thinks he's a big deal. He worked

as a diplomat or something for a bunch of countries no one's ever heard of."

I doubted the citizens of those countries would agree.

"And he decided that girl didn't live up to his standards." Victoria dropped her head into her hands, staring down at her desk. "So, everything has to be absolutely perfect. *I* have to be perfect. And now the planner's quit because I was too 'demanding' that he do his job *apparently*, and the baker only works with *him,* and now I have no dessert."

She dug her fingers into her hair. "Whatever, this isn't your problem, just go. Enjoy your weekend grooming your eight cats, or whatever you do."

My adopted family. I corrected myself mentally—family. Just family. They were great—normal, good jobs, content with life. My parents hadn't been able to conceive, so they'd adopted me, and then, as often happens, a couple years later had my sister out of the blue.

The three of them were peas in a pod. So completely normal and perfect. My sister still lived in St. Louis, three blocks away from my adopted parents—there I went again.

They had dinner together every Sunday night and went to Cardinals games together. They loved me, and I loved them, but I just didn't fit. I felt so much like an outsider that I couldn't stop myself from thinking of them as my adopted family.

I often wondered if I'd be a pea in a pod with my birth parents. Anyway, I knew what trying to fit in felt like—like trying to squeeze into jeans two sizes too small. Uncomfortable, tight, and you could never relax. I could see it in Victoria, and I felt for her. I rolled my eyes at myself. *Stupid empathy*.

"You know, Victoria." It was almost painful to get the words out. "I do bake."

She lifted her head slowly. "You do?"

I had to close my eyes to keep from rolling them. I brought baked goods into the office literally three mornings a week and made a special cake for each person's birthday. "I made you a birthday cake, remember?"

"Oh right. I didn't eat any, I don't do sugar." She raised her brows. "So what?"

I huffed. "So... if you need someone to make a cake and eighty cupcakes, I could help you out."

She blinked. I could see the wheels turning in her head. She opened her mouth, her eyes hard, then stopped. She swallowed and said in a softened tone, "You'd really do that? I mean, it's super last minute."

"Yeah." I nodded. "I'd do that."

"I'll pay you." She sat up straighter and wiped her eyes with the back of a perfectly manicured hand. "I'll pay you what I would've paid that other J-hole. Is three thousand enough?"

3

THE PLAN

I tried for a poker face. I knew I didn't have one—I could feel my eyebrow twitching with the effort to hold back a gigantic shriek. Three thousand dollars? Three thousand dollars! I wanted to jump around her office screaming. Instead I took a deep breath, willed the corners of my mouth to stay down, and said, while picking at my nails, "Yeah, I think that should just about cover it."

"Hey."

I looked up.

Victoria pointed a finger at me and gave me a leveling look. "You know, if you're doing this to suck up, it won't protect you from layoffs, right?"

I blinked. "Layoffs?"

I replayed weeks of office talk and scanned my memory. I couldn't think of anyone mentioning layoffs. *Dang!* I needed that job.

Except, after I got that three thousand dollars from Victoria tomorrow, I wouldn't actually. I'd have enough to open my bakery—enough for the lease, the build out, the marketing. I'd accounted for it all and it'd taken me seven years, but I'd finally saved up enough.

"Uh, earth to Imogen."

I snapped my head up. Victoria stared at me, one brow raised, her eyes ringed in mascara and still she somehow looked elegant. I'd need to do my best work to live up to her standard of perfect.

"Listen, I uh—" She swallowed. It looked difficult, like she might be sick. She cleared her throat several times, and finally managed to spit out, "I really appreciate this. Thank you." I think she actually gagged a little after she said it.

I grinned. "I'm happy to help."

"Well, I am paying you, you know. And I expect to get my money's worth."

Back to the good ol' Victoria I knew. I pulled up a chair next to her and for two hours—two hours!—we reviewed the guests' various allergies and preferences, her collection of possible recipes, concept art for the cake and cupcakes, and photos of other wedding desserts until I wanted to claw my eyes out.

Instead, I sat quietly and nodded, and in my head formed my own ideas of what I'd make for her. Victoria claimed she hadn't eaten the cake I'd made her for her birthday, but I'd caught her pick up just a crumb and savor it with eyes closed. It'd been a carrot cake with cream cheese frosting. I nodded to myself. That would be my little gift to Victoria. Something she actually enjoyed.

"Well, I think that just about covers it. I'll call to check on your progress in the morning."

By the time I got to my building, the mist had turned to rain. I held my jacket over my head to keep water out of my eyes, a bottle of wine in one hand. I'd stopped by the liquor store on the corner and bought the cheapest red they had, my first splurge in months. *Whoa, big spender.* I dropped the jacket and tucked the wine under my arm, fumbling for my keys.

"That you, Imogen?"

I looked up. My neighbor, Mr. Hendricks, stood beside me with an umbrella.

"Hello. How are you tonight?"

"Drier than you, it seems." The old man held the umbrella as high as his stooped back allowed. I ducked under and smiled at the sweet guy.

"Thank you so much." I shook my purse, listening for the telltale jingle of keys.

"Oh, don't bother, I've got mine." The rain came down harder now, tapping against the fabric of the umbrella and casting a hush over the whoosh of cars at our backs. The lock in the iron gate turned with a groan, and Mr. Hendricks pushed the door open for me. I stepped in under the overhang. As he shook out his umbrella, he nodded at the wine in my hand.

"Special occasion, young lady?"

I smiled brightly. "Got a job baking a rehearsal dinner cake."

He nodded and gave me a wink. "Good for you. Smart customer, too."

"Thanks." I smiled, and he waved me up the stairs, saying, "Ladies first."

I left him at the next landing. As I rounded the corner, he called up to me. "See you tomorrow at the market."

Mr. Hendricks always did his shopping at the Saturday farmers' market where I had my little baking stall. Shoot! The market.

"Oh, actually, not tomorrow. I'm going to be baking that cake all day."

His face fell.

"But I'll need someone to test it... if you're around?"

The lines around his eyes crinkled deeper as he gave me a huge grin and nodded. "Sure will."

The dim lights in the wall sconces flickered as I padded down the hall to my apartment. The door groaned as I shouldered it open. I left my keys and coat on the hook and locked the door behind me, flicking on the lights. *Home, finally home.*

I surveyed the entire 250 square feet of my closet-sized space. Cozy and simple, it suited me just fine, and the rent was actually cheaper than the room in that four bedroom I'd had before this. Plus, the only things I really cared about were a usable kitchen and a comfy bed, which in my case doubled as my couch.

I padded over to the small kitchen. I'd painted the cabinets white when I moved in, and hung my wood cutting board and rolling pins on the wall. The open shelves held my mixing bowls, and a white ceramic pitcher next to the stove held my wooden spoons, whisks, and spatulas.

I grabbed a pan and set it on the counter, right below the leak in the ceiling. *Ping! Ping! Ping!* I shook my head. The landlord had promised to fix that last month. I pulled up on the wood window frame above the sink and opened it a crack, taking a deep breath. I loved the smell of rain. I loved the smell of my kitchen in general, the butter, sugar, and chocolate scent that always filled the tiny space. Rain just made it better.

A police siren wailed nearby. *Ah, the sounds of home.*

I opened the half-sized refrigerator and stood pondering

the selection. Eight eggs sat in a bowl—what was left of a gift from a farmer last week at the market. The market!

Before I could forget, I texted a friend who sold honey at the stand next to mine and asked her to cover my booth tomorrow. She lived down the street and we'd covered for each other on occasion. Then I got back to business. I grabbed the half-full (I'm such an optimist) Chinese take-out container of noodles, smelled it, deemed it acceptable, and grabbed a fork. I plunked down on my bed, too tired to heat the food up.

I shoved a mouthful of noodles and baby broccoli into my mouth and pulled my notebook off the side table beside me. I flipped through all my scribbles and opened it to a dog-eared page filled with rows of figures and dates. I looked at this book every night. I already knew how much sat in my savings account, but I couldn't help reading with pleasure.

I'd scrawled my target goal of $110,000 across the top of the page and circled it, doodling cupcakes and loaves of bread all around it. I'd eaten like a starving college student, worked seven days a week (the weekends at the market), lived in a tiny closet, basically had no friends because I could never afford to go out—all to get to $107,000 seven years later.

I know, woe is me. All of my pain was self-inflicted. I could've gone out more with my coworkers and friends from the market, but I was usually either too tired, or just had more fun working toward my dream. After seven long years though, I was ready for a change. I'd thought it'd be a couple more months before I hit my goal, but with Victoria's cake tomorrow, I'd be there sooner than I'd thought possible. *Finally.*

I moved to the kitchen and popped open the bottle of

wine. I needed to bake for the market tomorrow, but before I did I held up my glass of wine (just a plastic cup, I did not have the budget for fancy glassware) and said, "To my future bakery!" As I sipped, it did not escape my attention that it made me a total loser to toast myself, alone. *And to a future where I have friends to cheers with.*

4
REHEARSAL DINNER

"You're late."

I whirled to find Victoria standing in front of me. I smoothed my hands over my dress and stood straighter, blowing my bangs out of my eyes. "Victoria. Hi."

Her blond locks cascaded over her shoulders in perfect curls, her shimmery golden cocktail dress matching her flute of champagne. She glanced at the table behind me.

"Dinner's about to start and you've barely begun setting up."

"Right. Well...." I considered explaining what my whirlwind of a day had been like. From rushing to the store to buy ingredients, edible flowers, and more cupcake carriers, to baking three different batches of batter till I got it right, to decorating a cake and eighty cupcakes, to transporting it all by myself across town. Once I'd arrived at the mansion, I'd made four separate trips up and down the slippery stone pathway that led from the street to the manicured garden out back. But one look at Victoria's on-edge expression, and I held my tongue. I tried to change the subject, lighten the mood. "This is... incredible, so beautiful."

Her arched brow pulled higher. "You're here as staff. The beauty is for the guests to enjoy. Get to work."

I burned with annoyance. "Right, will try my best *not* to enjoy the beauty."

I unpacked a carrier of cupcakes, setting an edible flower atop the cream cheese frosting of each one. The cake table sat at the back corner of the peaked white tent, a little removed from the guest tables, the string quartet, and the dance floor. Victoria edged closer, speaking out of the corner of her mouth. "My parents divorced when I was five, you'd think they could figure out how to be in the same five-hundred-foot radius of each other. But no, I have to play go-between." She heaved a great sigh as she scanned the tent and lush garden beyond it. "Ugh, and Ben's psychic grandfather isn't even here yet."

Without thinking, she picked up one of the little white-topped cupcakes and scooped a fingertip of the frosting into her mouth. I watched her reaction with trepidation, biting my lip. She closed her eyes and sighed. No longer speaking, she peeled away the crisp white wrapper and took a huge bite of the little cake, a soft moan escaping her lips. I opened my mouth to tell her a white frosting mustache lined her upper lip, but she tilted her head back, closed her eyes and let out a low groan. My cheeks grew hot, and I debated if I should interrupt my boss's sensual encounter with my cupcakes to let her know that an old man with bushy white brows stood a few feet away, watching her. When he cleared his throat and Victoria startled, I pretended to be engrossed with arranging flowers on the cake. The old man took a few steps closer. He held out a hand, and when she offered hers, he held it to his lips instead of shaking it. My brows lifted. I didn't know anyone actually did that.

"You must be Victoria." His voice rumbled deep from

inside his chest. He wore a deep blue velvet suit, and his eyes twinkled.

"And you are?" Her tone walked the fine line between civil and icy.

The old man chuckled. "Why, I'm Ben's grandpa, Arthur."

I sucked in a breath and sensed Victoria stiffen next to me. The psychic diplomat grandpa she cared so much about impressing?

"Of course!" Her voice went up an octave. "Silly of me, of course. So good to meet you, I've heard so much about you."

"I'm sure you have."

The silence stretched on too long, and I glanced over my shoulder. Victoria's blue eyes blinked rapidly, and she opened and closed her mouth several times while her fiancé's grandpa watched, his head cocked to one side, a bemused grin twisting his lips.

Finally, Victoria spat out, "I'm sorry, when you walked up, I was just testing the baked goods. I wanted to make sure they were up to stand—"

The old man cut her off with a wave of his hand. "I like a person who can truly enjoy themselves now and then, you know?" He smiled at her, his eyes twinkling under his bushy brows. "I'll leave you to your taste testing, but I'm glad to have met you and look forward to getting to know you more in the future." He turned to go, but paused and eyed the cupcakes strewn about the table. He raised his eyes to mine. "May I?"

I smiled. "Of course, sir." I'd only had time to place flowers on top of some of them. I searched one out and handed it to him.

He gave me a nod. I watched him wander off a few steps, peel back the wrapper, and take a bite. He then stopped and turned back to me, a question on his face. He cocked his head to the side, opened his mouth to say something, then glanced at Victoria and seemed to think better of it. He gave me another nod and wandered off toward the tables. What was that about? I watched him disappear into the crowd.

Victoria turned, her face blank with shock. "He said he wanted to get to know me better... in the future... as if... there will be a future, with me and Ben."

I smiled. "I think you're in."

Her face softened, and her lips tugged into the first genuine smile I thought I'd ever seen her give. "I passed the test." She giggled, a sound so startling from Victoria that my brows shot up under my bangs. It seemed to startle her too, because she covered her mouth, then giggled again. Even more shocking, she grabbed my hands in hers and held them tight. "Thank you, Imogen."

I swallowed. "For what?"

"I don't know exactly, but I think you've helped me out, quite a lot in fact." She gave my hands another little squeeze, then turned and scanned the crowd. She gave a squeal, another foreign noise coming from my boss, and waved someone over, bouncing on her heels. She turned to me, smiling. "Here he comes."

Okay, who are you, and what have you done with Victoria?

5
THE CONTEST

A tall, handsome man in a tuxedo strode toward us, looking from Victoria to me to Victoria. She took his face in her hands, pulled him down closer, and gave him a kiss that had my cheeks burning. I suddenly found my shoes very interesting. After a few moments, my boss pulled away from the man I assumed (hoped) was her fiancé, and turned to me.

"Imogen, Ben. Ben, Imogen. She made the most delicious cupcakes."

Ben eyed Victoria with a mix of doubt and wonder, his brows pulling together. "You ate... a cupcake?"

Victoria nodded emphatically, threw an arm around me, and pulled all three of us into a conspiratorial huddle. "Don't tell my trainer." She burst into giggles.

Ben asked, "Have you... uh, had some drinks?"

Victoria, mouth full with another dessert, shook her head, then said around her food, "No, bug id sounds lige a goo idea." She took a hunk of cupcake and pushed it toward Ben, who looked at it cross-eyed, then opened his mouth and chewed. The more he chewed, the more glazed his eyes got. He took Victoria's hands. "Dance with me."

Had I accidentally spilled a bottle of rum in the batter? I glanced at my desserts strewn about the white-linen-covered table. They seemed innocent enough. I looked back at the frolicking couple and smiled. Probably just love. Halfway to the dance floor, Victoria pulled Ben to a stop, their kissing and giggling drawing stares and then indulgent smiles from the other guests. She pulled her fiancé back to me as he fished around inside his jacket.

"Didn't want to forget," she explained as Ben pulled out a checkbook and pen. He scribbled something, ripped out the check, and handed it to me.

"I added a little extra," he said in a low voice. "I don't know what you put in those cupcakes, but they're pure magic—I've never seen Victoria like this." He winked and off they went, literally skipping to the dance floor, where they somehow managed to shimmy to the string quartet music, pulling other friends and couples up to join them. I sighed. Once I opened my bakery, would it be enough? Victoria and Ben stared into each other's eyes. Or would I still want someone to share everything with?

I flipped the check over and read $4,000. What? A *little* extra? My mouth fell open, and I pressed the check to my chest, letting out a high-pitched squeal that probably only dogs could have heard. Four thousand dollars! *Thank you, baking gods.* And now, finally, I really, truly had enough money to open my bakery. The realization nearly knocked me over.

After dinner and speeches, a waiter announced that dessert would be served. Time flew by as I sliced and served cake on little glass plates and said, again and again, "Yes, the flowers are edible," and "No, I didn't put in any liquid courage." Apparently, Victoria wasn't the only one whose spirits were lifted after eating a few bites. Soon, the entire party danced and swayed and laughed all over each other. People rushed up, smiling like naughty children, and dashed off with a cupcake in each hand. Champagne flowed, cocktail glasses clinked, and couples from their twenties to eighties snuck off into the shrubberies. What had gotten into everyone?

The string quartet, persuaded into playing the conga, churned out the familiar song as a middle-aged man sat next to them, an upended ice bucket between his knees, playing the "drum." The line of guests snaked between tables. I peeled my eyes away from the conga line as a beautiful guest sauntered toward me.

She smiled, her teeth bright against her dark skin. Her hair, tightly curled and piled atop her head in an enormous bun, bounced as she swayed her hips to the music, her snow-white gown catching the candlelight from the tables.

"Cake or a cupcake?" I asked for the umpteenth time. I smiled and held up one of each.

She tapped a slender finger against her lips as her dark eyes darted from one to the other. The diamond bracelets she wore slid up toward her elbows as she threw her hands in the air. "Oh, ow about zem both, eh?"

I grinned and handed over the plates. I loved French accents. Not that I'd ever been to France, or anywhere really. Before I'd moved from St. Louis, I'd never even been out of state.

"Are you ze baker?"

I nodded.

"I've been earing all night about ze desserts." She stepped closer and lowered her voice. She smelled like jasmine. "I eear they're just bearsting weeth mageeck." She winked, then held the cupcake up to her mouth, gingerly taking a bite around the wrapper. She moaned and bent her knees, sinking halfway to the ground. "Incredible. Just incredible. You should enter ze contest, you reeally should. And I don't do false flattery, believe me."

I raised a brow. "The contest?"

She looked me up and down. "You reeally don't know? Ze Water Kingdom's holding a contest for ze new royal baker. Last one died recently." She looked around and leaned closer, her voice hushed. "Ze official word is she died of a 'art attack, but if you ask me, eet was dark mageeck. Somezing underhanded, you know? Murder." She leaned back and straightened. How much had this woman had to drink? "Zat shouldn't scare you zough. I reeally zink you should enteer, zhere's steel time. I probably 'ave a flyer somewhere." She set the plates down and fished around in her sparkly white clutch. "Zey've been distributing zem all over ze kingdoms. Anyone can apply, anyone at all... well almost, no shifters, ze usual, but ze'll take emigrants like you." She poked around some more in the tiny clutch.

Pretty sure if you haven't found it by now, it's not going to suddenly appear. The bag looked like it could barely hold a credit card... maybe.

She looked at me and shrugged her slender shoulders. "Can't find one." She glanced around and then winked. "Don't usually break ze rules when traveling on visa, you know. But I am here as ze date of ze retired ambassador, so if I geet in a beet of trouble, he'll just geet me out."

I scanned the conga line. Did she mean Ben's grandpa?

A small sound, a zap, like snuffing a candle out with wet fingers, made me turn toward her again. In her hand she held a large, brown sheet of paper. "We'll just keep zat between us, eh?"

Goose bumps prickled up the back of my neck and arms. I looked between the paper and her face. Where had it come from? It was too large to fit in her bag without folding, yet it was completely smooth and crisp. She handed it to me. The oddly thick paper seemed to be coated in wax. I sniffed it and smelled honey.

"Well, I'm off." She lifted the plates. "Thank you for ze delicious treats. So good to have met you."

I nodded, not sure how I felt about this strange and beautiful woman. "You too."

"Think about eet." She lifted her chin toward the flyer in my hand and danced her way back to the party.

I held the waxy paper up to my face and read, "The Magnificent Contest for the Water Kingdom's Next Royal Baker."

6

CELEBRATION

Ping! Ping! Ping! I lay in bed that night, listening as the rain leaked through the hole in my ceiling and landed drop by drop in the pan on the kitchen counter. Ping!

I stared up at the cracked ceiling and willed my eyes closed for the umpteenth time. *Go to sleep, Imogen. It's late. You're tired.* Except, I wasn't. Not even a little.

A huge grin on my face, I bolted upright, threw off my quilt, and slipped on my fuzzy slippers. I practically bounded the few steps to the kitchen. I should've been tired, especially after all the trips up and down the steps at the mansion, followed by more up and down the stairway in my building to unload all my cake gear. But I absolutely vibrated with energy. I felt as if I'd eaten the entire cake and was flying high on the sugar trip of my life.

I pulled the window in the kitchen up a crack, inhaling the clean scent of rain. A car whooshed by outside, its tires splashing through the flooded streets. Nothing else stirred. My phone read 3:00 a.m. I grinned wider. Same time I'd be waking to start the first batches of the day once my bakery opened. Might as well get some practice in.

I moved to turn on some lights, but decided it was a special occasion, after all. I wandered back to my front door. I'd dumped all the trays there, along with the stubs of about a dozen candles.

Victoria had told me to take centerpieces, whatever I wanted at the end of the night. I'd taken the biggest candles I could find. I never had money for little luxuries and I'd been happy to discover they were beeswax, my favorite.

I gathered up the candles in my shirt, then arranged them all over the counter, along the top edge of the stove, and standing on tiptoe, placed some on top of the fridge. I set little plates and scraps of paper under them to catch the drips. I fished out a matchbook from the back of a drawer and lit them all. The warm, woozy scent of honey mixed with the smell of rain drifting in the open window, made the most delicious perfume in the world.

I donned my frilly apron then padded back to my purse and fished out the four thousand dollar check. It marked the beginning of me fulfilling my dreams. It was probably safer to leave it in my purse, but I wanted to keep it close. I tucked it carefully in the pocket of my apron.

Now for the other slip of paper. I fished the thick, linen-like flyer out of my purse and carried it to the kitchen. I leaned my elbows on the countertop and held up a candle. The wax coating made the flyer stiff and thick.

An idea occurred to me, and I crumpled the paper up, then folded it into a cup shape. No matter how I moved it, it held its shape. *Interesting.* I flattened it back out, new wrinkles crisscrossing its surface, and read. Across the top, in bold, wood block letters it spelled out,

"The Magnificent Contest for the Water Kingdom's Next Royal Baker."

Below the title, in smaller, curly letters it said,

In anticipation of the Summer Solstice Festival, held every year between the Water and Fire Kingdoms, as a symbol of our two peoples' unity and loyalty, the Water Kingdom invites all peoples* to enter the contest.

A little asterisk next to "all peoples" led to the clarification at the bottom of the page that this excluded "shifters and Badlanders." *Shifters and Badlanders?*

Please bake a signature dessert, a delicacy so delectable, so delightful, so definitely representative of your immense talents, as to convince our celebrity judges, Francis Valhaven and Rhonda the Seer—

I frowned. *Never heard of them.*

—of your deservedness of the high position of Water Kingdom's royal baker. All entries must be received by midnight on June 8th, with contestants to be announced the same day. If selected, entrants are responsible for securing their own transportation, though appropriate visas and stamps will be provided, to Bijou Mer, capital of the Water Kingdom, in time for orientation on June 11.

I checked my phone. As it was after midnight, technically it was June 8. The end of the day marked the contest's deadline. No way could I get this to wherever it needed to go in time. Come to think of it, how would I ship a baked good to these "celebrity" judges? I had to flip the flyer over to get the details. Outlined in block letters was a list.

"Three Easy Steps. 1—Bake. 2—Wrap baked good in this flier. 3—Wait for results!"

I flipped the flyer over several times. Just wrap it in the flyer? But where would I send it to?

Under the numbered list I scanned through all the

contest fine print and found an outlined rectangle that held an address: Royal Bakers Contest, Judges Quarters, Royal Palace, Bijou Mer, Water Kingdom. I frowned. Not even a zip code.

I looked up and searched my memory. Was it a joke? The woman who'd given me the flyer had seemed sincere, if a bit different. I looked back down at the flyer. Quite an elaborate joke, if it was one. Maybe French addresses were different... if this was French. It sounded French, right?

My elbows leaning against the cold tile counter, I tapped on the flyer with one finger, in time with the leak dripping into the pot. Though I couldn't quite puzzle out the reward for winning the contest, earning the title of royal baker certainly sounded impressive. Maybe the winner got to meet French royalty?

I imagined a beautiful framed plaque on the wall of my bakery, proclaiming me "honorary royal baker." I might get some media coverage. That would certainly help get the word out about a new patisserie. I smiled. Well, I might find some way to express ship something and get it there in time. In any case, I felt like baking to celebrate saving up the funds, so might as well enter the contest with whatever I made.

7

SEALED

I stood up and patted the flyer, my mind made up. I'd enter. Why not? And since the contest began in just a few days, if I made it in, it wouldn't delay the opening of my bakery.

I stood on tiptoe and lifted a few white ceramic mixing bowls off the open shelves above the sink, plunking them down on the countertop. I opened the fridge and pulled out a couple of half-finished cartons of fresh berries, leftover from last weekend's farmers' market.

Oh! I made a mental note to thank my friend for running my stall. I peeled off the lid of a tub of mascarpone, swiped a fingertip of the cheese to my lips, and savored the rich, salty sweetness. *Yum.*

Once I had everything I needed, I set the butter out to soften and happily closed the fridge door, shutting off the bright, artificial light. I let the warmth and romance of the golden candles scattered about the kitchen envelop me. What a magical morning.

I pulled out my loose collection of recipes—calling it a book would have been giving it too much credit. I kept the loose sheets of full-sized paper, note cards, even a few Post-its in a ratty pale yellow binder I'd had since high school. I flipped through it till I found the recipe I had in mind—shortcake, filled with mascarpone and topped with fresh strawberries and blueberries and a syrup made from some of the fruit. My mouth watered just thinking about it.

Humming a random little song I made up, I mixed flour and salt and the dry goods together, opting to do it by hand instead of using my mixer. With the softness of the candles, the curtain hush of pouring rain, and the dark early hour, it just seemed like a time for quiet—the whir of something electric would've broken the spell.

I mixed and hummed and danced around the kitchen, tasting this and that, practically bursting with joy. This was going to be my life.

I imagined myself in my bakery, doing this every day. A happy tear dribbled down my cheek and fell into the bowl of batter tucked under my arm. Oops! Should I start over? Probably... although as long as I kept my blood and sweat out, a tear was probably okay. The health department might have disagreed, but I'd worry about that when I had a real bakery.

It was nearly five when I finished. The entire counter lay under a white dusting of flour, as did my cheeks, the kitchen towel I'd tossed next to the whisk, my hands, and apron.

I pulled up a tall wooden stool and sat on the other side of the counter, staring at my creation. The little shortcake glowed a light golden brown, a few pieces of the top just starting to crisp. Inside lay buttery goodness and sweet and salty mascarpone. Berries and purple syrup tumbled over the top and down the sides.

I sighed, pleased. Then yawned, stretching my mouth so

wide, it almost hurt. I blinked my watering eyes a few times. Humph. Guess the late night had finally caught up with me.

I shook my head trying to clear it. Right, now what? I looked at the flyer. Maybe I really could just wrap the shortbread directly in it? I vaguely recalled reading that a long time ago, in the Middle Ages maybe, people had used waxed pieces of oilcloth to preserve goods, kind of how we might use plastic wrap.

I lifted my shortbread, set it carefully in the center of the paper, and then gently folded the sides up around it. I molded it protectively around the little cake and it folded neatly, so that the address ended up right on top. I smiled. *Perfect*. But how to keep it sealed?

I stood and fished around in a drawer until I found my red-and-white striped bakers twine. I sliced off a long piece with a knife and crisscrossed it around the flier, then tied a bow on top, like a present, careful to not obscure the address.

I sat back down on the stool and admired my handiwork. I'd take it to the shipping store as soon as they opened in a few hours.

Outside the window, the streets remained quiet and the sky dark. Soon though, I knew, lights would turn on and people would begin to go about their day. I yawned, groaned, and lay my head on my arms, resting them on my open recipe book.

I eyed my little creation by the soft golden light of the dying candles. Should I even bother going to sleep, or just stay up? I yawned heavily again; my eyes squeezed shut.

I let them stay closed, breathing in the sweet, bready smell of the cake and listening to the soft rush of rain coming in through the cracked window. I'd just let my eyes rest while I decided....

I woke up groaning, an ear-splitting, high-pitched peal driving a spike into my brain. I blinked. My eyes stung. I took a breath and coughed, and coughed harder. My lungs burned and ached. I squinted, trying to focus, and lifted my head off my arms.

I must have fallen asleep at the kitchen counter, but even knowing that, I could make sense of nothing else. Where was my kitchen?

In front of me stretched a dense cloud of black smoke. The electronic wail of the smoke alarm registered. Oh God! My kitchen was on fire!

My heavy head bobbed and I reeled, stumbling off the wooden stool and knocking it sideways. I leaned against the wall for support, burying my face in the crook of my arm, coughing and coughing until I could drag in a bit of breath.

I lifted my head and dashed into the smoke, waving my arms, trying to clear it, but it did no good and a flash of bright orange flame sent me stumbling back, the heat blistering my cheeks. My mind reeled. I looked around, saw the recipe book I'd been lying on, gathered it into my arms, and ran out of the apartment.

My phone! I went to dash back in so I could call the fire department, but another, bigger flash of flame made me stumble back, terrified.

I ran out the door, coughing and gagging. My apartment sat at the end of the hall, so I began pounding on doors and screaming, as loudly as my dry, scorched lungs would let me.

"Fire!"

8

THE FIRE

The cool mist beaded on my dry, cracked cheeks. I barely registered it or anything else around me. Firemen in dirty yellow gear bustled by, dragging hoses to their trucks.

A few of my neighbors sat in the back of a paramedic truck, blankets wrapped around their shoulders, legs swinging. They were all right. All my neighbors had gotten out, I'd made sure of that. That was a blessing.

I should've felt grateful, but honestly, I felt nothing at all. A numb emptiness settled over me. I seemed unable to peel my eyes away from the apartment building. Black smoke had billowed out the top floor windows, but now just a gray haze hung there. Black soot scorched the area around my shattered apartment window.

What *had* been my apartment, I corrected myself. The firefighters had informed me that nothing remained, just the skeleton of my iron bed frame. I had nothing but the pajamas I wore, my frilly apron, the recipe book I still clutched to my chest, and the rough woolen blanket someone, probably a firefighter, had placed around my shoulders. And I probably had to give that back.

My landlord, who lived on the bottom floor, stood talking with a man in slacks and a tie. Every now and then my landlord scowled my way. I shrunk within my blanket, my stomach tying into even tighter knots. I might be sick.

The guy in slacks left my landlord and approached me. He shifted his clipboard under one arm and held the other out. "Hi, I'm Tom Shear, assessor for the property." I shook his hand. *I'm supposed to say something.*

"Your landlord informed me that you're Imogen Banks?"

Oh, right, my name. I nodded, my eyes drifting down to the man's shoes.

"I understand the fire began in your apartment?"

He said it kindly, a matter-of-fact statement more than an accusation, but I couldn't help the silent tears that ran down my cheeks and fell onto my fuzzy gray slippers. I nodded and burbled out, "I'm the arsonist." I couldn't remember my own name, but that word popped into my head?

"You did that on purpose?" Tom Shear, property assessor, tried to catch my eye.

"What? No, of course not." I shook my head.

"Here." He handed me a folded white kerchief, and I took it with a trembling hand, dabbing at my cheeks. When I pulled it away from my face to hand it to him, it was stained a sooty black. It took me a moment to realize that my entire face must be blackened, and I cried harder. "I-I ruined it." I'd ruined everything. "I'm sorry, I'll-I'll get you a new one." My vision blurred, and I choked on big, gulping sobs.

I felt a warm hand on my shoulder. "Don't cry, miss, I have a million of those. Keep it, okay? Just don't cry."

I nodded, but kept sobbing, my whole body shaking. What a mess I'd made.

"Listen, I know now's not a good time, but do you have renter's insurance?"

Did I? Yes, my landlord had insisted I have it when I moved in. I nodded, still staring at my feet.

"Do you know who it's with?"

It took my sluggish brain a long time, but I remembered the name of the company and told him.

"Okay, I'll get them on the line. They'll help us sort out the liability for the accident, and sometimes there's provisions in case of something like this for hotel accommodations, a new wardrobe, that sort of thing."

I pressed the man's kerchief to my face and sobbed. I just wanted to wake up and have this all have been a terrible dream. Yeah, maybe it was all a dream.

I slapped myself across the face, hard. Well, that hurt like a mother, but I didn't wake up. And now I just seemed insane. I cried harder.

A firefighter had informed me earlier that one of the candles I'd left burning had caught a kitchen towel on fire, and it spread from there. Maybe the wax paper I'd wrapped my shortcake in had ignited. He'd told me they hadn't found anything like that, but that everything had burned very hot and it had likely disintegrated.

The fireman had said I'd done a brave thing, sticking around, getting everyone out. But I didn't feel brave. I felt like an overly excited idiot who'd endangered my neighbors' lives, destroyed a building, and ruined an innocent handkerchief.

The insurance guy, Tom, came up to me, a cell to one ear, his finger holding the other closed to hear better over the din. Spectators had gathered outside the police tape to gape, the firefighters called to each other over the clatter of loading up metal ladders, and the fire engine's motor hissed and whined now and then. Tom came to my side and lifted his spectacled face to mine. I lowered the kerchief.

"Do you know your ID number?"

I sighed, my heart sinking, and shook my head.

"No," he said into the phone, then listened. "Okay, they're going to ask you some identifying questions to verify your account."

I nodded and he passed the phone over. I spoke with the woman from the insurance company, and could hear her tapping away at her keyboard as I answered her questions about the name of my first dog and my mother's maiden name.

"All right," she said. "I'm going to pull up your policy and take a look at your coverage. This'll be a few minutes."

I stood in the cool morning mist, the flash of police lights bouncing off the wet street, and waited. After a few minutes she came back on the line. "Miss Banks, still there?"

"Yes." My voice came out a dry rattle.

"Good news is that you do indeed have fire damage coverage. However, you have a high deductible plan."

That didn't sound good.

"How high?" I croaked.

"Your deductible is $50,000."

9

SPECIAL DELIVERY

The world spun. Only Tom leaping forward and catching me by the shoulders kept me from sinking to the ground. I breathed in shallow gasps on wobbly legs.

"After that your plan will cover a portion of the damages, but because the fire was caused by negligence—"

The word "negligence" cut me to the core. I was negligent. Tears tracked down my cheeks again, my eyes so swollen and wet I could barely see. The woman from the insurance company explained that I would need to pay a certain percentage up to $100,000, plus fees, for a total of $107,000. All of my savings. I wanted to crawl into a hole and die. Hands trembling and numb from the cold, I handed the phone back to Tom.

"Do you get reimbursement for temporary lodgings?"

I shook my head slowly, numb.

"Do you have someone you can call?"

I squinted at Tom. What a kind question from someone I barely knew. I tried to pull myself together, and plastered a wavering smile on my face. "Yeah, yeah of course. I'll be okay. Thank you. Really. Thank you."

"You sure you'll be okay, miss?"

I nodded again, putting on my best "of course, don't be silly" face. "I'm cool as a cucumber."

The space between his brows creased, but he gave me one last searching look, then nodded and turned, taking his clipboard back to the scorched building.

With his back turned I let my smile and my shoulders drop. I had no one. I had no friends. I'd sacrificed everything for years to save up enough money for my bakery, and the night it finally was within reach, I'd literally burned the whole thing down.

It would take every single last penny I had to pay the damages for the fire, everything I'd saved up for my bakery. I had work tomorrow. Maybe my adopted—I mean, parents would wire me money? That would require explaining that I had none of my own. A guilty pit ached in my stomach.

I'd never told them about my dreams for a bakery. I didn't know exactly why I'd always hidden that from them, and I felt the wrongness of it. They'd support me, I knew they would. But... but it would be with words of caution, and backup plans and looks shared between my mom and dad and sister that said, "Let's be there for her when this doesn't pan out." They viewed any career outside a regular nine to five with suspicion.

I whimpered as I stared at the still-smoking building.

With the rough blanket wrapped around my hands, I sunk to the curb and sat with my face buried, my whole body shaking with my sobs. I was sitting there, willing the rest of the world to melt away and leave me be, when I heard a gentle *Ding! Ding!*

I lifted my hot, swollen face and blinked. In the middle

of the all the chaos of firemen, flashing lights, hoses, and groups of neighbors in blankets stood a man in Lycra pants, holding a bicycle at his side. He pulled an envelope from under his arm, scanned the address, and called out, "Imogen Banks?" He looked around, and I buried my face in the blanket. "Imogen Banks?" he tried again. I groaned. *Go away*.

I heard someone say, "That's her, over there, the lump in the blanket on the curb."

I groaned again. That was the perfect way to describe me, the lump on the curb, and that's exactly how I wanted to stay. The whir of bike wheels clicked to a stop in front of me. He cleared his throat.

"Imogen Banks?"

I lifted my head and his brows jolted up. Between the soot and the crying, I was sure I looked a mess. He held the brown paper envelope out to me. "Delivery for you."

I frowned at it, then at him, making no move to take it. "If it's some insurance document informing me I owe them my firstborn child, just take it away."

He shrugged. "I'm just the messenger." He pushed it a little closer, and with a roll of my eyes, I extricated an arm from the blanket and took it. He swung back onto his bike and peddled off, swerving around the police tape and through the crowd of onlookers.

I pulled my other hand free and turned the large envelope over. It crackled in my hand as I checked the return address. My heart stopped.

Royal Bakers Contest, Judges Quarters, Royal Palace, Bijou Mer, Water Kingdom.

No. How could this be possible? It was the address for the contest. The contest I'd never entered because my shortcake burned up in the apartment fire. With trembling hands, I tore open the package and slid out a single, oversized sheet of parchment. Across the top, scrawled in huge letters, it read: Congratulations! My head spun.

You've been chosen to enter the contest for the new royal baker of the Water Kingdom. Enclosed you'll find your passport to the kingdom. You must arrive by June 11, 9:00 a.m. sharp at the Old Miller's Quarters, back garden, Royal Palace, to begin orientation. Bring your own flame, or one will be provided for you. If coming by land, the nearest human town is St. Rael, on the coast of France. If by sea, locate the ferry dock on the south side. If by air, use the royal landing pad.

I lifted my head and looked around, expecting a camera crew to leap out and scream "gotcha!" But no one did. I reread it. My own flame? Was that a jab at the fire I'd lit? But how would anyone know about that and about the contest? Could I really have been chosen? But how could that be possible?

Goose bumps rose on my arms, and the hair on the back of my neck lifted.

My cake had to have burned in the fire. How could I have entered? And how could this package have gotten to me so quickly? It'd been only hours ago that I'd drifted off and the fire had started.

Fresh chills ran up my spine as I realized I'd never even written down a return address. I blinked back the dizziness that threatened to topple me over. None of this made sense.

And even if, somehow, this was real, I had no way of getting to France. Not now. Everything I owned lay in a pile of ashes and all the money I'd saved had to go to paying off the rebuild costs. I sighed heavily.

The dream of the contest, like my dream of the bakery, was over before it even began. I folded the paper up slowly, tears trickling down my face again. It would've been nice, though. The coast of France, a baking contest, maybe meeting royalty. Like a fairy tale.

I pulled my arm inside the blanket and felt around my hip for the apron pocket. As I slipped the note inside, the corner of another piece of paper poked my finger. I frowned. I pulled it out and held it in front of my face.

Victoria's check!

10

THE AIRPORT

I stared at the check in my hands. It'd be enough for some clothes, a deposit on a new apartment... I looked down at my fuzzy slippers. A pair of shoes. The ray of hope turned into a heavy weight on my chest.

I'd be starting all over again, fighting to rebuild a life that I'd been eager to escape. I sighed. It'd probably take me a year to get back to the status quo, then another seven to save for the bakery. I buried my face in my hands. Maybe after a good sleep, rebuilding my life wouldn't seem so daunting. *You tell yourself that.* I stuffed the check back in my pocket and as I did so, my fingers connected with the packet the bike messenger had delivered. An insane thought entered my brain.

I *could* use my last several thousand dollars to do sensible things, like salvage my life.

Or, I could buy a plane ticket to France and enter a baking competition. I wasn't sure of the time difference, but it'd be possible to arrive in time for the orientation. I might win a big cash prize, or maybe royal baker wasn't an empty title, but an actual job.

Speaking of jobs, I'd never once used my sick or vacation days, and had a bunch saved up. I could leave without risking my position—have a plan B back here in Seattle. When I pictured the rolling hills of the French countryside, the Eiffel Tower, bakeries, my heart felt light, in spite of all that'd happened.

I looked up at the charred building, the flashing police lights, and the gray low-hanging sky. I imagined staying and rebuilding—the sensible thing to do. I felt like I might be sick.

I took a shaky breath. If picturing my future made me queasy, that had to mean something. I stood, a tingling lightness dancing around my body. *I'm entering the competition!*

I strode past an ambulance, feeling sassy, and threw my blanket into the back. It hit one of my neighbors, and I backtracked to apologize.

I lifted the police tape, ducked under, and pushed my way through the crowd to the corner. I shivered in my T-shirt, flannel pants, apron, and fuzzy slippers as the light rain beaded on my arms. I waved down a taxi.

"Where to?"

By the time we reached the airport, I'd told the driver the whole crazy story.

"So good to meet you, Kirk." I smiled, ducking back in to shake his hand as he turned around in his seat.

He grinned. "No, Imogen, pleasure's all mine. You win that contest, you hear?"

I reached into my pocket and froze. I had no money! My mouth dropped, open and I blinked rapidly. "Oh no, my wallet burned up."

"Yeah, I kinda figured that might be the case."

My heart sunk. "I promise I didn't make that up to get a free ride."

His lips quirked to the side, and he nodded at my apron. "You're covered in soot, your hair's singed, and you smell like a campfire. Even if you had, I'd have to give it to you for committing."

I glanced down at my outfit, then back at the driver, still mortified. "Listen, I have that check. I just have to find an ATM to cash it. Oh, wait." I looked down at my feet, mumbling my thoughts. "I don't have a debit card." My face crumpled. "I'm sure I can find a check cashing place. Leave the meter running and I'll be back soon, I swear. I-I can leave something as collateral, my...." I pulled my slippers off. "I'll leave you my slippers." I pushed them toward him, my feet cramping on the cold sidewalk.

He laughed. "Ride's on me."

My heart swelled. "No. I couldn't."

He waved a hand. "I insist. Now, go get 'em. I want to hear about you on the news. For the contest, not for burning down more buildings."

I gave him double finger guns. "Right."

He grinned. "I almost offered to get your bags for you."

I chuckled, my shoulders shaking. "But I don't have any. Everything I owned burned up in a fire."

We laughed together.

I had completely lost it. I thanked him again, then passed through the sliding glass doors to the terminal. Men and women pulled rolling suitcases past me without a second glance, while airline workers in navy sweater vests chatted in little groups and pointed passengers to their destinations.

Feeling self-conscious in my pajamas, scorched apron, and slippers, I padded to the nearest ticketing counter. With only a short line, I soon stood before the middle-aged ticket agent in a blue sweater.

"How can I help you?" When she looked up, her brows jumped. I probably should have gone into the bathroom and checked a mirror.

I smiled my brightest. "Ticket to France, please."

She swallowed, gave me a careful look, and then tapped away at her keyboard. "Which airport?"

Uhhh... I supposed that was a normal thing for a traveler to know. I scanned the acceptance letter. "As close to St. Rael as I can get."

She tapped away at her computer. "Looks like Paris is the closest international airport."

"Okay." I grinned. "Paris it is."

She nodded and hit some buttons. "Departure date?"

I stood taller. "Whatever today is."

She glanced up briefly, frowning. "I can get you out on a flight leaving in an hour and a half...."

"Perfect, I'll take it."

"Return, or one way?"

I swallowed. Good question. I didn't know how long the contest would last, though I supposed that depended on how well I did. "One way."

She frowned deeper. I think I knew one girl who'd be getting the extra pat down at security. *A soot-covered woman buying a one-way with no baggage doesn't seem suspicious at all.*

"Passport, please."

"Ah." I closed my mouth and my eyes. How to put this? "I don't have one." I tilted my head. "Is that going to be a problem?"

Her face turned stony. Guess that was a yes?

"Wait!"

She startled.

"Sorry. But, I might...." I fished around in my apron

pocket. "Might have something." I pulled out the brown paper envelope, its stiff paper crinkling as I unfolded it.

From it, I pulled the special passport the letter had mentioned. I hadn't even thought to look it over yet. Embossed gold letters spelled out "Temporary Passport to the Water Kingdom" across the sea-glass-green cover. I flipped it open and nearly dropped it in surprise.

Inside, a picture of myself stared back up at me. Those were my big blue eyes, red curtain of bangs, winged eyeliner, and toothy grin. Goose bumps prickled up my arms. How was any of this possible? I'd never even entered the contest.

The ticket agent cleared her throat, and I jumped. "Oh right, sorry." With shaking hands I slid the passport across the counter to her. "I know this is unconventional, but...."

11

THE LEAP

As soon as the ticketing agent lifted the passport, she perked up. "This will be more than sufficient, Miss Banks." She gave me a toothy smile, her eyes open wide, but glazed. The knot of tension in my stomach loosened.

Whew, thank goodness for that passport. Maybe everyone else had heard of this place besides me. Had to admit, my knowledge of geography wasn't great.

She tapped away at her keyboard, copying information from the document. I leaned forward, standing on my toes. How did it have my height and weight? Though my birthday was wrong. *Odd.*

"That'll be $2,932."

I choked, my throat raw from inhaling so much smoke.

"How much?" I gasped.

She repeated the figure. That meant spending nearly all of my money. I'd only have about a thousand dollars left when I landed for a bus ticket, lodgings, and to get back home at some point. But, as I didn't see any alternatives, I handed over the check, hoping my good luck streak would continue and she'd accept it. Well, the streak that started after I burned down my apartment building.

She frowned.

"Yeah, I know. I burned down my home this morning." I made little fireworks with my hands, forcing some laughter. "Poof. Everything I own, gone. Ha ha. So I don't have my debit card, but could I write this over to the airline?" I clasped my hands and squinted. "Please?"

She licked her lips. "For someone traveling on your special passport, I'm sure we can make an exception."

I blinked. "Really?"

She nodded, and I signed it over. Then she handed me the change and my boarding pass. I shuffled through security, placing my slippers in the gray plastic bin. Hey, at least they were easy to get off and on again.

On the other side of security, I milled about, taking in the crowds, the whir and peal of airplanes lifting off, and the click-clack of rolling suitcases. I popped into the women's restroom, gasped when I saw my reflection, then whimpered.

No wonder the cab driver had believed me. I had a black line of soot across my forehead, and more smudges streaked my cheeks and chin. I pouted as I reached up and touched the bun on top of my head. Clouds of ash floated off my normally bright red hair, the bun stiff and crunchy. I pumped a length of paper towel out, ran it under water and scrubbed.

When I'd finished, my face stung from the rough treatment, but it was clean. Just the other 90 percent of me remained filthy. I noticed a white-haired woman standing in the reflection behind me, staring. I gave her a watery smile.

"Are you all right, dear?"

Before I could answer, she came forward and held out a

pass to me. "My husband and I always fly first class, better for our circulation you know, and we get these guest passes to the lounge. They have showers in there. Take it and get freshened up."

I looked down at the pass and then back to her face. I burst into tears. "Thank you."

"Don't cry." The tiny woman patted my shoulder. "They've also got complimentary drinks." She winked. "You look like you could use a stiff one."

On my way to the lounge, I popped into a souvenir store. I browsed past the neck pillows and bought a pair of stretchy pajama jeans, a white T-shirt with a unicorn on it that read, creatively, "Seattle," and a cami with a built-in bra to substitute for an actual one.

Holding my bag of purchases, I got into the lounge without incident. I'd expected more of a huff over my slippers and apron. I dashed down a hallway lit by wall sconces before they could change their minds. A large room opened up before me with a bar, breakfast buffet, and a half dozen men and women lounging in recliners. Okay, quick shower, then that buffet was calling my name.

Once in the women's locker room, I stripped down. I bundled my clothes up, gave them one last look, and shoved them in a trash can. Then I stepped into a steamy, near-scalding shower and scrubbed so hard at the black smudges all over my body that by the time I finished, my skin glowed bright red from forehead to toes.

I toweled my hair dry, put on my new jeans, cami, and T-shirt, and blew my hair dry. By the time I'd finished and stepped back into my slippers I felt semi human again, though my head spun with exhaustion.

After my third trip to the buffet, I felt more clear-headed. I should probably let some people know about my plans. Luckily, the lounge had free computer workstations.

First, I logged into my e-mail and used the Internet to call Victoria.

"Who is this?"

"Imogen Banks." I tried to put a smile in my voice.

"You realize I'm getting married today and have about a million things to do?"

Ah. Good old Victoria was back. "Congratulations! So, I accidentally burned down my apartment last night."

"What?!"

I glanced back. A few passengers looked my way with raised brows. "Sorry," I mouthed. I turned the computer speakers' volume down. "Yeah, everything's fine. Well, I'm basically homeless and destitute, but besides that. I just wanted to tell you that I'm going to take some vacation days. You know, to uh, get everything back in order and to—" I cleared my throat and tried to rush through the next part. "—go to France. So that'll be okay, right? I'll be back in a couple weeks, probably."

"Imogen." Victoria said my name slowly, enunciating each syllable. "You have always been a great employee, despite what I may say in my quarterly reviews—that's just to keep you motivated."

Right.

"And, I don't know what magic you worked last night, but it was the best of my life, and I will always appreciate that."

Okay, nice Victoria hadn't entirely disappeared.

"But, as I mentioned the other day, the company's about to enact some massive layoffs."

"I know it might not look great to take time off right now, but—"

"It's more than that. Imogen, they want anyone who can be spared, and there's no better way to say 'I'm unnecessary' than to leave for 'a couple weeks, probably.' You have to decide. If you stay, I promise you'll have a job. If you go, I'm sorry, but you'll be laid off."

I took a deep breath. *Geez.* I looked down at my unicorn shirt and slippers. *What am I doing? I'm throwing away a normal life, a good job, a boss who going forward might actually be pleasant to work with, benefits, and a chance to work toward my dream... slowly... so slowly.* I took a deep breath.

Or I could take the adventure of my life. If I did this, if I went to France on my last dollar, it'd be the craziest, biggest leap I'd ever made. Bigger than moving away from home by myself to Seattle, a city I'd never even visited. Crazier than saving up for seven years for my big dream. This would literally be all or nothing.

"Victoria, I hope you have the wedding of your dreams and an even better marriage. I'm going to France." Just like that, I quit my job.

A short silence followed. Victoria cleared her throat. "Go get your groove back, or whatever you're doing in France. Good luck, Imogen."

I clicked the button to end the call. There was someone else I should probably call. I pulled up the number in my contacts, then decided to write an e-mail instead.

I sent my adopted family a short note explaining that I was taking a vacation and would be out of touch for a few weeks, but not to worry. I told them I loved them, and hit Send.

I sighed. I did love them. They deserved a more honest daughter and sister. I just didn't feel like I could open up about that side of me. I worried they'd think my dreams too impractical. And since a part of me agreed with them, I didn't think I could handle hearing it in their voices.

I drowned my sorrows with another plate of eggs and biscuits and a complimentary mimosa, 'cause what the heck. Then I headed to the gate and boarded the plane.

France, here I come!

12

FRANCE

With some help from the people at the information desk in Paris, I boarded a bus headed for St. Rael and settled in for more sitting. *Urg*. In Paris, the sun sat high in the sky. I had no idea what time my body thought it was, but it certainly didn't think it was noon. I couldn't stop yawning.

For the next four hours I leaned my elbow on the narrow window sill and gazed out at the idyllic countryside whizzing past. We sped through crumbling stone villages with red tile roofs. Green fields stretched out to the horizon, divided into neat squares by rows of darker green bushes and trees.

Our bus stopped at one point to allow a herd of sheep to cross the single-lane road at their own leisurely pace, while leaves floated down the small stream that bordered the road.

The late afternoon light bounced gold and white off the blue sea when we reached St. Rael, the closest "human" town to Bijou Mer, as the letter had put it. Whatever that meant.

The bus let us off at the only station in the center of the small town, a tiny stretch of street bordered by gray stone buildings one or two stories high. With a hiss and a whine, the bus pulled off.

Now what? I turned in a circle, taking it all in. It took about ten seconds. Yep, seen it all—about fifteen buildings and a couple of pale faces peeking out at me from behind window curtains. All righty then.

"Beautiful, ain't she?"

The Scottish voice startled me, and I looked around. On a second-story balcony above me, I spotted a thin, middle-aged woman standing before an easel, a paintbrush in her hands. She looked from the ocean to her easel, and back again, dabbing away with her long brush.

"Is that Bijou Mer?" I pointed at the mountain that rose from the marshy reeds some distance away, stone peaks at its summit.

The woman kept her eyes on her work. "Mm. You here for the Summer Solstice Festival?"

Some knot in my stomach relaxed. Someone else had heard of the festival. I looked again at the city on the mountain, flocks of seagulls circling it. "No. Well, kind of." I smiled, a hand raised to shield my eyes. "I'm participating in the baking contest."

The woman squinted at her painting, blowing a curly gray lock out of her face, as the wind whipped her ponytail across her back. "Never heard of it."

I stopped. Was I in the right place? She had mentioned the festival at least. "Um, it's for the festival. For the next royal baker," I called up.

"Hmmph."

I waited for her to speak again, but that appeared to be the only answer I was going to get. I cleared my throat, then scratched at my head. "Is that the way to Bijou Mer?" I gestured at the marshy wetlands beyond the town.

"It's one way. Hope you're not planning on going now. You'll never make it before the tide comes up."

"The tide?"

She looked at me for the first time, her dark eyes searching my face. "You don't know." Her brows knitted together, then she turned back to her painting. "When the tide rises at night, Bijou Mer becomes an island. You won't make it before then, and anyway, if you did, you'd miss the ferry back. And there's no place to lodge out there for our kind."

"Our kind?" I blinked rapidly.

She turned suddenly and glared at me. "Unless you're one of *them*?"

I stepped back. "One of who? I'm not one of anyone."

Still glaring, she turned away. "Well, you'd better find a place to stay back in town then."

"Yeah, I guess I should. Is there an inn?"

She dabbed at the canvas. "You're looking at it."

I stepped back then and noticed the wooden sign hanging below the balcony. It read "Caving Cottage Inn." The slanting building did appear to be caving in.

"Mustn't think of staying the night out there," she said. "Strange goings-on in Bijou Mer. No good can come of mixing with that."

"What kind of strange goings-on?"

Shaking her head, she muttered, "All kinds of things. Floating lights, strange music, odd animals. It's unnatural."

I felt torn between laughter and fear at this odd warning. She seemed weirdly fascinated, painting a place she seemed to distrust so deeply.

I met the woman, Lois, and her shaggy white dog in the

empty lobby, and she set me up with a room in the attic. My attic room, with its peaked ceiling and dormer windows that looked out to Bijou Mer, made me want to stay forever, in spite of Lois's hard manner.

For dinner, she ladled me out some soup she'd made the night before with vegetables from her garden out back, as her dog rested its head on my thigh under the rough wooden table. I gobbled every bite down, and when I held the bowl to my lips to tip the last drops in, I caught Lois almost smile. *Almost.*

Not long after the sun set, she bid me good night, and I tromped up to my own bedroom, exhausted.

I awoke in the middle of the night, bits of a song I'd been humming in my dreams still floating off my lips. I rubbed at my tired eyes and blinked them open, then lay very still. No, I still heard it.

I walked barefoot across the rough wood floor and pushed open the stiff window. I gazed out at Bijou Mer, now an island surrounded by the dark water reflecting the pinprick light of the stars. A slim moon shone in a sly smile above the town.

I squinted and leaned halfway out the window, the breeze catching my red locks and playing them about my face. Were those lights floating below the surface of the water? I rubbed my bleary eyes again. No, they had to be the stars reflecting off the moving surface of the water... didn't they?

And that music. It gusted toward me on the wind now and then. Beautiful and eerie—could it be wind chimes? Or whales? In any case, lights lined the streets of Bijou Mer, the whole city glowing and twinkling out on the water. For a place that had no lodging, it certainly came alive at night.

Back in bed, I left the window open. I wanted the breeze and the strange music inside with me as I drifted off to odd and wonderful dreams.

13

BIJOU MER

The next morning I woke early and slipped on the only clothes I owned. Lois fed me a warm breakfast and eyed my slippers when I announced I was off to Bijou Mer.

"What size shoe do you wear?"

She told me to wait, and fetched me a pair of black leather boots. "We're nearly the same size. These are old, you can have 'em."

When I threw my arms around her in a big hug, she waved me off. "Don't go gushing over a pair of old shoes, after all." But her pale eyes twinkled. She warned me, twice, not to miss the last ferry back, then I took off to explore.

As I trekked across the marsh to Bijou Mer, I felt grateful for my new shoes. I kept waiting to feel the squish of water between my toes as I plunged my foot into mud puddle after mud puddle, but the boots did their job. No duct tape needed on those babies.

Seagulls cawed and flocked overhead, their white-and-gray bodies like clouds in the clear blue sky. Spires rose from the top of the mountain, while stone buildings spiraled all around its sides. What a lovely idea—a town on a mountain, becoming an island each night. I rubbed my chilled arms and let the wind play with my hair.

When I finally reached the base, my legs ached from the walk. I grinned in delight to find that I had to enter the tall stone city walls by drawbridge, passing under a stone arch and the dangling iron spikes of a portcullis. *Of course, because this town couldn't get any more charming.*

Once inside, I forgot all about my aches and bounded forward, unable to stop myself. A maze of streets opened before me, all impossibly narrow, the tall thatched buildings leaning in to nearly meet above the cobblestone streets. Shop signs and wrought iron lanterns dangled from their sides. I passed souvenir shops, a wine cart, and several taverns, closed up for the morning. Up and up I wound, losing all sense of direction as I explored.

As the day went on, the streets filled with men, women, and children, echoing with the sound of chatter and footsteps, while the seagulls cawed overhead.

I passed through streets where the buildings on the first floor had no windows or doors, only solid stone foundations, with stone steps leading from the street up to the front doors high above. Stone archways passed over these strange roads, stained and covered in lichen. Fish sculptures poked their gilled heads from the stone walls, mouths wide open, fins splayed, globular eyes pointing in different directions.

I grinned at every new narrow alley, at every black cat that darted across my path, at the cawing gulls, at the hot sun and the cool shade cast by crooked, latticed buildings.

After a few happy hours of wandering, I came across a courtyard where a crowd milled. I meandered past some bistro tables and eyed a baguette sandwich—the crisp, golden brown bread calling to me, leaves of basil and big white mounds of mozzarella poking out the sides.

I pulled the letter out of my pocket and reread the instructions. "Old Miller's Quarters, back garden, Royal Palace." Someone had to have an idea of where that was. Hopefully, someone who spoke English. I didn't need to be there till tomorrow morning, but I wanted to locate it today so I knew where to go. But, I probably had time for lunch.

A few minutes later and few euros lighter, I sat at a table under a white umbrella, crunching happily away at my sandwich. I licked up every last crumb, then sat in the sun, the occasional sea breeze making its way between the tightly packed buildings and rustling my hair.

I watched people go by, tourists mostly, gazing up at the tall buildings or at the wares lining the shop windows. The odd person strode past more quickly and directly, eyes ahead instead of gazing about like everyone else. *Locals, I bet. Maybe shopkeepers.*

Or could they work in the royal palace? I'd gathered from a map I picked up that the palace perched atop the mountain. I'd been winding my way up and up and had no idea how close I might be to the top.

After a couple of hours lounging and people watching, I roused myself and began again to climb. I popped into a soap makers, smelling every single bar, some like nothing I'd encountered in my whole life. I couldn't even guess if it were herb or nut or flower. The shopkeeper indulged me for a while then asked me to please stop putting my nose on everything.

I popped into a shop that sold tea leaves out of bulk barrels and another shop located in an alcove in the stone, lined with shelves of handmade pottery. If I'd had enough money I'd have bought one of everything.

As I wound higher and higher, the crowds thinned until, instead of bumping shoulders with every step, I went minutes before passing another soul.

I'd just passed by a narrow, shaded alleyway when the earthy smell of baking bread wafted into my nose and made me backtrack. I followed my nose down the alley's twists and turns, past stacked wooden crates and a hissing patchy cat. The sounds of the hustle and bustle faded away, until only my footsteps scraping over the stones kept me company.

My ears pricked at the tinkling of wind chimes nearby, and as I rounded a sharp bend between overhanging buildings, I spotted an uneven wooden sign above a doorway sporting a faded painting of a loaf of bread. As the heavy door closed behind me, I blinked, letting my eyes adjust to the murky light inside.

A few candles burned in wall sconces. The large front window lay in shade, and the thick layer of dust and cobwebs coating the window further diluted the dim light. I walked to the center of the shop. The space behind the counter stood empty, the till unmanned.

"Hello?"

I listened for an answer.

A crash sounded and some muffled shouting, then another shout. I cleared my throat loudly, trying to announce my presence, but the argument continued. *Awkward.*

I turned to leave, and an unusual assortment of eggs in baskets along the counter caught my eye. In front of each, a little label announced their type: tiny, spotted robin eggs, brown-and-white speckled chicken eggs, white swan eggs, bright Indigo eggs the size of my head labeled miniature dragon eggs. I paused at that one and grinned. Maybe they were dyed ostrich eggs for the tourists? Next to the huge eggs sat teeny, tiny ovals labeled snake eggs.

Another crash made me jump. A deep voice boomed, "Glenn." A sound of disgust. "Why, our Maple will knock him down a peg or two, I tell ya that." Another metallic crash sounded, like baking sheets clanging together. "He'll think twice about saying those things about our guild when one of our own is the next royal baker."

14

THE FERRY

A stocky bald man with beefy arms rounded the corner and came toward the till, calling back over his shoulder, "Oak, grab the list, will ya? Oh!"

He jumped when he saw me and smoothed his large hands down the front of his stained apron. "Oh, I'm sorry, I didn't hear you come in, miss. I, uh, hope you haven't been waiting long?" He swallowed and glanced over his shoulder a few times. "Oak! That list?"

I shook my head. "Oh no, it's all right." *Geez, I'd hate to get on this guy's bad side.* "I did overhear you mention something about the royal baker?"

His blond brows shot up his head, red splotches flushing his cheeks. "I, uh, I'm not sure what you heard but—"

"I've been chosen to be part of the contest." I leapt in to help ease his confusion. "But I'm not sure where to go, can you point me in the right direction?"

He lifted his chin. "You are, eh?" He squinted at my unicorn shirt and folded his enormous forearms across his chest. "You from the Earth Kingdom?"

I blinked at him, my brows drawing together in confusion. "Earth Kingdom? No, I'm not from any kingdom."

He slammed his broad hands down on the counter, rattling the baskets of eggs. He shook one finger at me, eyes narrowed. "You a Badlander then, eh? Out!"

I jumped back. "No, I'm from the US."

He frowned. "An immigrant? Where you originally from?"

I shrugged. "I grew up in Missouri, but I was adopted, so I'm not sure where I was born."

"Hm." *Apparently he finds that answer acceptable?* "My daughter's in the contest too, ya know."

I smiled. "Really? Does she know the way to the place we're supposed to meet, the, uh—" What had the letter said? "The Miller's Quarters, at the Royal Palace?"

The man thumbed over his shoulder. "Maple's already up there, but it's not too hard to find. You staying on the grounds as well?"

"Oh, um." The letter hadn't mentioned lodging. I thought back to Lois's warnings—she'd said that travelers stuck on the island at night had never been heard from again, or their bodies had washed up on shore the next morning, or they'd gone mad, ranting of voices and faces below the sea. "No, for now I'm staying in St. Rael. In an attic," I added, though I had no idea why.

His brows lifted again. "Well, if that's the case, you should head back down. Ferry's leaving any minute now."

I jumped. "Really? Any minute?"

He nodded. "Go out, head right down the alley, two twists, three right turns, and you'll hit the main road. Just head down and you'll find it... but I'd run."

I jogged backwards, bumping into a table filled with unsold bread, cobwebs catching on my jeans.

"Oh, and when you see Maple, tell her her papa says hello and good luck!"

I nodded. If she were anything like her quick-tempered father I'd do my best to stay as far away from her as possible.

I skidded down the alley, already darkening in the setting sun. The hazy darkness caused me to stumble over the uneven cobblestones. Not the easiest place to find, that bakery. No wonder there'd been no customers. After banging my shin on a crate, I hobbled out onto the main road, empty of all people. I sped downhill without seeing anyone, my chest tight from my racing heart and a creeping sense of something being very off.

Dong! Dong! Deep bells rang out. The map had indicated several temples with bells in Bijou Mer, the largest and oldest one at the top of the mountain. Dong! The sound of time running out.

As dusk deepened, and darkness settled around me, I burst forward out of a narrow road and slammed into a waist-high stone wall, the vista suddenly open to the sea below and everything beyond. The sea crept up the sides of the stone walls bordering the base of the mountain, the water level nearly covering them. Many twists and turns of the road below, I made out the rectangular ferry, beaded in white string lights, and the line of passengers boarding up the gangway. "Wait!" I shouted at the same time another bell rang out. I bounced on my heels, anxiety constricting my chest. They probably couldn't hear me from up here anyway.

I pushed off the cold stone wall and dashed back out to a wider road. I sprinted down, hoping I wouldn't break my neck on the uneven cobblestones. Torches sprang to life all around me, as did lamps and string lights, though I still passed no one. Dong!

I ran faster, a stitch pinching my side. Strange shadows flickered against the wall to my side, and I looked around but saw no one. A chill crept up my spine. I had to get to that ferry.

I slipped on a slimy stone and skidded into a stone wall. I jumped when a trickle of water dribbled from one of the stone fishes' mouths above my head. *Great, fish drool on my head.* I dodged to the side as the dribble spluttered, then turned into a gushing fire hose.

I looked up and down the passageway. Every twenty feet or so, another fish poured water, and I realized I wasn't standing in a street, but a canal. A canal that was now filling rapidly with water.

I splashed on, the water swirling up around my ankles. In the dim light I searched for a way out. The canal walls stretched far above my head and the smooth stones felt too slick to climb. My breaths coming in frantic pants, I waded through the calf-high (and rising) water, and nearly cried with relief when I found a stone stairway set into the wall.

I sloshed up the stairs and doubled over at the top, trying to catch my breath. When I straightened and looked around for a path down to the ferry, I found myself another tier higher than I'd been before, with no clue how to find the main street. I whimpered, picked a direction, and dashed on, my feet squishing in my wet boots. Dong!

Lights sprung on in shop windows and taverns. Voices and laughter trickled out into the night air, but still I saw no one. When I came face-to-face with a gaunt young man, I recoiled, gasping. I pressed a hand to my chest when I realized it wasn't an actual person, but a very lifelike drawing of one plastered to the side of a building.

"Wanted: Horace, leader of the Badlands Army."

The young man's hooded blue eyes seemed to bore into

mine. I backed away from the poster with the eerie feeling that it watched me. When I spun away, I noticed scores more posters lining the street. I'd have sworn they weren't there a minute ago.

A huge splash had me turning toward the now full canal to my left. My stomach clenched as a huge, iridescent green tail lifted out of the water and splashed back down again, the canal water glowing from below.

I spun and raced down, not stopping for the strange shadows, the watchful posters, or the haunting music that emanated from the canals. Dong! Dong! Dong! The bells rang with increasing frequency.

On and on I went, my thighs aching, toes throbbing from being jammed into the toes of my boots. I rounded a corner and found myself on a road that skirted the edge of the town. I realized the road was actually just the top of the city border wall, which now sat totally submerged except for the top foot or so. I could see the lights of St. Rael across the water and spotted the dock up ahead.

I waved my arms. "Wait!" I screamed. I tried again with my hands cupped to my mouth. "Wait!"

The ferry had already pulled away from the dock but was only about fifteen feet out to sea. They could still turn back. I sprinted on, willing myself faster and faster until I reached the docks. An older man pulled the folding iron accordion gate closed.

He looked up at me, his white mustache twitching. "Just missed it, I'm afraid."

15

THE RISING TIDE

Lois's warnings swam through my head. "I can't stay here," I yelled over the howling wind.

The older man locked the gate then came over to me. "Don't have lodging?"

I shook my head.

"All the rooms are booked for the Summer Solstice." He shrugged. "You're young. S'pose you could stay up all night at one of the taverns?"

I swept my hair back from my face, looking out to sea. For a moment, I considered the ludicrous idea of swimming out to the ferry, but the water had turned choppy and rough.

"Ah, lassie, we best be movin' to higher elevations. Tide's rising."

The churning sea lapped over the dock and licked at the stone road we stood on. I jumped back from the encroaching shoreline and followed the mustached ferryman up a set of switchback stairs carved into the rocky cliff. I looked over the edge.

The water already covered the gates the man had just

locked. *Climb faster, old man.* We made several more twists and turns before stepping out onto a narrow lane.

I jogged up the cobblestoned road, skirting the cliffside. My soggy boots scuffed along the uneven stones. The sea clawed its way up the street, flowing nearly up to our heels and then ebbing away.

I looked at the retreating waterline, then at the ferry man.

"Best to pick up the pace a wee bit."

I gasped when a cold spray licked up my back, soaking my shirt and the hair at my nape. The ferryman looked over my head and muttered, "Oh dear."

That couldn't be good.

He grasped my wrist and yanked us both into an alcove. A wave of water rushed by, soaking me up to my waist. The pull of it as it ebbed made us both brace against the sides of the stone alcove to avoid being dragged with it down to the sea. We looked at each other wide-eyed.

"Quick, while it's out."

We dashed back into the street.

"I know a shortcut."

I followed the older man up the street. I glanced back, and my stomach quaked as a huge wave coiled up. We dashed past a few more buildings, then made a quick turn into a shallow alley. He pointed at an iron ladder bolted to the side of a building.

"Climb!"

I hoisted myself up as quickly as I could, though my wet boots slipped on the rungs. The ladder rattled with the ferryman's steps. A giant wave frothed up the street, barreled into the alley below us, and churned around in the tight space. I shimmied up and up, my heart pounding in my chest as the whoosh of the sea below told me the water continued to climb.

Finally, I dragged myself onto a flat roof and turned, reaching an arm down. The ferryman grasped it, and I helped haul him up. We sat, panting, until the rising sea slowed down and then calmed. Only the top few feet of the ladder remained visible.

"Whew." The ferryman stood, dusting off his soaked blue work trousers and lifting his cap to run his fingers through his white hair. "That was a close one."

The sea had swallowed up entire buildings, leaving just the peaked roofs visible.

You don't say.

I followed the ferryman across a swaying rope bridge to a street a tier higher. We stopped at the edge of a broad street, standing in the shadows of an alley. Laughing crowds passed down the brightly lit road. Where'd all these people come from?

"This is the main street. You can stay up all night here and walk back in the morning."

I recalled the baker's words about his daughter staying on the royal grounds. "You don't know how to get to the palace, do you?"

"Why?"

"I'm in the baking contest."

His mustache twitched. "Well, why didn't you say so? Pssh. I'll take you there."

"Really, it wouldn't be a bother?"

"Not at all, not at all." He gestured toward the bustling, bright road. "We'll take Main Street all the way up. Where you from?"

We walked as I told him my story.

Silhouettes moved about inside brightly lit windows. A group of teenage girls bounced down the street, giggling. With flower crowns—and was that a cloud of moths fluttering above their heads?—they looked like forest fairies. Two older women, short despite the boost from their tall thong sandals, stood in a doorway. The bins outside their shop overflowed with glowing blue ice and fresh fish. They smiled as we passed, their faces round and wrinkled.

By the time I finished my story, the ferryman simply muttered, "Well, I'll be."

Ahead of us stretched one of the stone arches I'd thought were trellises. I saw now that they formed bridges over the canals. Water poured from the mouths of the fish sculptures, like a filling bath. I followed the ferryman out onto the railing-less bridge and peered down at the water.

Glowing orbs floated by under the surface. What could those be? A kind of bioluminescent fish? A shimmer flashed below. Had I just seen a tail? A large tail? The smiling face of a woman shot up out of the water, her wet, purple hair matted to her head and shoulders.

The woman looked around, saw the ferryman, and waved. He waved back. She turned to me and smiled, her face shimmering like glitter and her teeth oddly small. Then she dove into the water, and her shimmering, scaled tail flipped up, the huge fin waving as it dipped back below the surface.

"What is this?" I scrambled back on shaking legs.

"Merfolk."

My head hurt.

"Ah, come on, I guess you'll figure it all out soon enough."

We crossed the bridge and passed a fortune teller sitting

at a table at the mouth of an alley. She wore a turban and laid out tarot cards. "Care for your fortune, Imogen?" I slowed, but the ferryman grabbed my elbow and dragged me forward.

"Charlatans." He muttered the word so quietly I almost lost it under the din of music pouring from taverns on each side of the road.

"But how did she know my name? Maybe she really is psychic."

He rolled his eyes. "Of course she's psychic, but does that mean she's going to be honest with you about what she sees?"

I marveled at that. Really psychic? Was no one else impressed by that?

We passed a tavern with an outdoor patio, wrapped in trailing vines and blooming pale lilac flowers that perfumed the air far out into the street. A group of young men raised their frosted glass mugs then poured the bubbling blue liquid down their throats. As soon as they thudded their mugs back down on the table, the liquid refilled. I stopped. How could that be possible?

"Let me guess, never seen magically refilling mugs either?"

I shook my head. *Magical?*

He huffed. "You're too used to human ways."

"Human?" I jogged after him, doing my best not to trip as I marveled at the strange sights all around me. "Aren't we all human?"

"We're magic folk—you daft, girl? If we were human we'd a been on that boat down there."

"I tried to get on it." A woman with twin fires blazing on her shoulders strode by. I gaped, turning to watch her.

"Oh, don't encourage 'em. They jus' love to show off their fires." The ferryman led me uphill. "The temple bells are enchanted to make sure all humans board the ferry back to the mainland by the last launch."

I gaped at him. "But... I was told stories, about people staying on the island at night and going mad."

"Sometimes, if a human's got magic somewhere in his or her veins, way down the line, they may have enough to resist the wards. It's only happened once or twice. They didn't go mad, the other humans just didn't believe their stories and assumed they had. It's hard for most humans these days to accept the reality of magic."

It became easier to concentrate on his words as we left the loud streets below and climbed into darker, quieter neighborhoods.

"In the old days, they believed it all too well," the ferryman continued. "Some lived with us peacefully, but many wanted to use us or hurt us for our magic. So eventually we formed the kingdoms. Some of our kind mingle with the humans, the ambassadors, you know, and tradespeople, that sort. You need special permits to come and go and most of us never bother with it. Never been to human lands before myself, though I'm mighty curious about a few things. How do they get from place to place, long distances I mean, without magic?"

Magic? He had to be joking, right? Then again, how else could I explain all I'd seen? The mermaids, the beer mugs, the fortune teller... for that matter, the contest itself and how I'd somehow entered without that being possible. I stopped short, my chest tight. I fought for breath, my mouth opening and closing like a fish out of water.

"I believe you." I shook my head at him. Then laughed.

"That probably makes me absolutely crazy, but I believe you. I believe in magic."

"And I believe in oxygen." He scowled. "Young lady, you'd best believe, you're part of a magical baking contest that starts tomorrow."

16

MAGIC

My smile dropped. "It's a *magical* contest? But... I don't have magic."

The ferryman motioned me forward and I followed numbly. "First of all, of course you have magic. You couldn't have even entered without it."

I held up a finger. "Actually, I never really entered. I baked a shortcake, wrapped in the flyer like it said to do, but before I could mail it, my apartment burned down."

He laughed and shook his head. "You're like a baby, that's how much you know. The flyer was enchanted, lassie, to transport your package to the address upon it. As soon as you wrapped up your cake, you sealed the spell and whoosh, off it went to the royal estate to be judged. So you definitely entered. And you would've been on that ferry if you didn't have magic. You're one of us, and you best accept that."

I blinked at him. Believing in magic was one thing, but believing I had magic when I had a lifetime's worth of evidence to the contrary was another.

We hiked on in silence. The crash of the waves, now far

below, kept a steady beat for us and bats swooped overhead whistling and squeaking. We passed over another stone bridge, the water below teeming with glowing orbs and glittering tails. I sighed. Between the tiny lights that hovered among the leaves of the trees, the mermaids, the soft music that seemed to emanate from the water, and the occasional deep ringing of temple bells, I found myself in love. This city buzzed with magic and life and beauty.

The road narrowed, the cobblestones even and better paved. We approached a tall, elaborately woven, wrought iron gate with gold leaf accents. Two guards in blue, green, and gold livery stood at attention. When we approached, they lowered their lances, forming an X over the gate.

"State your business."

The ferryman leaned toward me. "Show them your competition materials."

"Oh right." I fumbled in my bag and pulled the documents out, handing them to the guard on the left. "I'm here for the baking contest."

The guard glared at my face, then looked over the passport.

I turned to the ferryman. "Do ticket agents and such know about this place? About magic? They seemed to recognize that passport."

He shook his head. "Lass. It's the spell. When a nonmagical person sees that document, it's spelled to make them as helpful to the person bearing it as possible. Then they forget all about it."

I grinned. "That's awesome."

The other guard spoke into a glowing earpiece.

"We're summoning the contest coordinator. She'll escort you to your lodgings, Miss Banks."

I sighed with relief. At least I'd found the right place.

"Well, this is where I leave ya."

I turned to the ferryman. "Thank you so much. I would have been lost without you."

He waved me off. "I know."

I grinned and reached out a hand. "Imogen."

He looked at my hand, then stuck out his hand in the same stiff manner, without taking mine. "Charlie."

I grinned, clasped his hand, and then shook it slowly. "That's how humans do it."

"Huh." He nodded. "Something new every day." He turned to go. "Say, Imogen, if you ever want to hear some local history from salty old barnacles like me, come by the Rusted Wreck. Won't see any of them fancy types there." He jerked his chin at the palace gates. "But they got a damn good clam chowder and cheap drinks."

I grinned. "The Rusted Wreck. I'd love that. And I can tell you all about human long-distance travel."

He nodded and waved goodbye. "See ya around. And good luck tomorrow." He froze. "One more thing."

I raised a brow.

"Be careful. I'm guessin' you don't know about the last royal baker. She was murdered, through and through, no matter what they tell ya. Someone's out for the bakers, so you watch yourself and take care, ya hear?" Charlie walked off with one last wave.

I gulped. The woman at Victoria's rehearsal dinner had said something along those lines, too. Did I need to be worried?

A woman in a pencil skirt with a swirling hem appeared behind the gate. Her white hair stood out against her dark, smooth skin, and her dark eyes looked off into the middle distance.

She nodded, "Uh-huh, uh-huh. Well tell her that all

contestants are treated the same and she doesn't get an en suite bathroom because no one else does either." She rolled her eyes. "Fine, I will." She turned back to me as the gates separated magically, letting me through. She pulled something like a glowing white gumball out of her ear and tucked it into her pocket.

"Amelia Tate, Contest Coordinator. And I hear you're Imogen?"

I nodded. "Hi."

She swept an arm toward the expansive green grounds behind her. "Welcome to the Royal Estate. I'll show you to your quarters."

17

THE LADIES' FLOOR

Singing coming from the room next door woke me up the next morning. Last night, Amelia had warned me about the walls being paper thin. I listened harder to make out the lyrics.

> *"As I toiled in the kitchens one morn, one morn,*
> *By the heat of the flames and the wet of*
> *the sweat,*
> *I spotted a rat steal an ear of corn,*
> *And I vowed when we met, that crime he'd regret.*
>
> *In a furious rage I cast a spell, a spell,*
> *Sent a fiery blast to cause the thief great grief,*
> *Cursed and lashed out all pell mell,*
> *And instead of the rat, I extirpated the beef."*

I chuckled into the sheets. The violent lyrics, contrasted with the girl's cheery tone, got me.

> *"The flames caught the curtains alight, alight,*

*I called on the heavens to redress the mess,
As the rain poured down, the rat gave me a bite,
And that's how I caught my plague-like illness."*

I had to meet this girl. I climbed out of the sleeping alcove that held my bed.

Last night, my mind whirring with magic and the competition, I'd been convinced I'd never fall asleep. But the down bed took care of that. I'd had the best sleep of my life.

I lowered my bare feet to the warm wood floor. French doors opened to a field that ended in a sharp drop off to the sea below. I threw them open and stood with arms spread wide. The rush of the sea met my ears, the air humid and salty.

I left the doors open and did a little happy dance as I turned back to my room. With tall ceilings, exposed stone walls, and the doors to the field outside, I was in heaven.

Though it was tiny, it felt cozy and airy. I liked the simplicity. Besides a desk, the only other furniture was an armchair and a wardrobe. Maybe it held some extra clothes in my size? I *was* in a magical kingdom; a girl could hope.

I opened the twin doors to find empty wooden hangers and below that two empty drawers. *Bummer*. I had on all the clothes I owned—jeans, a cami, and a unicorn T-shirt. I pulled on the socks and boots Lois had given me. Amelia had promised to send her word that I was all right and staying in Bijou Mer.

I picked up my complimentary toiletries and headed left down the hallway. An enamel sign on the last door read Toilette. I knocked, three short thuds.

"Occupied."

I waited... and waited some more. Finally I knocked again.

"What?"

I didn't want to get off on the wrong foot with a fellow contestant, especially if she was the baker's daughter and had inherited his burly arms and temper. "Hi. I'm Imogen."

"Yes?"

"Well, Amelia said there's only one bathroom on the women's floor, so I don't mean to rush you, but if I could just brush my teeth, I'll be out in a jiffy and you can have it back, if you need more time?" I winced, scratching at the tendrils at my nape while I waited for a reply.

"That's true. Only one bathroom, so we'll all have to learn to share."

I forced myself to wait before replying, so as not to say something I'd regret. "Sharing *is* caring. I'll just wait then, I suppose. Right here. Outside the door."

"Patience is a virtue," sang the high-pitched voice.

A creak down the hall alerted me to another door opening. A blond girl, rubbing roughly at her eyes, emerged. I couldn't be sure, but it looked like she came out of the door next to mine.

She wore pink flannel pajamas patterned with horses that magically galloped around the fabric, over her shoulder, and down her shins. I grinned and lifted my hand in a tentative wave. She looked behind her as she made her way toward me, then flashed me a shy smile.

"Hallo." She winced at the bathroom door. "Occupied?"

I nodded.

"Is it Pritney again?"

I shrugged. "I don't know anyone yet."

She folded her arms. "How long has she been in there?"

I whispered, "Ages."

The girl huffed. "Pritney then." She leaned against the wall beside me. "I'm Maple."

The baker's daughter! Not the burly Amazon I'd expected. "Imogen. I met your father yesterday, he told me to tell you good luck from him."

"You met my pa?" Maple groaned and buried her sleep-lined face in her hands. "Urgh. He means well, but he's so... so embarrassing." Maple let her hands drop and she frowned at the bathroom door again. "I seriously might wet myself, right here in the hall, if she doesn't hurry." She scooted closer to me. "I'd tell her so too, if she didn't terrify me."

I grinned.

Another door opened next to Maple, startling us both. A gray, wiry mop of hair poked out the doorway. A wrinkled face with tiny squinting eyes blinked at us.

Maple grinned at me. "Lillian, this is Imogen. Imogen, Lillian."

I waved hello.

"Why you two young things hangin' around outside my door?"

Maple raised her brows and sighed, poking a thumb at the bathroom.

She shuffled into the hall in a stained nightshirt, a large hole at the seam revealing a bony shoulder. She scratched her side. "When you get old, your bladder ain't what it used to be. When I need to get to the toilet, I need to get there fast. Which is why"—she shuffled past us and balled her bony hand into a fist, then bellowed—"it does not fly to have young things occupyin' the toilet to do their hair and makeup."

I cringed, covering my ears. Lillian continued to pound

at the door. At that rate she'd wake up the entire women's floor and maybe the men above us, too.

The door flung open and Lillian jumped back, fists still raised to pummel the door… or maybe the person behind it. A tall, impeccably dressed blond stood huffing in the doorway. She stared daggers at Lillian with her piercing blue eyes. Her straight nose flared at the nostrils and her thin lips peeled back in a snarl. "Done. You satisfied, you old witch?"

Lillian dropped her fists and gave the blond a cheeky grin. "Very." She shouldered past, turning to Maple and me. "Cutting ahead. You girls understand." She slammed the door behind her, leaving us alone in the hall with the tall, fuming blond. She shook long, pale locks out her eyes.

"Hi, I'm Imogen." I reached forward to shake her hand.

She looked me hard in the face. "You said already." She walked away, leaving me hanging. Her perfume filled the whole hallway with its cloying scent.

Maple gave me a nudge with her shoulder. "She's like that with everyone."

"Oh, and Imogen?" I turned to find Pritney poking her head out her door. "I really like your shirt. Very brave." She slammed the door shut before I could respond.

I glanced down. *What's wrong with a unicorn tee?*

Maple put a hand on my shoulder. "I like it, personally. What is it?"

I pulled the hem of my shirt down so she could see it clearly. "A unicorn."

Maple's blond brows jumped up her forehead. "That's not what any unicorn I've ever seen looks like."

"You've seen a unicorn?"

Lillian threw the bathroom door open, and to Maple's pleading look, I waved an arm. "Go for it."

18

ORIENTATION

I did eventually get to brush my teeth and hair. I piled a big round bun on the top of my head and did my best to smooth down my red curtain of bangs. I then grabbed my collection of recipes and headed down the hall, toward the sound of voices. I stepped through a small crowd gathered at the front door and joined Maple outside on the lawn.

"So, these are the other competitors?" I glanced at Maple, who nodded. "Have you met them all?"

"Briefly." Maple sighed and tilted her head to the side. "I'd like to get to know him, I mean them better." She blinked lazily, and I followed her gaze to a tall, dark-skinned guy. He had black curly hair and a neatly sculpted black beard. With his arms folded across his chest, an intricate brown tattoo was visible, wrapping around his right hand and forearm. *Intense.*

"I can see why." I grinned. "What's his name?"

"Wool." She barely breathed it.

"Where's Mr. McHottie from?"

Her cheeks flushed bright pink. "Fire Kingdom."

I laughed. "Of course, where everything's *hot*."

Wool looked up, and I followed his gaze to the field. Three people walked toward us. I recognized Amelia with her short white hair, but I'd never seen the other two before. More contestants?

Maple edged closer. "The judges." Her voice came out as a squeak.

Amelia raised her arms "Contestants, welcome! Congratulations on making it into the competition. Today, we'll give you a tour of the grounds, the rules of the competition, and a chance to get to know each other. As you all know, I'm Amelia Tate, Contest Coordinator. If you need anything or have any questions, I'm the one to ask."

A dark-skinned, stocky guy shot his arm into the air.

"Let's hold our questions until after I've explained a few things." He nodded but kept his arm raised. Amelia's nostrils flared. "Glenn, just put your arm down."

Glenn? The name sounded familiar.

Maple leaned in. "Glenn's on the Earth Kingdom's Baker's Guild board."

Recognition slipped into place. Her father had been shouting about Maple beating Glenn. "So, he's your mortal enemy?"

Maple rolled her eyes, but grinned.

"As I was saying," Amelia continued. "The competition will begin tomorrow. Each day, you'll face a trial, as determined by our judges. At the end of each day, one contestant will be eliminated, for the first seven days. The remaining three will move on to the final. The winner will earn the title of Royal Baker for the Water Kingdom, a prestigious and lucrative position, and can hire two from the pool of contestants on as staff. We hope this contest will foster friendship and cooperation among the kingdoms in preparation for the Summer Solstice. Speaking of which, the new royal baker will be charged with creating a special bake for the Summer Solstice feast to be held the day after the final."

Glenn raised his hand but when Amelia gave him a sharp look, he dropped it.

"Next, I'd like to introduce you to two people, who likely need no introduction." Amelia stepped to the side and swept her arm out in a grand gesture. "Francis Valhaven, vampire celebrity personality with an exquisitely refined palate."

The tall vampire loomed above us, narrow shoulders squared, long black hair slicked back, eyes lined in charcoal like an Egyptian. He bowed. I frowned. Was anything I thought I knew about vampires correct? Francis hovered in the sunshine, so they could clearly venture into the light. And if he were judging a baking contest he ate things besides blood.

Unless all of our bakes were to be blood cakes with blood frosting. I shuddered. *Gross.*

"And Rhonda the Seer, celebrity psychic and renowned baker."

The dark girl with a halo of shoulder-length tiny braids stepped forward, smiling beatifically. Suddenly, her body jerked, and she threw her head back to the sky, slapping a palm over her eyes. I leaned forward as a golden circle of light glowed on her forehead. Just as suddenly, she relaxed with a gasp, dropping her hand.

"I have just received a vision," she announced in a slightly stuffy voice, as if her nose was plugged. She pointed at the tall, dark-haired young man with the large nose. "You there. You shall *not* marry a princess." Rhonda smiled, looking very pleased with herself.

The guy froze for a moment, his thick brows lifted. Then

he shook his head slightly. I leaned closer to Maple and whispered, "Yeah, and I shall *not* turn into a spider." I chuckled at my own joke, but Maple gave me a serious look.

"She's never wrong, like ever, and she has a *lot* of visions."

I swallowed, my laughter dying. "Really?"

Maple nodded.

Amelia smiled at the blond bathroom hog. "Why don't you all introduce yourselves to each other and the judges? Pritney, how about you start us off?"

She perched on a stone windowsill as if she were posing for a magazine shoot. "I'm Pritney. I apprenticed under the last royal baker."

Wool spoke next, his voice low and his accent seductive. I nudged Maple, whose cheeks glowed pink. Then came Zeke, a scruffy, pudgy guy with a long brown ponytail and bushy brown beard. "I'm Zeke. Grew up in the Earth Kingdom, then moved to the Air Kingdom. I believe in natural living, so I hope to show you that baked goods can be healthy and delicious." He nodded several times, grinning and brushing his hair out of his eyes. Maybe it was the way he sounded like a surfer, but there was just something instantly likable about Zeke.

Next came Bern from the Air Kingdom, a tall, bald guy wearing glasses. He worked as a magicneer, and brought a technical mind to baking. Then Lillian introduced herself—it involved a lot of wild laughter. Then came Glenn.

"I'm on the council for Earth's Baking Guild, the most prestigious guild in the kingdoms."

Wool snorted.

A man named Sam shifted nervously, shrugging as if his clothes fit too tight. His voice, when he spoke, startled me, for the low drawl didn't seem to belong to the chinless man with large ears and glasses.

Then came the tall, brooding guy with the overlarge crooked nose, who according to Rhonda would *not* marry a princess. "I'm Hank and I'm from the Water Kingdom."

Next, Maple stammered her way through introductions, and I went last.

"Hi, I'm Imogen. So, I've just discovered magic exists—"

"What!" Amelia stalked toward me, her gray eyes round. "Repeat. Repeat what you said. You just discovered magic? What do you mean by that?"

I swallowed, and smiled brightly out of nerves. "I always thought I was human... until yesterday."

"Your parents didn't tell you you're a witch?" Amelia panted.

You're a witch, the childish part of me wanted to retort.

Even Maple blinked at me in surprise.

I rubbed my neck with both hands. "I never knew my parents, my birth parents. I was adopted." *I should probably clarify.* "By humans."

Amelia staggered a few steps back. She held the gumball earpiece thing and spoke into it. "We have a situation."

19

VISIONS

Amelia waved at me to follow her. "Talk amongst yourselves."

I felt the other contestants' eyes on me as the judges and I followed Amelia to the back of the house. I felt like I was being led to the principal's office.

We stopped under a massive tree.

"What do you mean, you just discovered magic?" Amelia's big gray eyes darted up and down the length of me. "You can't compete if you don't know magic. Oh geez, we're going to have to get an alternate in here." She pressed the white gumball thing to her ear. "Smit, I'm gonna need you to call up our list of alternates and see who can be here by this afternoon." The wind shook the heavy boughs above us.

The tall vampire raised his dark, lined eyes to mine. "Hold on, Amelia," Francis drawled in a deep voice. "I tasted her bake. It reeked of magic. The girl may not know how to control it, but she possesses magic, I'm certain of it."

I still didn't believe I possessed magic, despite the vampire's confidence. Next to him, Rhonda the young Seer held up her hands, neon pink and green nails flashing.

She nodded, sending her shoulder-length black braids bouncing. "I had a vision, you know, that she would do quite well in the competition."

Really? Or was she just trying to help me out? Exasperated, Amelia lifted her eyes and said to the person on the other end of her ear gumball, "Forget it. Imogen's staying."

Francis literally floated back into the shadows, his feet hovering an inch above the ground. Rhonda, though, smiled and walked up to me. "You'll figure it out. My visions are never wrong." She suddenly threw a hand over her eyes and lifted her glowing forehead to the sky. "I'm getting another vision... two."

The spot at the center of her dark forehead glowed golden, her whole body seeming to suspend and stay still in a way that didn't seem humanly possible. Then again, apparently Rhonda wasn't human—and neither was I.

Suddenly, the glowing circle disappeared and Rhonda gasped in a huge breath of air. She grinned. "Woo. Doozy." Her smile dropped, and she said in her stuffed-up sounding voice, "You'll be intimately involved in a murder investigation."

My eyes blinked wide open. "Come again?"

"You'll be intimately involved in a murder investigation," she repeated, louder and slower.

I'd heard her. I just couldn't make any sense of it. Maybe her visions weren't time specific. Maybe, in the future, I became a detective or something? That seemed unlikely.

She lifted her chin, then dropped it. "In the next ten days during the competition."

"Whose murder?" Amelia gasped, her face full of horror. "She can't be in the competition if we know she's going to murder someone." She threw a wild look my way, and I hugged my collection of recipes to my chest like a shield.

"Don't know who dies. It's a gift, it reveals what it reveals and nothing more, nothing less." Rhonda held her hands with their brightly painted nails palm up and shrugged. "But you can't remove her from the competition, because I see her in it. Definitely in it. And I didn't say she killed anyone, I mean she might, she's just involved in the investigation. But I would tighten security, yeah, for sure."

Amelia looked like she wanted to strangle Rhonda but stepped back a few paces and began hissing at someone through her ear device. Rhonda turned back to me.

"The second vision...."

I didn't want to know.

Rhonda smiled. "Don't worry. It's good news." She stepped closer. "That bowel movement you've been waiting for is on its way. Soon, I'd say, very soon, you'll have relief."

My mouth dropped open.

"Don't be embarrassed, travel always messes up my rhythm, too."

The word rhythm had never sounded so gross.

Rhonda, a few inches shorter than me, patted my shoulder bracingly and lowered her voice. "Around two thirty, three o'clock-ish, I should find myself near a toilet if I were you."

We rejoined the others, and Amelia led us across the green grounds toward the tent where we'd be doing our baking. We passed by a cypress hedge and a tall stone wall behind it.

"On the other side of this fence is the Water Temple, the biggest and oldest on the island. Just beyond that is the Royal Palace. All of you will be invited to attend the Summer Solstice feast, but with heightened security due to threats from the Badlands Army, I'm afraid we won't be able to tour the palace beforehand."

"They normally do tours?" I tried to peek over the hedge, my curiosity piqued.

Maple nodded. "It's beautiful, I've gone a few times."

We reached the tent, the long white fabric peaked in three places, and one side rolled up. We entered it through the rolled-up side, and as we did I felt a shimmery cool tingle fall across my skin. I looked around, but saw nothing.

"You know, if you've rolled the sides for airflow," Bern said, peering through his glasses at the flaps, "it'd work much better if you lifted the other side as well."

Amelia nodded. "That side is rolled up because that's where the bleachers will go."

"Bleachers?" Maple paled.

Amelia gestured to the grass just outside the tent. "We've invited spectators to cheer you on. And...." She pressed her lips together and raised her thin brows high. "There'll be some very special guests at tomorrow's opening day." She looked around. "Any guesses?"

Glenn's hand shot up.

"No? I'll tell you then, it's the Water Kingdom's royal family!"

Maple gagged and pressed her hands over her mouth, and Hank, who'd seemed so cocky and sure up till now, turned white as a cloud.

"Oh, don't let the pressure get to you." Amelia's smile dropped, and she practically growled, "Seriously. Don't. That's an order. Tomorrow has to go perfectly. The royal family's watching."

Maple slumped against me for support.

"Anyway." Amelia plastered on her smile again. "Each of you will have a station." The tent was divided into two rows, one closer to the open flap, the other set back. Each row contained five butcher-block countertops, with a sink set into each one, a pizza oven, and a cupboard.

The stations were staggered so that people in the bleachers could easily see all ten contestants working away. Watch their every move. I was not usually one to cave under pressure, but even my stomach turned at the thought.

"Some of you have expressed special needs and concerns." Amelia shot Glenn a flat look. "Pritney, we've arranged for a cushioned mat for your feet." She raised a brow at Pritney's stilettos. "Zeke, you'll have the table in the northeast corner, as requested."

Zeke grinned and nodded. "Nice. Thank you very much." He addressed the rest of us. "Best spot for vibrational energy reasons, hope y'all don't mind."

"And Glenn," Amelia continued, "we understand that you have a severe allergy to snake venom. Obviously none will be allowed in the tent, but we're also banning snake eggs, just to be on the safe side, as the yolks can be a source of venom. You'll also be required to pass through a magical protection field—you may have felt it on the way in. It'll scan you for anything contraband—poisons, black magic, snake eggs, etcetera, as well as reveal shifters."

Sam devolved into a coughing fit, and Lillian pounded his back. Francis drew himself up taller, hovering another couple of inches above the ground. "How singular." His dark eyes bored holes into Amelia.

She cleared her throat. "The spell forces shifters to reveal their second form, so if any had been among us, they would have transformed into their animal."

The vampire's full lips peeled back, revealing fangs. Amelia shrank back. "So I shall have to enter as a bat each day? Wonderful." Francis huffed. "And if a shifter should be revealed among them"—he swept his arm toward us—"they'd be disqualified?"

Amelia scratched her ear and looked away from Francis. "You obviously didn't turn into a bat, Francis. We made sure the spell excluded vampires. And as for a shifter, yes, he or she would be disqualified. The contest rules clearly excluded shifters from entering."

Francis hissed like a cat, and Amelia shrunk back. The vampire snarled, "Everyone seems to forget that vampires are a form of shifter and that as such, I too suffer when the magical world shows shifters such distrust."

I glanced at Maple. "What's all this about?"

"He's right," she said in a small voice. "Shifters aren't treated equally—people fear how deceptive they can be. Think about it—other kingdoms have shifter spies, people who can turn into bees and butterflies and cute little cats. It's hard to feel totally safe when a shifter's around."

I could see that point. But then again, with everyone possessing magical powers, weren't there a lot of things other folks could do to be sneaky also? Seemed unfair to single out shifters.

"Last, but not least," Amelia continued, a few steps further away from Francis, who continued to glare at her. "You'll be given the afternoon to practice and get the hang of your baking stations. I'm assuming everyone brought their own flames? Yes?"

I raised my hand and shook my head.

Amelia sighed heavily. "Right. Where are we going to find you a spare flame?"

Pritney piped up in an overly sweet voice. "Why doesn't she partner with Iggy?"

Amelia's brows drew together. "You think he'd go for it?"

Pritney smiled widely and batted her lashes. "Absolutely."

"Who's Iggy?"

Maple shrugged. "At least you'll have a flame though."

I frowned. I had a feeling I was in way over my head.

20

PRACTICE MAKES SOMETHING

Amelia folded her hands. "Tomorrow's challenge will be a showcase bake—something that shows off your skills. It can be anything you like. I suggest you spend the next few hours practicing. Also, I'd like to introduce you to our medic, Natsu." Amelia motioned to her left. A tall, golden-skinned man with dark, thick brows waved. He wore a navy-blue jumpsuit with a crest embroidered on it.

"You can call me Nate. And while I'd like to meet you all, I hope it's not because you've blown a hand off."

I grinned, and he flashed a bright white smile.

I turned back to Amelia, though it was difficult to pry my eyes off the handsome medic.

"He'll be on hand in case anything goes wrong or you're not feeling well. All right then, carry on!"

I swept a hand over the long butcher-block counter. I'd never had so much space in my life. In the cabinets below I found ceramic mixing bowls, spoons, whisks, and tin baking sheets. Now what to make? I drummed my fingers on the butcher block and looked around the tent for inspiration.

Everywhere, something fantastic caught my eye. Fire danced up Wool's arms and wrapped around his neck. As Lillian rolled out dough, little blue birds flew into the tent, perching on her shoulders and in her nest of hair, chirping away.

Bern bent low over his table, peering through his glasses. Reams of papers littered his table with drawings of molds and cakes. He muttered to himself, "It may take a few flying buttresses to maintain the integrity of the...." As he spoke, a feather quill danced magically across the papers, jotting down his specifications and outlining the drawings.

"That's incredible," I murmured.

"Oh, hmm?" He looked up at me over his spectacles, then down at the quill. "Ah, yes, quite handy. You charm it to jot down exactly what you do, so you can replicate it again, or tweak things for the next time."

I sighed. "That would be useful."

Bern straightened. "I can show you how if you'd like?"

I brightened. "I'd love that."

The middle-aged man came over to my station. "Do you have a recipe book?"

"I do!" I procured my folder of loose papers.

He nodded. "And a quill?"

I bit my lip. "I don't."

Bern looked around. "Maybe someone has a spare or—oh! That'll do. Lillian?"

The older woman looked up, birds flying round her head like a mobile.

"Might we borrow a feather to make a quill for Imogen?"

She grinned, showing off a few missing teeth. "Borrow? You going to return it to the birdie then?" She cackled, and with a flick of her wrist, a bright blue feather loosened itself from a bird and floated over to us. Bern plucked it out of the air. "Now we just need a bit of wood and metal."

I darted just beyond the tent and picked up a stick. "Will this do?" I felt like a Labrador playing fetch.

"Perfect." Bern collected it from me. "We could create all this from scratch, it just requires more effort to do so. The only thing you can't conjure from nothing is food, of all things. Now for a bit of metal."

"Oh!" I reached up into my bun and fished out a bobby pin. "How about this?"

Bern peered at it through his glasses. "Should work." He laid the feather, bobby pin, and stick on my station, then moved to his. He returned with a leather-bound book six inches thick.

My mouth hung open. "What is that?"

He grinned sheepishly and pushed his glasses up his nose. "My spell book. I've been accused of being overly thorough."

He flipped through the book. "Q, Q... ah, here it is, quills." He marked his place on a page covered in words and diagrams. Bern held his other hand over the ingredients. "Turn in a clockwise manner, okay."

He swirled his hand over the ingredients, then read from the book. "Metal for the nib, wood for the shaft, feather for the frill, magic make quill." A little flash of light followed, then a popping noise, and suddenly a quill lay on my table where the individual parts had been a moment ago.

"Thank you, that's amazing." I picked up the quill and pretended to scribble in the air. "And very practical. No 'hocus pocus' or 'alacazam'?"

He gave me a shy smile. "No. Afraid my spells are rather boring."

I smiled back. "How do I get it to write for me?"

Bern consulted a subcategory of his "quills" entry. "Why don't *you* try this one?"

My stomach turned with a mix of anxiety and excitement. "I'm not sure I can."

"It's the only way to learn," Bern said gently. "Hold the quill upright."

I did.

"Next, you draw on power from deep within. It's kind of like taking a deep breath, pulling magic up from your toes. Then you say, 'Quill, jot down all my recipes, true and right.'"

The quill vibrated in my trembling hand. I took a deep breath, imagined pulling magical energy up from my toes to my lungs and said, "Quill, jot down all my recipes, true and right."

I looked to Bern for confirmation. He nodded at the quill. Slowly, carefully, I pulled my fingers back and—it dropped to the tabletop. *Hmmph*. Disappointment sat heavy in my stomach.

"Try again," he said gently.

I did, again and again. Lillian counseled me to stand barefoot in the grass. Maple suggested I sing the words to a happy tune, and Zeke offered a wand. Hank helped by muttering, "Can't even do a simple spell, and they call this a competition." I wanted to kick him in the shins, but he was right. What was I doing here?

Bern ended up enchanting the quill for me. I stood over my table, happy to let everyone disperse to their own bakes while I calmed my nerves. I wanted this bad. Not only to win, but to learn to wield my magic. I had nothing to go home to.

Okay, I had a loving family in St. Louis to go home to, and

it was unfair to discount that. I leaned my head against my hand. But it made sense, why I'd always felt I didn't belong. I literally wasn't even human. I was... a witch. And not like Pritney was a witch in the personality sense of the word, but an actual, magic-wielding, cackle over a cauldron witch. And I had better learn how to be a darn good witch, or I'd be flying an airplane, instead of a broomstick, home tomorrow.

I heaved a great sigh. Well, I could always do poppy seed cake the traditional way. Maybe the judges would find my human techniques charming and quaint.

I flipped to the recipe in my book, the magical quill hovering at the ready. We had full access to the royal gardens behind the tent. Maybe they grew some edible flowers I could adorn the cake with.

As I walked to the pantry I passed Hank, who didn't look up, but huffed as I went by. I glared at him. Tall and sharp-jawed, he might have been handsome, despite that large crooked nose, if he weren't scowling all the time.

A frosted glass jar of cream flew past my head, the cold of the jar stinging my cheek. I jumped and looked back. The jar floated softly onto Sam's table. He raised a hand. "Sssorry!"

Shaky, I raised a hand back and nodded. *It's okay that you almost decapitated me with a jar of cream.*

I dipped into the pantry, a small room lined floor-to-ceiling with shelves. I touched a frosted jar of syrup and yanked my fingers back from another jar wrapped in a band of flames. The liquid inside bubbled. I guessed with magic you didn't need refrigerators to keep things cold, or slow cookers to warm them. *Handy.*

Ducking under a bunch of dried herbs hanging from the ceiling, I gathered a carafe of cow's milk, a jar of butter, plucked a couple of speckled chicken's eggs from a basket, and grabbed a small burlap sack of poppy seeds.

When I returned to my station I moved to set my oven to three hundred and fifty degrees, but didn't see a dial. A sneaking suspicion caused my chest to grow tight. I threw open the cabinets. No electric mixer either. I patted around the tabletop and sides of the counters, my breathing coming faster and faster.

21

SICK BURN

Rhonda the Seer rushed up to me and put her hands on my shoulders.

"What are you looking for?" Her eyes searched my face.

"There's no electricity." I needed to sit down.

"I'm not sure what you're talking about," Rhonda said. "Let's ask Amelia. AMELIA!" she screamed. "AMELIA!"

Outside the tent, Amelia stood talking with a small group of men with hammers and long boards of wood thrown over their shoulders. She held up a finger, said a few more words to the men, and then stalked over, a tight smile on her face. "Yes? What?"

Rhonda pointed a neon-green-and-pink fingernail at me. "Imogen needs licktricity."

Amelia turned to me, eyebrow cocked.

"Electricity. I— That's what I cook with at home."

"Oh right, the flame." Amelia grabbed a handful of grass, spoke a few words into her palms, and then blew the blades into the air. As they fell onto my table they caught fire, growing into a bright orange-and-gold flame. "There. Anything else?"

I blinked at the fire, which miraculously wasn't spreading. "How do I cook with it?"

Amelia threw an arm toward the oven below the counter. "Put it in the oven." She pressed a finger to her earpiece. "Be right there." She dashed off.

Rhonda the Seer gave me a double thumbs-up, then skipped off.

I turned back to the flame sitting on my table. "Okay, how to get it into the oven."

"It? Rude. Maybe I'll just call you 'it.'"

I staggered a few steps back. My fire had just spoken. I looked around the tent, but no one had seemed to notice. Or maybe they just didn't find it that remarkable. "You can speak."

"Oh, we've got a real genius here." My fire had a very low, droll English accent, and a face, two round eyeballs with black dots in the center and mouth that gaped open when it spoke.

"I'm Imogen." I reached out a hand in greeting, then pulled it back when the flame roared higher and hotter. "Right. Fire. Will burn." I chuckled nervously, rubbing my arm.

The fire continued to stare me down.

"What's your name?"

"I'm only telling you because I don't wish to be addressed as 'it.'"

I nodded. "Sorry about that."

"Iggy. My name is Iggy."

"All right then. Iggy." I plastered on a smile. "Could you — I mean, would you mind—" I swept both hands toward the oven.

Iggy's eyes grew small.

I stood there waiting, my palms open. I gave him a toothy grin. "Maybe we can work together?" I was pleading with a flame. A flame who continued to glare at me. Warmth rushed to my chest and cheeks. I could see my bad luck with fire was only continuing. I stomped my foot. "Get in there!" I jabbed my finger at the oven.

Iggy gave me a cruel smile and slid over the counter into the mouth of the oven, leaving a charred black trail behind. "As you command."

I took a few calming breaths. Maybe that had been a little rude of me. Okay, a lot. I crouched down in front of him, worried my eyebrows might be in danger of being singed off.

"We got off on the wrong foot."

"I don't have feet, witch."

I closed my eyes for several moments, willing the anger inside me to simmer down. "Figure of speech. We started off badly. But I'd like it if we could start over."

He said nothing.

"Could you, please, heat the oven to three hundred and fifty degrees? I'd very much appreciate it."

His eyes flashed and a slow grin spread across his face, until he burst into laughter, his fire gusting with each deep-throated chuckle.

I shifted, balancing on my toes. "What?"

He continued to laugh. "Do you think I'm a thermometer?"

Maple came to stand by me. "Flames are tricky."

I rolled my eyes toward Wool, whose fire danced along his arms. "Doesn't seem tricky for anyone else."

"Wool's had his flame since birth." A pink blush spread over her cheeks. "It's why the Fire Kingdom has such good bakers. The Earth Kingdom may have the best ingredients and training, but the Fire Kingdom people spend their lives developing their relationships with their flames. It takes time, and trust. Maybe try to get to know him?"

"I'm so behind," I muttered.

Maple stood taller. "Whenever I felt discouraged by not being as good as someone else at something, my nana always said, 'They had to start where you are. Everyone starts at zero.' Just remember that, all right?"

I nodded. *Yeah, but what if I stay at zero?* "I'm used to cooking with set temperatures. How do you bake with a magical flame?"

Maple brows knitted together. "We simply tell them what we want. For instance, 'cook this pie until the crust is golden brown and you can see the filling bubbling up.' Something like that."

I cocked my head to the side. "So the flame, theoretically at least, helps you?"

"Oh, yes." Maple shook her head, blond waves skimming her shoulders. "I don't know how I'd get on without mine. She was my nana's flame, actually. Knows all her recipes."

Maple moved back to her station, pausing once to give me an encouraging nod. I crouched back down to my flame.

"Iggy, I'd very much like if we could work together."

"I'm sure you would," he drawled.

I tried not to let him rile me, and considered Maple's words. "Can you heat this oven evenly at a medium-hot temperature? Just the right one for baking a poppy seed cake?"

Iggy considered a moment, then nodded. "Yes. I can."

I grinned. "Wow. Thank you." I stood up and gave the

counter a happy little pat. Well, good. I frowned. Though it seemed too easy.

I mixed up my cake batter. As I added almond extract, the blue feathered quill hopped onto the open page next to me. Its feather bobbed as it crossed out 1 teaspoon and wrote 1 1/2 teaspoons. I grinned, delighted. I then buttered a beautiful silver Bundt pan and poured the batter into it.

I crouched down in front of the oven, the heat stinging my face. I smiled at Iggy and gently slid the pan into the opening.

"Can you cook this until it's baked through, not too dark, just a very light golden crust around the outside?"

Iggy grinned slyly. "Indeed, I can."

"Thank you. I think an hour should just about do it."

I stood and turned over a magical hourglass that Zeke had explained ran out at whatever time you ordered it to. "One hour." Maybe baking without magic wouldn't be as much of a challenge as I'd imagined—not with everyone's help.

The tent took on a mix of beautiful aromas—sweet sugar, bitter chocolate, and tart raspberry. My nose was in heaven.

I made a few trips to the pantry, returning the pouch of poppy seeds and the jar of milk. When I returned, the stinging scent of smoke reached my nose. I sniffed a few times, looking around the tent, before I realized it came from my oven.

I dropped to a crouch. "Oh no!" I fanned my hand, then grabbed a kitchen towel and fanned away more black smoke. "Iggy! Iggy, stop burning!"

"Oh, now you want me to just extinguish and die, I see."

"No, I mean, stop burning my cake."

The flame pulled to the back of the oven, and with red

mitts over my hands, I pulled the pan out, turning my head to avoid the smoke. I coughed through it, shoving the torched bake onto my countertop. Zeke dashed over and waved his wand at it. The smoke cleared immediately, but black, charred cake remained.

"Is it a volcano cake?" Zeke grinned at me through his scruffy beard. I wanted to laugh, but just didn't have it in me. Zeke mouthed "Sorry" and retreated back to his station. I gritted my teeth together and dropped down.

"You said you would bake it till it was golden brown."

"No," Iggy purred. "I said I *could*, not that I *would*."

"Urg! You are—" I pressed my lips tight together, stopping myself before I cursed at him.

"Infuriating?" Iggy opened his fire eyes wide.

"Yes!" My chest heaved.

"You could always quit."

22

DINNER ON THE LAWN

So, practice went well.

I stood with the others on the lawn in front of the house, trying to stay on my feet in spite of my exhaustion.

"I need not remind you the royal family will be present tomorrow, so let's do our best." Amelia opened her gray eyes wide, looking at each and every one of us. Nerves tightened my chest. She then clapped her hands. "Dinner will appear soon. See you here, on the lawn, tomorrow morning at eight sharp."

She turned to go, but Glenn raised a finger. "Have my dietary needs been considered for dinner and breakfast and all our meals? If we want snacks, where do we get those?" He looked around the group, grinning. "Sometimes I get a bit peckish in the middle of the night, you know. Don't worry, I'm not sleepwalking if you see me roaming the halls, just looking for a bit of cheese and bread, or some hot cereal, or a slice of chocolate cake." He licked his full lips, eyes closed. "Hmm, I could go for a bit of chocolate cake right about now, couldn't you? In fact, how about—"

"Glenn!" Amelia shrieked, stopping him short. She flushed, hands balled into fists. "Yes, your dietary needs have been considered for meals, as I've already told you four previous times, and there is a small kitchen on the first floor next to the library. We've stocked it with snacks."

Breathing heavily through her nose, Amelia turned her wide eyes on the rest of us. "Any more questions? No? Good. I'll go put out the other eight fires I'm sure have started while I stood here talking to you lot." Off she stalked across the lawn, speaking to someone through her ear device.

"How about we all eat together, outside?" Zeke spread his arms wide. "It's beautiful out." A breeze rustled the trees.

Wool and Hank conjured chairs from the kitchen, and I assumed, everyone's rooms. They floated out the front door to the lawn, bobbing and hovering into a rough circle, and then plopped down on the dewy grass.

The sun had mostly set by this point, only a dull orange glow peeking above the water on the horizon. Wool held out his palms together and slowly drew them apart, revealing his flame between them. "Would you mind being our campfire for the evening?"

The fire jumped from his palm to a pile of logs Hank dumped in the middle and set them alight, crackling and popping and providing a pleasant golden glow. Everyone milled about, picking out their seats from the mishmash of armchairs and kitchen chairs.

I sat and waved Maple over. She took the seat to my left, settling herself between Wool and me. She gazed into his oblivious face. *Like a moth to a flame.*

Hank, scowling as usual, stalked up to what had apparently been his chair, but found Maple in it. He looked around, and finding the one on my right the only other empty seat, he plunked into it, his body angled away from me.

I twisted my lips to keep from smiling. I scooted closer to him and he inched away. "I don't bite, you know. Usually."

He turned to me then, eyebrows raised. He blinked a few times, then his face softened. "No, of course not." He ran a hand through his floppy thick brown hair and turned his body slightly closer to mine. Had I embarrassed him? I opened my mouth, not even sure myself what I was about to say, but a veritable feast materialized out of thin air.

Silver-covered dishes rattled into place before us, along with a white ceramic gravy bowl, a wooden bowl of hot string beans, and a three-tiered platter of petit fours. I startled, then giggled at my own jumpiness. I lifted the lid on the large dish that hovered before me and peeked under, moaning as the scent of roasted duck reached my nose.

The floating dishes began to parade in front of us, floating slowly past as if on a conveyor belt. I'd wondered how we'd eat without a table, but magic took care of that. Plates of various patterns distributed around the circle, hovering at the perfect height for each person, along with a set of cutlery. My dish had pink frolicking bunnies lining the edge, while Maple's had a vine blooming with purple flowers.

I looked left and right for direction. Maple was no help. The food simply passed her by, her mind too full of Wool to notice. I glanced Hank's way.

He sighed and gestured at the dish with his large hand. "You tell the dish how much you want and it'll serve you."

"Oh." I smiled at the bowl of greens beans. "One big scoop, please."

The wooden spoon lifted up and deposited a large scoop of beans on my plate. I flushed with delight.

"You don't have to say please, it's just a bowl." Hank waved the floating dish before him away.

"Yeah, well, I've never had to be polite to a fire before either." I kept my eyes on the dish of steaming baked potatoes before me, but out of the corner of my eye caught Hank do a double take. Then a grin spread across his face. It shouldn't have pleased me so much to have caused the first smile I'd seen on his face all day.

"Touché."

I nudged Maple and snapped her out of her stupor. She began to dish food onto her plate, though she barely picked at it.

"My stomach's all full of butterflies and moths," she muttered to me. "I'm afraid I'll toss it all up, if I eat. And then I'd just die if I did that in front of him."

The evening passed pleasantly, and though I didn't con any more smiles out of Hank, he gradually edged closer and closer to me and we ate in friendly silence, with a little comment here and there.

After dinner we milled about, Sam and Zeke volunteering to get the sponges and the soap going on cleaning the dishes.

I joined a little group over by Bern, the magicneer from the Air Kingdom. He asked me how I liked Bijou Mer, and when I told him I thought it was the loveliest, most sparkling place I'd ever seen, he told me that his grandfather had helped design the Levaquifer system that filled the canals.

Glenn cornered me at one point and talked at length about not only the food and seasonal allergies he had, but also listed all the ones he didn't have. *Why?*

After twenty minutes, my patience wore thin. I tried to flash my eyes at Maple, blinking out "help" in Morse code, but she was too busy gawking at Wool, who stood talking with her and Hank.

Hank intercepted my SOS though, and to my complete surprise, pulled away from his conversation. He strode over to where we stood a little ways away from the fire.

23

THE LIBRARY

Hank put a large hand on Glenn's shoulder and said, "I think Zeke was asking for you in the kitchen."

"Oh? Oh really? I wonder what for. Maybe he'd like help with the dishes, though I should think he and Sam should have that under control, don't you? Or perhaps he has a question about a certain ingredient or technique used by the Earth Kingdom. Did you know he's originally from Earth? Why anyone would leave, especially for Air, I certainly cannot fathom. Can you? Or maybe—"

Hank loomed over him. "Why don't you go to the kitchen and ask him yourself?"

Glenn gulped. "Oh. Oh, all right." And with that, the short round man power walked back inside the house. I watched him go with relief.

But when I looked up into Hank's face, a different sort of anxiety stirred in my stomach. I looked quickly away, and stared instead at his broad chest. Nope, not the place to look either, on a dark starry night, in the shadows of a flickering campfire.

"Thanks for that. He's a nice guy, but I don't think I said one word. Literally." I grinned and nodded a few too many times. "Well, should we join the others then?"

Hank stood too close for me to take a full breath. It was as if he were sucking all the air out of the dark and starry sky. He smelled salty and herbal, like lemon thyme maybe. I felt as if the air itself made me woozy.

Instead of moving toward the group, he took a half step closer. I gulped and felt like I had to throw my head all the way back to look up into his face. But when I did, my breath caught, and I stumbled back. He gazed down at me intently. The expression alone would have surprised me, but what sent me reeling back, was that his face had changed; his features were different.

I squinted. Was it the firelight that made his eyes now appear blue instead of black? His hair shorter than it'd been a minute ago? His nose, still large, but straighter, without that crooked bump in the middle? His chin dimpled and square, where it'd been sharper and pointy before? Could the flickering light change so much? His expression changed too as I continued to blink and stare and recoil.

"What is it?" His hands reached to his face, patting around. His thick eyebrows jumped up, his lips parted, and he turned away.

I tried to peek around his broad back, but he kept his face hidden from me, muttering to himself. When he turned, I blinked in surprise. He looked like he had before. Dark eyes, pointy sharp jawline, crooked nose. Had I just imagined the change? Had it been the firelight and shadows?

He swallowed, his throat bobbing. "Why don't we, uh—" He gestured to the group and strode back to the fire, not even waiting to see if I followed. I stood still for a bit, reeling.

Finally I shook my head. There was so much in this world I didn't understand.

So much about Hank I didn't understand. Earlier, he'd seemed to hate me, then at dinner he'd warmed to me, I thought. Now... now I had no idea. And what did I think of him? I took a deep breath. It wasn't something I had to figure out this moment. Tomorrow the competition began, and there was something I'd been meaning to do.

I said my good nights, then headed down the hall. Amelia had mentioned a library. I opened the door beside the kitchen and entered a room lit by glowing wall sconces and a fire burning bright in the hearth. I wondered if it were a flame with a personality.

"Hello, fire?"

But nothing answered. I briefly wondered how Iggy was doing in the tent. He'd insisted on staying behind in the oven. That was fine by me. I didn't need his insults keeping me up all night.

I moved about the two-story-tall room. The huge fireplace took up one wall, with a large, magically moving painting of the sea above it. In front of the fire stood four stuffed armchairs and a wooden coffee table on a dark red rug. All around the other three walls, from floor to ceiling, stretched shelves packed with books. A spiral staircase wrapped its way up to the mezzanine on the second floor, which overlooked the great room below.

I browsed, gathering up about a half dozen books in my arms, and plunked them down on the coffee table. I settled into the armchair closest to the fireplace and pulled a soft white blanket over my legs. I dove into the first book, entitled *Magical Ingredients in Baking and Cooking*. I figured it'd help to study up as much as I could.

One, I was excited to discover new plants, herbs, and

flavors for my bakes. But also, to avoid doing things like mixing baking soda with dragon's bane, which I learned if inhaled would cause permanent baldness. When I came to the chapter on venoms, Glenn's allergy made more sense to me. I read:

Snake venom can be extracted from fangs, snake shifters, and is found in smaller quantities in snake eggs. The venom has medicinal purposes as well, and when used with the proper enchantments, it can block specific pain signals in the brain, with no observed side effects. Used improperly or in greater quantities, the venom can be deadly. Doubly so for those with a rare allergy to the venom.

I raised a brow. *I guess Glenn has a legitimate worry there.* I cocked my head to the side. *Not that he needs to tell us all about it twenty thousand times.*

I must have drifted to sleep, because I yawned and blinked sometime later. I sat up and stretched, trying to focus in the dim light of the fire, which had dwindled to embers. A movement outside the windows caught my eye.

I blinked and leaned forward in my chair, dropping my feet off the coffee table. Out on the lawn, a bent figure snuck across the grass. It disappeared into the line of cyprus trees before I could move to the window for a better look. *Strange.*

Too tired to puzzle out what it meant, I crept back down the dark hall to my room and collapsed into bed.

24

THE COMPETITION

The sun rose bright in a beautiful blue sky as we ate breakfast on the lawn before the competition. Maple, sitting next to me, turned a light shade of green.

"Too nervous to eat too?" I nudged her with my shoulder.

"My dad's coming today. Sent word he was able to get tickets."

I tried to sound upbeat. "He's being supportive, right?"

Her nostrils flared. "You'd think. But he's so caught up in this rivalry with Glenn."

Across the circle from us, Glenn detailed to Bern all the ways in which he was clearly the superior baker. "In the Earth Kingdom, apprentices train for years, and to get to my level on the council, it takes heaps of experience and talent, you know?"

I jumped when he looked up and caught my eye. Maple tried to hide her face behind her bowl of oatmeal.

He shook his finger at her. "You're Roger's daughter, right?"

Maple lowered her bowl a fraction and nodded.

"I was just telling Bern that to rise up to a level like mine, or like Nan's—" He turned to me. "She was the last royal baker, Earth rest her bones. It takes lots of time and paying your dues. Glad to see you're still at it— Was it Maggie?"

My friend gulped. "Maple."

"The humiliation you must've felt." He clicked his tongue. "But I'm glad you're still trying your hardest. Good for you."

Maple turned bright red and hid behind her bowl. Confused, I looked from her to Glenn.

"Her dad tried to get her hired on in the royal kitchens. Nan was one of us, from the Earth Kingdom, and she didn't accept her application. Well, Roger took great offense to that, thought someone from the Water Kingdom ought to be in the Water kitchens, but when you're talking at that level you've got to be realistic. And between you and me"

—*And everyone else who can't help but eavesdrop, you're so loud*—

"only the Fire Kingdom's guild even begins to approach our standards in Earth." Glenn brushed nonexistent dust off his sleeve. "With my connections, I could introduce you to some master-level bakers looking for an apprentice when the competition's over."

I glanced at Maple, whose bright red face and downcast eyes showed the extent of her embarrassment. *Glenn*. I didn't think the dope intended to be rude and annoying, it just came naturally.

"Thanks, but who knows—I may already have a job when it's over."

Glenn blinked at me, then his eyes grew round. "Oh! You mean—if you win?" He chortled. "My girl, you're up against some very experienced bakers here, and you don't even know how to use magic."

I nodded, smiling through my annoyance. "True, but Amelia did say that whoever wins can bring on other contestants as staff." I put an arm around Maple's shoulders. "And I've got my fingers crossed that Maple might choose me."

Glenn's mouth hung open.

Maple knocked her shoulder against mine. "Thank you," she whispered.

After some magical tidying up, we followed Amelia to the tent. Behind it, wooden bleachers rose up from the lawn, adorned with waving flags in blue, green, and gold. A couple hundred people sat on every available inch of the benches and at the top, in boxes separated from the rest of the crowd, sat the royal family. An older man and woman with dark hair and twisting golden crowns sat in the center, surrounded on both sides by young couples.

"Maple!" Maple's dad stood and waved from the benches, with who I assumed were her mother and some younger siblings. Maple winced and raised a hand.

If my family could see me now, what would they think? Could they even process the existence of magic? I blinked as an idea occurred to me. Had they known when they'd adopted me? *No.* They couldn't have kept something like that from me all these years.

Amelia stood before us with Rhonda and Francis. She raised her arms, and the crowd quieted down.

"Welcome to the competition for the next Royal Baker of the Water Kingdom. A day made even more special by the royal family gracing us with their lofty presence. To the health and prosperity of the Water's royal line!"

A great cheer of "Huzzah!" rang out. The crowd bowed their heads and Maple dipped into a low curtsy beside me. I lifted my brows. *Oh yeah, royalty.* I bent my knees, grateful that my jeans were so stretchy. Hank, standing to my left, suddenly jolted and folded forward into a low bow. *What took him so long?* I, at least, had the excuse of being unfamiliar with the customs. Maybe nerves had gotten the best of him. He did look pale and twitchy.

Maple murmured, "I wonder where Prince Harry is?"

"Hmm?"

"Oh." She leaned closer and whispered. "There are five royal sons."

I lifted my eyes. Only four young men sat in the box seats.

"Strange." Maple pulled her lips to one side.

"Why strange?"

"He's actually a big supporter of baking. He's been pushing for years to try to get the Water Kingdom's baking guild up to par with Earth's and Fire's. Seems like the kind of thing he wouldn't want to miss."

I stood as everyone else rose. "Kind of odd for a prince to be into baking, isn't it?"

She heaved a great sigh. "It makes him even dreamier."

I raised my brows and grinned. "Oh? Dreamy, huh?"

She swallowed, catching herself. "That's just what all the girls I know say."

Amelia turned toward us and commanded, "To your stations."

As we made our way through the tent, she turned to the crowd, announcing, "The bakers will have exactly one and a half hours to complete a showcase bake, something that demonstrates their skills and personal style. Ready, bakers? Begin!"

Amelia gathered up a pine cone from the ground, tossed it into the air, and when it came down, it transformed into an hourglass the size of the woman herself. White grains of sand poured into the bottom half.

I took a shaky breath as I donned the white apron provided for all of us contestants. I nodded at Bern to my right, smiled at Zeke to my left, then looked down at my butcher-block counter. *Breathe*.

I pressed my trembling hands to the tabletop and opened my collection to the poppy seed cake recipe. As I did so, the blue feathered quill sprang to life and hovered at the ready.

I ducked past flying glass jars and baskets until I'd gathered all the ingredients from the pantry. Now the hardest part. I plastered on my brightest smile and crouched in front of the oven. Iggy dimly glowed in the back.

"Hey, Iggy. How are you today?"

The flame coughed black smoke. "You do have eyes? I'm nearly extinguished. You left me with hardly anything to eat."

He did look dim. "I-I didn't know you needed anything to eat."

The flame rolled his eyes. "Do you know anything?"

I blew my bangs out of my eyes. "I'll get whatever you need if you'll please heat up the oven for poppy seed cake? And less hot than yesterday?"

"Bring me some decent logs, and I'll consider it."

Okay, now where to find some firewood? I glanced around the tent and saw Sam feeding some logs into his oven. I dashed over to him.

"Sam. Hi."

He jumped. "Oh, Imogen," he said in his low, lisping

voice. "You sstartled me." He blinked at me with his milky blue eyes.

"Sorry." I cleared my throat. "Just wondering where you got the firewood?"

"Ah." He pointed behind the tent. "There'sss a pile jussst out there."

"Thanks, Sam."

I staggered with an armful of wood to my station. Life would certainly be much easier if I could master some simple magic. Come hither, logs. That sort of thing. I dumped the pile on the ground and fed a log into the oven. Iggy uncoiled himself and climbed onto it, crackling a little louder.

I grinned in spite of myself. He looked so content, like a kitten curling up on its favorite chair. "That better?"

The flame's eyes shot open. "Tolerable."

I'd take it. "Let me know when you're ready for more."

"Ah, right, because you don't know how to cast an auto-feed spell."

I bit back a retort and straightened, working on my batter. Most everyone else was already pouring their bakes into pans or laying their crusts into pie tins. I was way behind.

I wiped a trickle of sweat from my forehead. Between the beating sun and all the cooking fires, I was sweltering. With both hands, I poured the batter from the heavy glass bowl into the Bundt pan, then carefully lowered myself down in front of the fire. A blast of heat reached my face.

"Iggy, my man. You ready for some cake?"

My attempt at buddiness fell flat. "I'm ready for nothing."

"Well, that's a shame, because cake's coming in. Let's not overbake it."

"As you command, master."

"Okay, thanks, buddy." I stood, balled a towel up, and pressed it to my mouth to stifle my scream of frustration. Of course, Rhonda and Francis chose that moment to appear at my side.

25

JUDGING

"How's it going, Imogen?"

"Uh, everything's going great." I brushed my bangs aside.

Rhonda nodded. "That was a celebratory scream into a towel?"

My voice raised an octave. "Oh. Yeah. I do that all the time when I'm happy."

"Right. Right. And what are you making for us today?"

"Poppy seed cake." I gave the judges a bright smile.

Francis took a long, lingering sniff from my shoulder to the top of my head. His tongue flicked out like a snake's. "Hmm. I love this one's smell of stress and doubt." The vampire groaned. "Love it."

"Good luck, Imogen." Rhonda and Francis moved on to speak with Zeke.

What next? Right, the edible flowers.

I dashed to the garden behind the tent. Raised beds dotted the space, with trellises and little stakes denoting each plant's name. I pooled my apron in front of me and used it like a basket to hold the rose petals and violets that I gathered, shielding them from the sea breeze that whipped my hair. I deposited the flowers at my station and crouched in front of the fire.

"How's the cake coming along?"

"How should I know?"

"I've heard fires can know as much, if not more, than the bakers themselves." *The more you know.*

"In your case, I should think a rock would know more."

I smiled brightly at him. *I will murder you.* At least my cake didn't look burned. I straightened and stirred together some sugar, milk, and almond extract with more force than necessary. A yelp startled me. I looked back.

"Ow. I've twisted my wrist." Pouting, Pritney made her way back to Nate. She swayed her hips side to side. Most injured people I knew didn't strut.

She presented her wrist to the medic. He ran one hand up and down her arm. *Hmm.* I wouldn't mind getting hurt if it meant Nate running his strong hands all over me.

Ah. There it was.

She was probably faking it to get him to do exactly that. After a few moments, Nate sent her back to her station. He must have felt my eyes on him, because he looked up suddenly.

I froze, embarrassed to be caught staring. But then a sly grin spread across his tanned face. He glanced at Pritney, then back at me and rolled his eyes. I flashed a smile back and turned, my cheeks flushing hot. I bit my lip and stared down at my glaze. *Focus, Imogen. On your baking, not the hot medic.*

Rhonda skipped back over to me. "I've just had a vision about you."

Please God, don't let it be about my bowel movements.

"What you think is hot is cold, and what you believe is cold is hot."

I cocked my head to the side. "What does that mean?"

"You're welcome," she sang, and off she skipped. She froze in front of Zeke. "Consider your judges." She pointed her fingers from her eyes to his and back to her own again. "Consider them well." He froze, muffin tin in hand. Then she grinned and skipped off again.

Zeke looked my way, a question in his eyes. I shrugged. You'd think visions would be more useful. I worked for another twenty minutes on the glaze and flowers, waiting as long as I could. Then I kneeled in front of the oven.

"All right, Iggy, bake time's up." Mitts on, I pulled out the cake.

It wobbled far too much for my liking. I inserted a toothpick into the center. If it came out clean, it'd be done. Instead, it came out covered in wet cake. Not good. I tried in a few other spots. Wet, again and again.

My hands trembled, and I blinked back tears. *I'm out. I am absolutely out.* How could I make it through this round with a raw cake? I slid it back into the oven.

"Hotter, Iggy, please!"

The flame just smirked. With trembling hands, I paced back and forth in front of my station. The other bakers put the finishing touches on their creations as I ate into my decorating time. With just minutes left, I pulled the cake from the lukewarm oven.

I flipped and lifted away the pan. The cake stuck and tore in places. I drizzled on the glaze. With no time to let the cake cool, the glaze pooled on the plate instead of hardening into white rivulets.

I hastily wiped away the tears running down my burning

cheeks and got to the business of arranging the flowers. I'd come this far, and I intended to see it through.

"Sixty seconds, bakers!" Amelia announced.

A jolt of adrenaline coursed through me. With shaking hands, I plucked up the remaining edible flowers and arranged them all over the top and around the base of the cake.

Amelia called out, "Time's up! Please send your bakes to the front table and step up behind them."

With trembling hands I lifted my cake and carried it to the long, wooden table that suddenly appeared between the tent and the bleachers. Everyone else's bakes floated magically into place. Maple slid up beside me, blond tendrils sticking to her damp forehead. I found her hand and gave it a little squeeze.

"Bakers, well done. You've completed your first task." Amelia turned to the crowd. "Let's give them a round of applause! Judges?"

Amelia stepped aside to let Rhonda and Francis take center stage. They started at my far right with Lillian and her chicken pot pie. As the judges spooned into the crisp golden crust, the crowd hushed, only the caw of the seagulls overhead and the flapping of the tent in the wind breaking the silence.

"Hmm," Rhonda moaned. "Delicious. Crust is nice and crispy. Perfection."

They loved Sam's millionaire's shortbread, Pritney's red velvet cupcakes, and the heat in Wool's spicy Qatayefs. I gave Maple's shaking hand another squeeze as the judges moved in front of her. They sliced into her loaf of lemon yogurt blueberry bread.

"I love the brilliant blue of the berries inside." Rhonda took a bite, then held her fork up to Francis, who ate off it.

"Tangy, but sweet." He chewed on it for a moment. "I quite like it."

Rhonda nodded and took another bite. "Me too."

They moved on to me. I held my breath. They sliced into my cake and poked at the inside with a fork.

Rhonda frowned. "Hmm, undercooked." Francis nodded at her. They each took a bite. My heart seemed to stop beating while they chewed on it. Their faces gave nothing away.

Finally, Francis spoke. "Flavor's good though."

Rhonda nodded. "I must say, I prefer the almond to the traditional lemon glaze. And very pretty with the flowers on top." She popped a violet petal into her mouth. "But it needed longer in the oven."

I nodded and swallowed against the tightness in my throat. It hadn't been the complete smackdown I'd been expecting. Zeke came next.

Zeke smiled brightly as he handed Rhonda a muffin. "Pineapple bran muffins. I want to prove that baking can be healthy."

Rhonda looked dubiously at the muffin, then handed it to Francis. "You go first."

He took a bite, then handed it back to her. They both chewed for a long, long time. Rhonda scrunched up her nose. "Well, I'm not tasting any pineapple. You?"

Francis shook his head.

"They're bland and dry." Rhonda cocked a brow. "I told you to consider your judges. I like desserts to taste good. If I want nutritious, I'll eat broccoli."

I gave Zeke a sympathetic look. He shrugged and gave me a tight-lipped smile. Which was worse, raw cake or dry muffins? After the judges had moved down the entirety of the line, they announced they'd need to deliberate. I reached out for Maple's hand to my right and Zeke's to my left to await the decision. After a few moments, Rhonda and Francis stood before us with Amelia beside them.

"We have thoroughly enjoyed meeting each of you, and it is with regret that we announce today's loser," Rhonda said.

I would have preferred "winning-challenged participant."

"I regret that...." Rhonda paused for dramatic effect.

I braced for the next words, sure that they would be, "Imogen will be leaving us."

"Zeke is out of the competition."

The crowd awwed and murmured. Rhonda came up to Zeke and gave him a hug. "You're a lovely guy. I just didn't get much flavor from your hippie muffins." She winked at me. "Got that term from the human world."

I didn't know whether to feel relieved or horribly guilty. "Zeke. It should have been me. I didn't even cook my cake. Kind of an essential part of baking, is actually, you know, baking things."

He chuckled. "It's totally fair. I knew going healthy would be a gamble." He wrapped his arms around me in a tight hug. "You get 'em tomorrow, all right?"

That night, we gathered quietly on the lawn for dinner. Hank turned in as soon as he'd finished eating, saying, "You all ought to go to get some rest if you're serious about this. It's only going to get harder."

Wool called through a cupped hand, "Thanks for the advice, grandpa."

I chuckled along with everyone else, and Hank waved us off, stalking upstairs.

Maple yawned and headed to bed. "I'm just happy to be here right now. If I were at home, Dad'd be making me practice all night." She yawned and patted my shoulder before shuffling to her room.

I supposed I should sleep too. Instead, I wandered again to the library, determined to learn as much as I could to ready myself for tomorrow. I fell asleep in the armchair in front of the big fire with a book on my lap.

26

TOAST

I stood at my station facing rows upon rows of spectators, the royalty at the top. Still no Prince Harry the hottie today.

I'd remembered to put extra logs in the oven last night, so Iggy still burned brightly, warming my legs. It also meant he'd have the energy for even zippier insults. *Oh goody.* I took a deep breath. *Stay positive.*

I found that difficult to do with the sky gray and cloudy today, my arms covered in goose bumps from the chill. I wished for a jacket. Heck, I wished for a change of clothes. I wore my unicorn tee and jeans for the third day in a row, which had not escaped Pritney's notice.

At breakfast on the lawn she'd lifted a brow and sneered, "You must really love deformed horses."

"You're a deformed horse," I'd muttered back. Not my finest retort.

Amelia stood before me with Rhonda and Francis at her sides. "Before you are all of the ingredients and tools you'll need to make today's surprise bake. No recipes may be used today, so please stash your books away."

I stuffed my loose recipes into their folder, then slid them onto a shelf under the counter. I replaced my hands on the countertop, and fiddled with the shimmering cloth that lay over a bunch of bumps and mounds. Everyone else had one on their table, too, except for Zeke's empty station to my left. I missed his cheerful, laid-back demeanor. I needed a little chill right now.

Amelia continued. "Most of the world's chocolate comes from just three different types of cocoa beans. But most of us have never tried the extremely rare fourth type, the Rico Bean. It's found only deep in the Amazon, and lucky you, competitors, you'll have the opportunity to work with its rich, creamy, completely nonbitter flavor today, to make—"

She took a deep breath for dramatic effect. The spectators in the bleachers leaned forward to catch her words.

"—tuiles! In two different shapes—can be curls, twirls, straws, bowls, and cones. Up to you. You'll have two hours to complete the challenge, starting now!"

The giant hourglass turned over, leaking sand in a steady trickle. The crowd burst into applause as the gauzy shimmering fabric dissolved, revealing the ingredients below.

I took a deep breath. Okay, tuiles, I could do this. I'd made the potato-chip-shaped biscuits once before for a cousin's tea-themed baby shower in St. Louis. They'd turned out cute that time—patterned like a target with concentric rings of brown chocolate and golden batter.

I eyed my ingredients. A small bar of chocolate labeled "Rico Chocolate." I bit my lip. Hopefully they'd given us a little extra so I could try a nibble. Next to it sat a carafe of thick white cream, a basket of eggs wrapped in a red checkered towel, jars of sugar, flour, and Rico cocoa powder, a vial of vanilla extract, and two sticks of softened butter.

I rubbed my palms together and sucked on my lips. My least favorite part, dealing with Iggy, needed to come first. I dropped down in front of the oven.

"Iggy. Good morning. Today we're making tuiles."

"I heard."

"Chipper as ever, I see." An ache in my neck throbbed. "Could you please preheat the oven to—" I caught myself. He said he didn't know temperatures. "A standard baking heat perfect for tuiles, same as you'd usually do for cookies, for example."

"Oh, very specific." Iggy chewed lazily at a glowing log. "These things taste like dirt."

"It is a stick." I swallowed and rubbed my neck. "I just got it from the woodpile out back."

"Hmph. How dignified. How would you like it if your food came from a 'pile out back'?"

"How'd you like it if—" I exhaled heavily through my nose, stopping myself. "Iggy. Please."

"As you command."

I straightened and rubbed my clammy palms across my apron. I unwrapped the chocolate bar and broke it into small pieces. I popped a shard into my mouth and savored the creamy, rich flavor. I groaned. *Best chocolate ever*. Maybe I could spare another piece. Sucking on another bite, I realized I needed to heat up a saucepan.

I looked around and found everyone else already had their flames going on their tabletops, as well as in their ovens. Oh great. I had to ask Iggy for even more favors. I crouched back down.

"Iggy, I need you to, um—split yourself up and have part of you up on top with me to heat a saucepan, all right?"

"As if I have a choice."

I held out a fresh log and Iggy's flames licked onto it. I

carefully brought it up to the counter, wincing when a gust of wind sent the tent sides flapping and nearly blew Iggy's flames out. He glared at me, but I ignored him and set him on the table.

"Okay, low to medium heat please." I poured in about half the carafe of cream and heated it until it just simmered, then pulled it off the flames and added the chocolate pieces, stirring continually until it all melted and the mixture stirred smooth and glossy.

I poured it into a bowl to cool, turning my tiny hourglass and murmuring, "Fifteen minutes." I then moved on to the tuile batter. At home I would have used an electric handheld mixer, but now I whipped the mixture by hand. Everyone else's spoons magically stirred themselves while they worked on other projects.

"Some magic sure would be nice right about now, hm?"

I glared at Iggy. "You are no longer needed outside the oven." Huffing, I shoved him back below, still stirring with my other hand.

When the batter turned into a thicker paste, I whisked in six egg whites. I tossed the shells to Iggy. Maybe he'd like them. I got no response, but a light smell of smoke. I arched a brow. I didn't know eggshells smoked. I added the flour bit by bit, folding it in carefully then beating it with a wooden spoon between each addition to add air and lightness.

I sniffed. The smoke smell grew stronger. I glanced around the tent looking for the source. Everyone else was already pouring their tuiles. *Shoot!* Panic tightened my chest. I needed to hurry up. I coughed, my throat burning with smoke. *Why are my legs so warm?* My eyes opened wide and I shoved my bowl onto the tabletop, jumping back.

"Oh no!"

Flames erupted from the shelves next to the oven. I

yanked up a kitchen towel and beat at the flames, tears stinging my eyes.

Rhonda rushed to my side. She whispered a few words and, as if an invisible bucket had upturned, a deluge of water doused the fire. The crowd gasped and pointed. I let out a shaky sigh and dropped to my knees, grateful to have my face hidden from the crowd.

On the other side of my station, Amelia addressed the spectators. "Minor fire. Nothing to worry about. Rhonda the Seer, always a step ahead, has already taken care of it."

With my towel I beat away the smoke. Rhonda crouched next to me and Maple appeared at my other side. "You okay?"

But I couldn't answer. Not yet. A sickening thought crept into my mind. With my stomach twisted in a knot, I reached forward and grasped the crumbling, scorched pages of my recipe book. "No." Tears poured down my face. I couldn't stop them. I gulped on a sob. As I pulled the book out, it disintegrated into ash.

"Why did you do this?" I wheeled on Iggy.

He frowned at me. "I did nothing, you dolt. You shoved that log with half my flames onto the shelf with your book. Now I'm at half power, and you have no recipes. This is all you."

27

UNDER PRESSURE

I wanted to strangle Iggy, but having s'mores for hands probably wouldn't help me any. Instead I buried my face in my hands and cried. Maple and Rhonda sandwiched me.

"It's-it's just...." I gulped and cried more snot onto Rhonda's overalls. "My apartment back home burned down, but I saved my recipes. Now I've burned them up, too. I have nothing left."

Maple hugged me tighter from behind and Rhonda took me by the shoulders, forcing me to look at her with blurry, swollen eyes.

"Sometimes, you have to just let it go, mate. Maybe you had to lose it all to get something new, right? And sobbing on the ground isn't going to help you win this, or your friend for that matter." Her dark eyes darted to Maple. A stab of worry pricked through my self-pity. Still sniffling, I turned to Maple.

"She's right. Thank you, but you have to get back to your bake."

"It's just a stupid bake, are you okay?" Maple's worried blue eyes searched my face.

I managed a smile. "It's not a stupid bake. You've got him to beat."

We all turned to see Glenn mosey over to Hank. Glenn popped a piece of Hank's chocolate into his mouth, oblivious to Hank's dark glare. "Mine are all in the oven, made pretty quick work of it, if I do say so meself." He wobbled his head side to side, very pleased with himself, and ate another piece.

Hank's dark eyes flashed. "Unhand my chocolate."

Glenn looked up, wide-eyed, then raised his chocolate-covered palms in surrender. "Hey, don't let me distract you." He sucked chocolate off a fingertip and turned to Bern. "What's cookin', Bern, my man?"

Maple turned to me and rolled her eyes. "I'll go, but only if you're all right."

Still feeling shaky, I let Maple and Rhonda help me to my feet. How I wished I had a station further away from the bleachers. But the crowd gave me a round of applause, and with burning cheeks, I waved Rhonda and Maple off, and got back to it.

I just needed to focus on this moment, this task. Sure, I didn't have any recipes, but I couldn't use them today anyway, and when it came to tomorrow, if I made it that far, I'd figure it out then. I brushed some loose tendrils of hair behind my ears and refocused.

I got my chocolate and tuile mixtures made with Maple's help—with no refrigerators, she chilled the bowls with a "frigus" spell for me.

"You know, you should be able to do this on your own."

I glanced behind me. Hank raised a thick brow.

"There aren't any rules about helping your friends out." Were there?

"Maybe not—" He blew his wavy hair out of his eyes as he directed his tuile mixture with his hands. It spooned itself into just the right oval shapes. "—but you shouldn't need so much help."

I turned, hands on hips. "And what does it matter to you? You're not exactly falling all over yourself to help me. I don't see why it'd put you out."

He cleared his throat, eyes on his task. "This is a competition. It should be fair. If I win, I want to do it fairly. You should too."

I shook my bangs out of my eyes. "Well, next time you want to compete in a human baking competition without magic, then you can talk to me about fair."

He glanced up briefly and our eyes met. For just a moment, his look changed, like it had the other night. His eyes looked blue, his nose straight. I felt a jolt of energy, heady and intoxicating. I swayed on my feet and blinked.

Just as quickly, the feeling passed and his appearance looked normal, except for the startled expression in his eyes. He watched me, lips slightly parted, until I turned back around and resumed my baking. What was that?

Baking, Imogen. Back to baking.

I worked hard for the next hour, barely stopping to breathe. Rhonda and Francis helped me with pouring out the tuile shapes without the molds I would have used at home—magic made them unnecessary. Unless you possessed magic but had no idea how to use it, like me.

Between the heat of the fires and the sweat I worked up from dashing back and forth from the oven to the worktop, molding the tuiles over rolling pins and around wooden spoon handles to shape them before they cooled, I couldn't believe I'd ever thought the day chilly.

When I heard a whine of pain behind me, I didn't have to turn to know where it came from. I rolled my eyes and glanced over my shoulder. Pritney made her way back to Nate, sucking a finger a little too deeply into her mouth. *Uh, stop deep throating your finger, Pritney.* She pulled it out slowly in front of him. *Gross.*

"Burned it." She presented her finger to the medic.

I glanced to her tabletop. As her hot tuiles were magically molding *themselves* around cones and into folded bowl shapes, I found that unlikely. I, however, had burnt every single finger during the process of molding the hot wafers.

Nate tended to her imaginary wounds with care. What a patient guy. I would've just sent her right back for wasting my time. I cocked my head to the side. Then again, it probably didn't hurt that she looked like a Swedish supermodel. I hissed and sucked on a burned fingertip as I finished shaping my last few tuiles.

"Hey, Imogen, right?"

I jumped, and found Nate, the hot medic, standing right beside me. His dark, almond-shaped eyes twinkled. I grinned back at him, stunned by the whiteness of his smile against his darkly tanned skin. I struggled to form words. "H-hey."

He swallowed and nodded at my tuiles. "Thought you could use this." He set a little jar down on my tabletop and opened the lid, setting it to the side. "It'll help with the burns."

I eyed the glowing, milky liquid dubiously.

"Here, let me show you." He gently took my left hand in both of his, his right hand cupping my wrist and his left cradling my fingers. He lowered my fingertips into the liquid. A tingling cold spread up my fingers, and I jumped. I had to laugh.

"Sorry, I'm a little on edge right now. That feels good though. You're so cool— I mean, it's so cool." *I'm such an idiot.*

I didn't know where to look. It'd be odd if I just kept staring into his beautiful face, wouldn't it? With the cooling liquid spreading chills all over me, I leaned closer to the warmth of him. His eyebrows lifted, and I realized that yep, I'd been staring too long. I dragged my eyes back to the jar. That seemed safe to look at. Would it cool my burning cheeks and neck?

"That's a lot better, thank you."

He nodded and released my hand. I dipped my other fingertips in, though I racked my brain for some reason to need his help with the second hand.

Afterward, he scooped up the jar. "I'd leave it with you, but it's the only one I have. If you need more later, I'm right back there." He gave me another megawatt smile and moved to the back. I watched him go, until I caught Hank glaring at me and turned back to my baking.

While the target-patterned tuiles cooled over the rolling pin, I raced against the hourglass to dip the rolled tuiles into the melted Rico chocolate. Using my last two minutes, I spooned dollops of chocolate mousse onto the potato-chip-shaped desserts, finishing just as the last grains of sand ran out.

As I carried my platter to the front table the other bakes floated past me. I noticed a plate of cracked tuiles next to a pile of crumbs. Oh no, whose was that? I looked around and saw Rhonda patting Lillian on the back.

The older woman walked with hands on her hips, bony elbows wide. "Amateur mistake. Tried to get too fancy." She shook her wild gray mop of hair. "Just my style though, you know. People see me, they think elegant, they think cutting edge, they think flashy."

I bit my lip. But when Lillian burst into cackling laughter, I chuckled with her. At least she had a good sense of humor. I deposited my plate.

"What happened?" I whispered to Maple, when she came to stand beside me.

She shook her head. "I guess she overdid it when she cast her shaping spell, and the cookies kept folding and twisting even after they hardened, so they broke." Maple sighed. "It's a shame. She tried spelling them back together, but the tuiles are so delicate, they just—"

"Crumbled," I finished. My stomach tightened for her. Lillian was a great baker, she deserved to stay in. But I guessed even the best had bad days. I was just hoping for a good day.

As it turned out, my tuiles weren't great—I sat squarely at the bottom of the pack—but Lillian's ambition cost her her place in the competition, and she was voted out by the judges. When it came my turn to say goodbye, I gave her a tight hug.

"You're an amazing baker." I pulled my lips to the side, attempting a smile despite the pit in my stomach. "I'm going to miss you."

Lillian threw her hair back. "Course you will, I was the life of the party." She winked.

I sighed. "If it's any comfort, I burned my own recipes to bits."

She barked out a laugh. "You're nearly as disaster prone as I am."

I grinned back at her.

Maple and I tromped back to the big house, side by side.

I'd made it through day two. How had I lasted this long? And would I make it through whatever challenge the next day had in store?

That night, we ate dinner on the lawn, me in my usual spot between Maple and Hank. After last night it had almost become like assigned seating. And as usual, the tall guy sat close, but hardly spoke, so I chatted with Maple.

"Well, I'd better turn in." I pulled at my unicorn shirt, covered in stains. "I've got to wash this in the bathroom and then hang out in my room while I wait for my clothes to dry."

Hank's fork clattered against his plate.

Maple grimaced. "I'm sorry I can't help." She'd tried to lend me some of her clothes, but she was a good three inches shorter and a full size smaller than me. And she'd told me clothes, like food, couldn't be magicked from nothing. Her family was going through a hard time and she didn't have spare thread and fabric to magically whip me anything up.

"No worries. Jeans and this T-shirt are sort of my new uniform." I grinned. It was kind of funny, except I usually wasn't really a jeans and T-shirt kind of girl. Left to my own devices, it would've been dresses, preferably with pockets. It really didn't feel like me, but hey, maybe this was part of my self-reinvention.

I washed my clothes in the bathroom and read some of the books I'd borrowed from the library in my room that night, snuggled in my sleeping alcove. Maple knocked on the wall a few hours later and called, "Good night."

I yelled back through the wall, "Don't let the bed bugs bite."

After a long pause she returned, "I'm going to assume that's a human thing and not a threat."

28

A GIFT

In the morning, I opened my door and just outside in the hall sat a package wrapped in tissue paper, tied with a navy-blue ribbon. A flurry of surprise and pleasure swept over me. Who didn't love presents?

I looked up and down the hall and saw no one. I pulled the package inside, lifted the small white card from under the wrapping, and read "Imogen" scrawled in messy black ink.

Intrigued, I pulled on the ribbon and the entire package sprang open, like it'd been spring-loaded. I shrieked and stumbled backward, crashing into my desk. When I opened my eyes and lowered my hands, my jaw dropped open in surprise. Clothes floated about the room, magically suspended in the air as if on hangers.

"What...?" I couldn't find the words as I moved through them, running my fingers over them. A pink sweater with a white collar, gray pleated skirt, a navy blue-and-gold peter pan collared dress. And jackets, flats, slippers, pumps, tights, jewelry, boots, pajamas, and a velvety pink robe. I giggled, pressing my hands to my mouth.

I banged on the wall I shared with Maple and then took another spin through the magically floating clothes. How beautiful, and how *me*. They all looked like they'd be exactly my size.

Maple's door scraped open and she shuffled in through my open door, scratching her blond mess of hair. I threw my arms around her, twirling her in a circle with me.

"Whoa!"

I pulled back and threw an arm out. "You are the best friend in the world. How did you do this?"

Maple gaped as she turned slowly around the room. "Where did these come from?"

I grinned and punched her shoulder. "Don't play coy."

She frowned and shook her head. "I definitely did not do this." She reached up and lightly touched the hem of one of the dresses. "This is nice stuff. Like, really nice, Imogen. I don't have one dress like this, much less a whole wardrobe."

Now I frowned. My arms dropped to my sides. "Who else could have sent this? Who else *would* have? And it's my size and style, too." I thought about everyone I'd met. "Ah, I bet it was Amelia. She probably wanted me to look more presentable with the royalty in the crowd."

Maple frowned at a hovering dress. "She went all out."

That morning I sat in the blue-and-gold dress with its puffed sleeves and full skirt. I felt like a princess. Next to me, Hank worked at his pancakes, though I could feel his eyes dart over to me again and again. Finally, I set my plate on my lap and asked in a huff. "Yes? Do you have something to say?"

He bit back a grin. "No. Just... nice dress."

I squinted at him. Something else hid just behind that smile, but I couldn't work out what exactly. Finally, I sighed and returned to eating. "You're impossible, you know that?"

He chuckled. "You need to learn to take a compliment."

"You need to learn to give one."

He burst out in a laugh, and I couldn't help but grin. He had a nice laugh, deep and real. But then he clammed up again, and after a few minutes of silence, uncomfortable just because I couldn't stop being aware of his presence, I turned to Maple to chat.

That day in the tent passed in a whirlwind. My blue quill jotted down notes in the blank journal I'd found in my room. My new recipe book. I made apple and berry tarts, wrapped so that the dough looked like roses. Maybe it was the confidence of a new wardrobe, but I actually felt on top of it.

With my tarts baking, I put ingredients back in the pantry. When I passed by Nate stationed in the medic's corner, I couldn't decide if I wanted to catch his eye or not, so I kept darting glances between him and my feet.

"Imogen."

"Oh, Nate. Didn't see you there." I smiled and tried not to trip over myself.

"How's your finger?" He flashed me that smile that oozed bad-boy charm. Maybe not bad boy, maybe just "I'm gorgeous, and I know it."

"I've got ten of them." *Why would I say that?* But he chuckled, actually chuckled, at something I'd said. *Play it cool, Imogen.* I grinned back.

"Once you put that away, why don't you let me take a look, make sure it's healing properly."

"All right." I walked as calmly as I could into the pantry, set down the jars of sugar and flour in my hands, then scrunched up my nose and wiggled around in a little happy dance. Calmly, I walked back out and presented my completely fine hand to him.

He turned it over, and ran his thumb down the length of my palm. My legs turned to jelly. He stared at it, though I had no burn marks or anything out of place except for a little cinnamon-sugar glaze on my fingers.

Nate raised his dark eyes to mine, lifting my hand closer to his face. "No burns, but you've got a little something there." He slid a finger up to the spot with the glaze. *Lick it off*. The thought came out like a shout in my brain and I worried I'd said it out loud. *Oh God, I didn't, did I?*

He slowly, slowly released my hand. *Oh, please hold it forever.* I pressed my cheek to my hand, the one he'd just been holding, savoring the warmth he'd left behind. I snapped out of it, shaking my head.

"Sorry, just a little tired, I guess. I'm gonna—" I jabbed my thumb over my shoulder to my station and backpedaled, keeping my eyes on his beautiful face for as long as possible. I was almost as bad as Pritney.

Speak of the devil... literally. She stared me down, her thin lips pulled back in a sneer. *Er, awkward.* I made a detour to Maple's station, which smelled of chocolate and sugar—basically heaven.

She didn't look up from frantically smearing a thick white frosting on round orange cookies. "I told you, Glenn, I'm too busy right now to— Oh, Imogen." She glanced up and sighed when she saw it was me.

I chuckled. "Glenn giving you a hard time?"

She rolled her eyes. "Just being Glenn." I followed her gaze to find him standing beside Wool. The tall man had his fire weaving up and down his arms, like he'd had on the first day, and even that and his dark glare wasn't enough to put Glenn off.

Glenn's loud voice carried over the din of the crowd, the clank of spoons and the crash of metal baking pans. "You know, those are quite good for what they are, though not a traditional cookie." He poked at one of Wool's cooling bakes.

The beautiful dark brown gingerbread hands had been decorated with a henna-like swirl of lace and designs. Wool's dark eyes flashed and his lip pulled back. Glenn continued, undeterred. "But when I think cookie, real cookie you know, I think chocolate chip, sugar cookie, shortbread, oatmeal, peanut butter...."

I turned to Maple, drowning him out. "He's the worst. What can I help you with?"

She handed me a thin spatula, and I helped her frost cookies. I'd actually gotten my tarts in the oven early, so it felt nice to be able to help Maple with something for once. She'd already helped me more times than I could count. Eyes still on her work, Maple said, "Still no Prince Harry. Did you notice?"

29

A SIGN

I glanced up toward the bleachers and saw the same king and queen and four princes and their wives. "Hmm, that's right."

Maple leaned closer. "*The Conch*, the Bijou Mer paper, is speculating that he's dating one of the contestants and doesn't want to appear for fear of showing favoritism."

I grinned. "But he could've come today, right? I mean, Lillian was eliminated yesterday."

Behind me, Hank coughed, then coughed again and again. I looked over at his flushed red face and desperately blinking eyes.

"He's choking!" Maple pointed at him.

"Oh!" Bern looked up. "What's the spell for choking?" He fumbled with his spell book.

"It's, uh— It's uh—?" Maple grimaced and shook her hands, bouncing on her feet. "I can't remember!"

I didn't know magic, but I did know the Heimlich maneuver. I dashed over, grabbed Hank around his surprisingly firm middle, and leaned back, lifting my fists in and up with all I had. A piece of dough flew out of his mouth and landed several feet away at Nate's feet.

The medic raised his brows. "Nice, Imogen. I was right behind you if that didn't work."

I nodded, panting. Hank slumped over, one hand on his table, and I slid my arms from around his waist. I came to his side.

"You all right?"

He kept his dark eyes down on the ground, but nodded. I waited a couple of moments. "You sure?"

He gulped, his throat bobbing, then turned to me. "How'd you do that?"

I blinked in surprise. "The Heimlich maneuver? Kind of standard first aid."

He frowned. "Is that a human thing? Heimlich?"

I grinned. "Yeah, Heimlich's a human thing."

He nodded and after another moment I turned to go. I stopped in surprise when he caught my arm. I turned, looking at his giant, warm hand.

"Thank you," he said gruffly, then turned back to his table, slowly sliding his hand away from mine.

I felt.... I wasn't sure what I felt. Light, and fluttery and confused. I returned to Maple. "That was... something."

"That was amazing! You saved him—and without magic." She grinned. "See, you can teach us a thing or two also."

I returned to my station to check on my tarts. And of course, Iggy decided to *be a tart* and burn half of them.

I stood in tears before my scorched pastries, hoping the judges would consider the half of them that weren't turned to soot, when a scream sounded out from the bleachers, followed by another and another. Spectators pointed into the tent, and I whirled.

A tornado of flying tools whipped around Bern's station. He cowered on the ground behind his table, hands thrown over his head, as magically animated scissors snipped through the air erratically, knives flew, and a wooden rolling pin hammered all over his table. I dropped to a crouch and waved Bern over to my station.

As he army-crawled over on his stomach, a rogue pan flew at his head, and I leaped forward, smacking it away with a pan of my own. Screams and the pounding of fleeing feet on the wooden bleachers filled the air.

"What happened?"

Bern pulled himself up to sit against the side of my station, adjusting his glasses. He blinked, face flushed and eyes wild. "I cast a sort of marionette spell, to get the tools working on their own, but they got out of hand, and now I can't get them to stop."

I peeked over the edge of the table. Rhonda and Francis stood in front of the fleeing crowd, beating off utensils with the magic they flung from their hands. I looked behind me to check on Maple, in time to see her scream as a knife flew at her.

A scream stuck in my throat, but Hank leapt in front of her, freezing the knife in place as he threw out his hands, sparks flying from them. My chest heaved with relief.

"Get out, everyone! Get out!" Amelia waved us toward the garden.

"What about the utensils?" Hank barked.

"The Royal Guard have been called. Get out, they'll contain it."

Hank frowned for a moment, then waved at me to follow. He and Wool stood beside the tent's flaps sending the rest of us contestants through. I turned and saw them dash through themselves, magically sealing the tent, as a knife and a potato peeler embedded themselves through the fabric where they'd just been standing.

I stumbled backward across the lawn, keeping my eyes on the tent, until I tripped and stumbled. A pair of strong arms broke my fall. I looked up to see Nate smiling down at me. He lifted me upright and turned me around. I could have stared up at that chiseled face with his scruffy beard forever, except that a harsh cough startled me.

Scowling, Hank stalked past. "We need to get to safety, away from here."

I followed him and the group back to the house, regretfully leaving Nate behind. We spent the next few hours tensely waiting for news. Hank stalked back and forth across the lawn so many times, he actually started to wear a rut in it. Bern sat crumpled in a chair. No matter how many times we told him no one blamed him, he only shook his head. "If anyone's been hurt...."

Finally, Amelia appeared after dinner. She stood with hands clasped, and we gathered around her, expectant. "Good news first. No one was injured, beyond a couple of sprained ankles from tripping while running, and a fractured wrist."

Bern moaned and Wool shook his shoulder. "It's all right, man. Could've been worse."

Amelia nodded. "Everyone injured has already been fixed up and is good as new." She exhaled heavily. "Bad news. Bern, this probably doesn't come as a surprise, but you're out."

"It's the least punishment I deserve." Bern removed his glasses and rubbed the tears from his eyes. My heart went out to him.

"No one blames you, Bern, accidents happen." Amelia

sighed. "Truly. If Rhonda were here, she'd threaten to beat you up if you didn't stop beating yourself up."

That got a chuckle out of him, but his eyes stayed fixed on the ground, his head hanging.

"Oh!" Amelia gasped, eyes round, and pressed a hand to her mouth. With the other she pointed at the sky behind us. I whirled and followed her gaze. More gasps, and Maple screamed. Somewhere, down the mountain in town, a siren began to wail.

Up among the stars and the drifting wisps of gray clouds, a shifting, noxious yellow symbol hovered. A twisting, writhing eel, with a gaping maw and leering expression wrapping around the globe of the Earth, about to swallow it whole.

"What is it?" I whispered.

"Everyone inside," Hank barked.

"Bern, come with me. Everyone else, stay inside till I tell you otherwise." Amelia and Bern dashed across the field, and we all ran toward the house.

Once inside, I gazed out the windows at the swirling spectacle. My heart pounded with fear. "What is it?"

Maple turned her pale face toward me. "The symbol of the Badlands Army. It always appears before they attack... and kill." Tears welled in her eyes. "I hope my family's all right."

I put an arm around her shoulders and hugged her close. With heavy hearts we retired to bed, unsure of what the next morning would hold.

30

EXTINGUISHED

We gathered on the lawn the next morning. Amelia announced, "First of all, everyone's all right. We've had no known attacks."

"*Known* attacks." Glenn raised a finger. He sounded way too cheerful as he said, "But we may discover a body in one of the canals or up a chimney, or half the sewer might still be blown away, or—"

Amelia cut him off. "Because our city appears safe, the competition will continue today. But we will have no spectators, making the competition less of a target for attack. This will also prevent someone from the BA from sneaking in as a member of the audience."

My stomach relaxed slightly, and I glanced at Maple. Neither of us had enjoyed the scrutiny of the crowd. That, at least, would be a relief. I also found comfort when I passed through the magic field around the tent, the cool tingle blowing over my skin. That lent us some safety.

Once behind our stations, aprons donned, Amelia announced, "It's bread day. You'll have three hours to bake an artisanal loaf. Sweet or savory, it must be impressive. Begin!"

I grinned, enjoying the noises of magic and baking, clanking pots and the thunks of glass jars on butcher block. Today, without hundreds of eyes trained on me, might be my day. I yawned, my jaw aching as I stretched my mouth wide. Well, might be my day, if I could wake up. I'd tossed and turned all night.

As I considered what type of bread to make, a trilling little song from an orange and gold bird sounded from a tree outside the tent. It reminded me of a bread I'd seen once, braided, with colored eggs woven in. I could wrap the braid to form a round nest and weave in some exotic eggs like I'd seen in Maple's bakery. I hoped Rhonda and Francis would find that impressive enough.

I passed Maple on my way to the pantry for ingredients. She looked more at home in the tent than I'd ever seen her.

I called to her, "Why's the baker the richest man in town?"

She looked up and frowned. "I dunno, why?"

"Because he's got all the dough."

She groaned, and I chuckled. *What a hoot I am.* As I passed Hank, he shook his head.

The deep bags under his eyes and the aggression with which he smashed his flour, eggs, and water between his bare hands made me give him a wider berth. *Geez, someone's not a fan of cheesy jokes.*

I puttered around the pantry for a few minutes, gathering eggs from the basket marked "Rainbow Thrush." The second I saw them, I couldn't resist. Roughly the size of a chicken egg, the shell twisted with deep grooves, almost like a soft-serve ice cream. Brilliant colors of purple, blue, yellow, red, and green swirled around the egg like, well, a rainbow.

I carried a large armful of ingredients back to my station. Hank had moved on to kneading, slamming the heel of his hand into the wet dough, dragging it forward, lifting the ball of dough, smacking it down, and repeating. I blinked and raised my brows, but took care not to meet his eyes. Someone had had a worse night than me, it seemed.

Maple sang a jaunty little tune as she kneaded. I smiled to myself and listened as I unpacked my ingredients.

> *"Flour the table*
> *And spread it round,*
> *Mix up your dough,*
> *Plop down the mound,*
> *Shape it and work it till,*
> *It's loosely bound,*
> *A making bread we go.*
>
> *Flour your hands,*
> *We've mouths to feed,*
> *Punch the dough,*
> *Do the deed,*
> *Fold and rock,*
> *And press and knead,*
> *A making bread we go.*
>
> *No rest for the wicked,*
> *No rest for the dough,*
> *Not too quickly,*
> *And not too slow,*
> *Knead it in rhythm,*

*And work it in flow,
A making bread we go."*

I BOBBED my head and hummed along with her. My enchanted blue quill scratched notes in my new recipe book as I mixed up my dough.

Oops! I needed to get Iggy preheating the oven.

I crouched down to speak with him, and my stomach clenched with panic. Instead of the usual heat warming my face, only a cold, dark oven opened before me.

"Iggy?" An edge of panic laced my words. "Iggy?" Where was he?

A small flame, like that of a candle, peeked over a charred stick.

"Iggy!" I jumped to my feet, panicked. "Help!" Surprised and worried expressions met mine as I whirled, looking around the tent. I wasn't sure what I needed, but I felt sure Iggy was moments away from extinguishing for good.

"What's wrong?"

I jumped at the gruff voice behind me, instantly recognizing it as Hank's. I turned and looked up at his tall frame. His glassy, bloodshot eyes softened as he looked at me. "How can I help?"

"It's Iggy, my fire, he's almost out." I pointed at the oven and Hank dropped down to look inside. I pressed my trembling lips together as tears rolled down my cheeks.

He rubbed one wrist with his other hand. "Get me some dry firewood and tell Wool to come over here."

I nodded and dashed off, going to Wool first. When I returned, skidding to a stop in front of my station with arms full of logs, I could tell by the heat on my legs that Iggy was already better.

I dropped the pile and fell to my knees beside Hank and Wool. Wool held his palms to the fire, eyes closed, humming and chanting words I didn't understand. His palms glowed red and fire danced up and down his arms and shoulders. I looked from him to Hank, who gave me a slow nod. "Iggy's going to be all right."

I slumped with relief, letting out the breath I'd been holding. "Really?"

"Yeah." Hank nodded. His thick brows knitted together. "You can't forget to feed your fire like that, though. He could've died, very nearly did in fact. You left him all night with no firewood and—"

I nodded, my chin trembling, and then buried my face in my hands and sobbed. He was right, of course. I'd been irresponsible, and if I'd had any magical talent at all I could've cast an auto-feed spell, or whatever Iggy had called it the other day. I cried harder, my shoulders shaking. I was a talentless failure who didn't deserve—

My thoughts and my body stilled as Hank wrapped his arms around me, tentatively at first, and then pulled me closer in a gentle embrace. Shock made me freeze. And then, after a few moments, I relaxed, resting my cheek on his shoulder. My tears wet his shirt.

I felt a warm, tingly wave of energy. A heady rush filled me up, from toes to head. I pulled back, surprised at my own reluctance to let go, and looked at him. My mouth fell open in surprise.

"Your eyes."

His dark eyes now looked blue, his jaw more square, and his nose straighter and— Before I could finish taking inventory of the many small changes that added up to a different face, he stood, leaving me tottering on my heels. "You've got this, Wool?"

It seemed more a command than a question. He strode past his station, where I'd assumed he was headed, to the pantry. I blinked after him. I'd felt something when he hugged me, tingly and warm and fluttery—had that been magic? Was it magic that made his face look different sometimes?

Wool finished chanting and turned to me. "Imogen?"

I nodded. "Yes? How's Iggy?"

"He'll be all right. As Hank said, you must be more careful with your flame. You could have lost him." He stood, his own flame still playing up and down his arms.

"Thank you." I pressed my hands together, still feeling shaky with worry. "Thank you, so much. How did you get him back?"

Wool's dark eyes twinkled. "We from the Fire Kingdom have a way with flames. It's good Hank told you to get me."

"I can't even...." I let out a tremulous breath. "I owe you. Big time."

Wool nodded. "I'll remember that." He headed to his station, and I glanced at Maple, who practically drooled as she watched him, slowly dragging the heel of her hand through her dough.

31

PROOF

I turned to Iggy, grateful that he blazed much brighter, some heat reaching my cheeks. "Iggy, I am so sorry. I can't even tell you—"

His eyes narrowed to tiny slits. "You abandoned me."

My chest tightened with guilt. "I'm so sorry. They told us to evacuate the tent, knives were flying and—"

"And you should have come back for me or asked someone to feed me."

"You're absolutely right." Another tear trickled down my cheek.

"I bet you want me dead, don't you?"

I recoiled. "N-no." I blinked frantically.

Iggy flared, sending me stumbling back, then turned his back to me.

"Iggy?"

I got no response. I sighed. I didn't blame him for being furious. I felt furious with myself.

"I know we don't always get along, but I would never want to hurt you. I promise. I messed up, really badly. I *should* have asked someone to check on you. Just, please know, I'm sorry."

He showed no sign of hearing me, so eventually I stood up and got to making my bread with a heavy heart. Even Maple's jaunty baking song couldn't put a spring in my step. I kneaded and worked my bread, then put a towel over it and took it to the pantry to let it rise on the shelves with everyone else's.

During the downtime that followed, I made half-hearted conversation with Maple and thanked Wool again, profusely. Hank looked like his normal self, and though I tried to catch him, to thank him and try to ferret out some information about the change in appearance I'd seen, he avoided me. Well, that and Glenn cornered him, making the possibility of anyone else getting a word in impossible.

As I half listened to Rhonda's visions of tomorrow's weather, I watched Hank and Glenn. I couldn't hear what Glenn said, but his hands flew in his usual bombastic manner, and Hank's face grew darker and darker. My stomach tightened with unease. Hank seemed edgy and tired, and Glenn couldn't be helping.

"And then, a rainbow." Rhonda spread her hands in an arc through the air, smiling. She grew serious as she pointed at Sam. "Watch how long you stand looking at it though, there's a certain seagull that's got a poopy present with your name on it. Left shoulder."

Sam blinked.

Something about birds pooping on people reminded me that I hadn't been the butt of any snarky comments or dirty looks for a while.

"Where's Pritney?" I asked no one in particular.

"I ssssaw her wander into the garden a little while ago." Sam pushed his glasses up his nose.

A metallic crash sounded, like a clap of thunder, and we all jumped.

"Stop!" Hank's growl raised the hair on the back of my neck. I froze as Hank jabbed a trembling finger at Glenn, who backed up, palms raised.

Glenn blinked his wide, round eyes. "Okay, Hank, calm down. Didn't know my detailed comparison of the strengths of the Earth Kingdom's Guild over the Water Kingdom's would upset you so much, but if you're so touchy that—"

Hank slammed his palm down on the table. I grimaced —that had to have stung. Hank's broad chest heaved and after a few moments of heavy silence, he slid his eyes across to our stunned group. His eyes found mine, and the anger in them faded. He lowered his head and stalked off past the bleachers.

That left us all staring at Glenn. The pudgy man raised his shoulders in an exaggerated shrug, then thumbed toward Hank.

"If you can't handle the heat, get out of the tent, as they say." He chuckled dryly, but when no one joined him, he cleared his throat. "I'm just gonna take a turn around the garden, fresh air and all that." He waddled outside, and Maple and I turned to each other.

"Awkward," Rhonda sang.

Maple cleared her throat. "Looks like it's time I checked my prove."

I nodded as she walked to the pantry, joined by Sam and Wool. They'd all gotten their dough into the pantry to rise ages before me. I fidgeted with the hem of my apron as the three of them carried their bowls back to their stations. I craned my neck to get a look. All of the dough balls had grown to twice their original size and had a nice shine. That would make good bread.

If I didn't take mine out soon, I wouldn't have enough time for the bake, but if I took it out of the pantry too soon, the bread would turn out flat and tough. I bit my lip and brushed my bangs out of my face, waiting as long as I could. After another fifteen minutes, I walked over to the pantry, doing mental calculations.

Okay, if I work it and braid it for ten minutes, then weave in the eggs, that'll take another five, and hopefully the oven's hot enough, I can bake for twenty-five minutes. Oh wait, I still need to brush the egg over the dough to get that shine.

In the dim pantry, I found my bowl beside the others, and walked back to my station. I dumped the bread out on my floured countertop. It had risen surprisingly well.

I pulled it into three equal sections, rolling and pulling each section into three long, skinny ropes. As I greased my baking sheet, the sound of voices made me turn.

"Well, I never, I mean—" Glenn muttered to himself as he entered the tent from the garden, wringing his hands and taking a few steps in one direction and then a few in another. He seemed confused or conflicted. Could he still be upset over his row with Hank?

Suddenly Hank threw back the flaps on the opposite side of the tent and stalked toward his station, eyes on the ground. Still muttering, Glenn shuffled to the pantry, and Pritney appeared just behind Glenn.

A shout startled me. What now? Glenn staggered out of the pantry.

"Who's taken my dough?" Glenn rounded on Pritney, jabbing his finger in her direction. "Was this you?"

Her heavy brow dropped low and her eyes burned. "How dare you!"

Glenn scowled and began stalking around the tent,

investigating everyone's stations. "You think this is some sort of prank?"

Had he looked hard enough at the shelves, there'd been three bowls left, one each for him, Hank, and Pritney. Unless.... Oh no.

I looked at my bowl and with a sinking stomach realized that the towel that had covered the dough was blue, where mine had been blue and green. I stepped back, hands in the air in surrender.

"Oh Glenn, I'm so sorry."

He looked up from poking around Maple's cabinets, while she looked on, horrified. He stiffened and stalked to my station. "What have you done?"

"I thought it was mine, honestly." I sighed, my throat tight. I just seemed incapable of doing anything right. First, I'd nearly extinguished Iggy, now this?

"I don't trust that anyone in this tent is honest anymore." Glenn threw his nose in the air and sniffed. He gathered up his bread then turned to Rhonda and Francis, who stood nearby, drawn by the commotion. "I want it noted that she worked my dough and any issues with toughness and texture are entirely her fault."

I swallowed. "It's true."

Amelia rushed into the tent from some errand. "What's going on?"

Glenn jabbed a finger at me. "Cheaters and liars all around. But most pertinent right now, is she's stolen my dough."

"It was an accident." My chest trembled as I fought to hold back tears. "Truly, the pantry is dim and—"

"And so are you!" Glenn barked.

I pressed a palm to my aching chest.

"You don't speak to her like that." I turned. Hank's dark

eyes looked rabid in his pale face. He stood very still, but a vein in his neck bulged and his knuckles looked blotchy as he gripped the edge of the table.

Amelia looked back and forth between him and me and Glenn. "All right, enough. I know we've been under a great amount of strain, but this is a baking competition, for great ocean's sake! Everyone, back to their stations, finish this up, and yes, Glenn, we've noted that she worked your dough, but let's complete the task and just sort this out during judging, all right? In the meantime, everyone cool it."

32

OUT

I took a shaky breath and slunk back to the pantry to get my real dough. I peeked under the towel. The measly thing had barely risen at all.

With a heavy heart I carried it past the medic corner where Pritney, pretending to be injured no doubt, stood huddled with Nate. I couldn't hear what she said, but her harsh and frantic whispers sounded angry. I tried to catch Nate's eye, but he kept his head down, eyes on Pritney.

I stood before my station, divided the dough, braided it, circled it up, and worked in six of the rainbow eggs.

"Iggy?"

I didn't get a response, and I hadn't expected to. I pushed the tray with my flat, lifeless bread into the oven and flipped my hourglass, muttering "Twenty-five minutes."

I tucked the thing in my apron, padded out of the tent and past the bleachers, and collapsed at the base of a giant tree. I leaned my back into its trunk, pulled my knees up close, and buried my face in my lap to cry.

I'm out, I'm absolutely out. Even if they don't end up disquali-

fying me for taking Glenn's bread, mine has absolutely got to be the worst of the group's. It's flat and dull, and that's assuming Iggy doesn't torch it or underbake it, and I'd hardly blame him for doing either. I cried harder into my apron.

After I'd cried myself tired, I leaned against the tree. The sea breeze ruffled my hair, and the waving boughs cast mottled shadows across my arms and legs. I'd miss this place. I'd come to love it here. It felt like home, like where I belonged. I leaned my chin on my knees. Maybe it was home. Had my parents been from the Water Kingdom?

Beyond what lay in the past, I had friends. I had Maple, I had magic and beauty and adventure... but I also had a temporary visa.

I'd asked Amelia about it earlier in the competition. I could only stay till the Summer Solstice, and then after that if I wanted to return, I'd have to apply for a new visa. If I'd won, I could've stayed on a work permit. But with security concerns about the Badlands Army and no magical records or knowledge of my birth parents, she'd told me to expect a lengthy, tedious process. And I thought that was her being nice.

In the meantime, I'd have to figure out a way to get back home on the funds I had left and try to get a new job. I brushed my palm over the lush blades of green grass. Ah well, I could only do my best.

I stood, brushed myself off, and went back to the tent. Even the delicious smell of baking bread couldn't comfort me much. Maple gave me a tight-lipped smile, and I gave her one back, mouthing, "I'm all right." She frowned, but nodded and went back to fanning her beautiful round twist loaf, filled with a sugary nut spread. I knew one person who'd be continuing on till tomorrow. That cheered me a bit. At least I could stay on and cheer for my friend.

I pulled my pan from the oven with just minutes left in the giant hourglass. Iggy had decided not to bake it at all. The dough had spread and when I poked it, it was still gooey and raw. I took a shaky breath and when Amelia announced, "Time's up," I carried the sad loaf to the front table on a ceramic platter.

Maple gave my hand a tight squeeze. Tears trickled silently down my cheeks. I didn't want to be crying, but I couldn't seem to stop. The judges and Amelia came to stand before us.

"I've got something to say."

I blinked the tears from my eyes and looked down the line to Glenn. Though short, he'd drawn himself up to his full height, chest puffed out. "I've been debating and debating, and I feel it's my duty to say something. I simply cannot let such flagrant cheating—"

My stomach clenched. How could he think I'd meant to take his bread? Well, I guessed my dough was awful, and someone in my situation might try taking someone else's. But if that were the case, wouldn't I have tried to be sneakier about it? And did he really think so lowly of me?

Before he could continue, Pritney, who'd been running behind, pushed her way between Glenn and Sam, turning as she did so. The bread she'd shaped like a coiled dragon opened its mouth and a curling flame shot out of it, catching Glenn's sleeve on fire.

"Ah!" He screamed and batted at it. Sighing, Amelia threw an arm out, magically dousing Glenn in water and extinguishing the fire.

Panting, Glenn looked around, panicked.

"Go see the medic, Glenn," Amelia ordered, pointing back toward Nate in the corner. His thick brows had drawn together in a deep frown. "You can finish telling us all about the flagrant cheating after he patches you up."

Glenn opened his mouth to speak, and Amelia barked, "Uh!" Then she pointed to the medic and Glenn hung his head like a puppy and trudged back to the corner.

Amelia let out a heavy sigh. "Right then. Thank the great sea goddess we didn't have an audience today." She waved the judges forward. "To it, then? You can come back to Glenn's when he returns."

Rhonda and Francis tasted their way down the line, Rhonda moaning over Maple's loaf. "Oh, this is divine. Absolutely divine." She ate an extra bite.

I came next. They stared blankly at my loaf.

"I can't eat that, it's raw. I'll have stomach bloat if I do, and I've got a hot date tonight, so...." Rhonda grimaced.

Francis sniffed it. "Completely inedible."

Rhonda shook her head. "Even if it had been baked, I can tell it didn't prove long enough. It should have at least risen some."

I nodded, my throat tight.

Rhonda gave me a sad smile. "Sorry, Imogen. We all make mistakes sometimes."

They finished their lap and about that time, Glenn rejoined us, his right forearm wrapped in white binding. Rhonda lifted off a hunk of Glenn's cheesy pull-apart bread, a long yellow string trailing behind. She chewed and chewed, looking right then left.

"Normally, mate, I'd say put bread and cheese together, you've got yourself a winner. And it's decent, but rather bland. Not enough salt, maybe."

Francis nodded, still chewing.

Glenn's dark skin flushed a deeper shade and he shot me

a fiery glance. He yanked off a hunk of the bread and popped it in his mouth. He chewed a bit, then said around the bread, "Well, uf she hodn't pulled it and worked it, it'd be softer, but you're crazy if you think id needs salt 'cause—"

He stopped and dipped his chin forward, blinking rapidly. He coughed, then coughed again, his breath wheezy. Glenn spit the bread out of his mouth and pressed both hands to his throat, while his face turned red and blotchy.

"What's wrong with him?" Rhonda turned to Amelia and Francis.

Sam put a hand on Glenn's back. "Are you all right? I think he'ssss choking."

"Medic!" Amelia shouted. "Nate, over here now!"

Oh no. I itched to help, but had no idea how. Nate cast an antichoking spell and Glenn, turning a deep shade of purple, shook his head. He slumped over and Nate, Sam, and Hank eased him to the ground.

"Give him some space," Nate ordered, his deep voice tremulous. He fumbled in his bag as everyone backed up, forming a wide ring around Glenn, who trembled and shook, his breath coming in short pants. Nate poured a vial of red liquid down Glenn's throat, murmuring some incantation. I held my breath, waiting for some change.

"He's not choking," Hank barked. "The spell didn't work."

"His allergy!" Maple cried. "Remember his allergy to snake venom."

"How could we forget it," Francis grumbled, hovering over Glenn with his sharp-featured stare.

"Suck his blood," Hank bellowed.

Francis shook his head. "Won't do any good."

Hank's eyes blazed. "Why not?"

Glenn went limp, his head lolling to the side, eyes open and unseeing. Maple shrieked and covered her mouth, and I pulled her close in a hug.

Francis pointed with a long, pale finger. "He's already dead."

33

THE INVESTIGATION

"Everyone, out of the tent." Amelia pointed with a trembling hand.

"B-but... Glenn." Sam looked from Amelia to the body on the ground.

Her gray eyes softened. "I know, Sam. But come on."

Once outside, Amelia shot a firework from her hands. It whizzed up high in the sky and erupted into the shape of a hand, index finger pointed straight down at us. The hand spun slowly, sparking and glittering in red and then white, alternating colors like a police siren.

"What now?" Hank asked, his voice gruff.

Amelia folded her hands. "We wait."

It didn't take the police long to arrive, minutes at most. They swept across the field, a team of about eight, cloaked in high-necked navy jackets with gold buttons, led by a short man with a tall blue cap.

"I'm Inspector Bon." The short man nodded at Amelia. "Where's the body?"

She stepped toward the tent, but he threw an arm out.

"Police personnel only." Inspector Bon spun on his heel, followed by his officers.

"How he'd know about Glenn?"

Maple pointed at the finger in the sky. "Different colors mean different situations. Red and white means... means someone has died."

I drew Maple into a hug and watched the officers crouch around Glenn, and then sweep the tent. We waited for hours, the police periodically questioning Amelia.

Maple and I sat in the shade of a big tree, neither of us, or anyone else for that matter, speaking much. Nate even sat near me among the roots, but I couldn't find the energy to care. Finally, Inspector Bon rejoined us, leaving a couple officers guarding the tent.

"You were right to call us." Bon nodded at Amelia. "The victim was murdered."

I gasped and pressed my hands to my mouth.

"No," Maple breathed.

"Mur-murdered?" Sam rubbed his shoulder and rolled his neck in discomfort.

"Hold on now." Amelia raised a hand. "Why are you thinking murder?"

"That man," Inspector Bon pointed back at where Glenn had died. Paramedics had carried his body off some time ago. "That man died of an allergic reaction to snake venom."

My stomach tightened with sympathy.

"He couldn't have," Amelia said. "We were aware of his allergy and banned snake venom from the tent. All of our contestants pass through a magical security field."

"Exactly." Bon shifted, standing with his legs spread wider apart, one thin brow cocked in an arrogant grin. "The victim's bread tested positive for snake venom."

I gasped, and Rhonda spoke aloud my own thought.

"Why would Glenn have put something he was allergic to in his own bread?"

"Unless, *he* didn't." Inspector Bon scanned each of our faces. "You lot were the only ones in the tent today, the only ones with the opportunity to kill."

Amelia scowled. "These are some very serious accusations, Inspector."

"Imogen could have done it."

My stomach seized. Pritney stood, pointing a slender finger at me. "She took his bread, remember? She had it at her station, played with it, had all those strange eggs—maybe one was a snake egg. She could've put the poison in."

"Hey!" Nate scrambled to his feet.

Pritney shot him a withering look. "She had the opportunity. And she had the motive. We all know she was being eliminated today. She was desperate to stay in, so she murdered Glenn to avoid being ousted."

"No." I could barely speak. I wanted to scream the word, but I couldn't quite catch my breath.

Maple put an arm around my shoulders. "Imogen would never do something like that."

"Besides," Hank came up and stood on my other side, "we all left our dough in the pantry. Anyone could have added the poison then. And again, we come back to the means. No one could have gotten snake poison inside the tent."

I couldn't quite manage a smile, but I hoped my earnest look let Hank know how much I appreciated him coming to my defense. He glanced at me and nodded.

"The Badlandsss Army." We all turned to look at Sam. He looked on the verge of tears. "The mark lassst night. We all sssaw it. Thisss could be them."

I hadn't even considered that. Could the mysterious, evil group be behind Glenn's death?

Amelia waved us down. "We don't even know for sure he was murdered, do we, Inspector? This could all just be a huge mistake."

Inspector Bon rubbed his hands together. "All I know for sure is that we'll be questioning each and every one of you individually. Starting now."

When it came to my turn, they asked me to recount the events of the day over and over again. Occasionally Bon and the two officers who sat with him would throw in a random question along the lines of, "Did you dislike Glenn? Did you want him dead? Why did you kill him?"

I think they intended to trip me up. They grilled me about taking his dough, and no matter how many times I told them it'd been an accident, they continued to act like I'd meant to do it. After an hour and a half, they let me go, and I stumbled back to sit under the tree, exhausted. Finally, after the sun had just set, they released us.

"Everyone is to stay on the grounds, tonight and for the duration of this investigation. Any departure, and you will be placed under arrest. Are we clear? We have a fairly good idea who the culprit is." Bon cast his eyes around the group, looking here and there, lingering on my face.

"So this is definitely a murder investigation?" Amelia cocked her head to the side.

"We're not releasing any information as of yet." Bon pressed his lips together smugly.

"Fine. Then what of the competition? If it's not officially a murder investigation, we should be all right to continue tomorrow?" Amelia raised her brow, hands on hips.

Bon spluttered. "Well— I— This is highly—" He stopped and swallowed. "I'll allow it, provisionally. And we shall have officers on hand tomorrow to keep an eye on all of you."

Oh goody. I felt more depressed than I could say. A man had died, and thanks to Pritney's accusations, I felt confident that I was now the lead suspect in a murder investigation.

34

IGGY

I swayed on my feet. I hadn't slept well for two nights in a row. The oven fires burned hot in the tent, making the air stuffy and thick.

I looked at the spot on the ground where Glenn had died. It didn't feel right to be baking today, as if nothing had happened. Then again, doing nothing would drive me crazy too.

I let out a heavy sigh as Amelia took her place in the front with Rhonda and Francis, all wearing mourning black. Inspector Bon stood to the side of them, eight more of his officers stationed around the tent, one just to my left. I hissed and scratched at my ankle as a mosquito bit me.

"Let's all take a moment of silence for Glenn," Amelia said, hands folded in front of her. It didn't escape me, the irony of taking a moment of silence for a man who had never stopped talking. But I folded my hands, lowered my head, and thought of Glenn.

I'm sorry, Glenn. You didn't deserve to die.

Amelia lifted her head. "Thank you. We will all miss Glenn. His... his larger than life personality, his...." She took a deep breath and opened and closed her mouth several times. She seemed at a loss. "Well, he'll be missed."

"Well said," Rhonda murmured.

I bit my lip to keep from cracking a smile. Just like me, too, at the most inappropriate times.

"But, the show must go on, as they say," Amelia continued. "We must all find a way forward, despite the sad and tragic events of yesterday. Glenn loved baking, and what better way to remember and honor him, than by continuing to do what he loved. So today, bakers, shall be pie day. Please make any pie, sweet or savory, that you desire. It must be lovely and tasty. You have three hours. Go!"

I took a deep breath, acutely aware of the man in uniform to my left. He stood stock still, which only grated on my nerves more.

"How interesting that you've time to relax."

I jumped. Inspector Bon stood across the station from me. He looked right and left. "All your competitors are already scrambling. Is there a reason you feel that you're safe? Perhaps you know you'll just 'take care of' any competition that gets in your way?"

I scowled, my hands balled into tight, clammy fists. "I just needed to collect myself. Now if you'll excuse me, I have to bake."

"Oh, don't let me interrupt. But my officers and I will be on hand, watching closely for clues, so don't let us get in your way."

I plastered on a bright smile. "Oh, I won't."

Bon moved on to speak with Sam, thankfully. Today was not the day to try anything fancy. I just didn't have it in me. So I'd do a classic. Cherry pie.

After a few trips to the pantry to gather supplies, and another to the garden to pick cherries, I mixed up my dough for the crust, divided it into two, and Maple cast a frigus spell for me to get the disks of dough cooling. Then I got working on the filling. I crouched down to speak with Iggy.

"Iggy. Can you please heat the oven up for a cherry pie?"

"Thanks for leaving me firewood this time." Iggy glowed red. "I see you're at least not trying to kill *me*."

"Is that in reference to Glenn?"

"You're not the brightest candle on the cake, are you?"

My nostrils flared as I tried to bite down on my anger. "I didn't kill him."

"Ha!" Iggy barked out a laugh. "I know that. He was poisoned with an illicit substance. You don't have the brains or the talent to sneak something like that past a magical field."

Heat flushed up my throat and chest and a muscle in my jaw jumped. "A man died, Iggy. Show some respect."

"A ha!" He barked out another joyless laugh. "Oh that's rich, coming from you."

I dropped to my knees. "What's that supposed to mean, huh? Why are you so hard on me anyway? You do nothing but insult me, but what about you? If you're so great, how come you can't bake to save your life?"

I shook my head, huffing. "You probably never baked a day in your life before you came into this tent. Someone thought it a great big joke to give Imogen the surly campground fire? Or maybe you're a dung pile fire, eh? Is that it?" My chest heaved with the vehemence of my anger, and I could feel my pulse pounding in my neck.

Iggy shook, his flame trembling and burning redder and redder. I thought he might explode, and I half welcomed it, when suddenly he dimmed and his mouth wavered.

"I was the royal baker's flame, you dolt." His voice held none of his usual bite, only sadness. "And you're not half the baker she is... was! None of you are." Iggy took a shuddering breath, his flames shrinking and dimming.

I swallowed, my throat impossibly tight, as a great round tear squeezed out his eye. *Flames can cry.* Then another tear squeezed out, and another.

"She was plump and lovely and kind and she always fed me linden branches, my favorite logs, even though she had to wander into the forest on the royal grounds to find them, with her bad knee." Iggy wept, his flames shaking with wracking sobs. "She's gone. She's gone, and all you lot care about is taking her job. But-but I miss her!" He dissolved into tears that fell upon the coals at his base, sizzling and steaming.

Tears welled up in my eyes, and I reached out before I knew what I was doing. The hairs on my arms curled up and I pulled my hand back. Oh, how did you comfort a flame? I sniffled as more tears ran down my cheeks.

"Oh, Iggy. Oh, don't cry, Iggy. You'll put yourself out." I squirmed, wanting so badly to do something for him. The flame continued to sob and gulp, small and dim.

"Iggy. Iggy, what was her name?"

Iggy sniffed and mumbled. "Nan."

"Nan sounds wonderful."

"She was."

Maybe talking about her would make him feel better. Now that I thought about the competition from his point of view, everything made sense. I'd feel the same way if someone I loved had died and I was forced, while still grieving, to partner with someone new who wanted to take their place. How awful.

"How long did you work with Nan?"

"Twenty-five years."

My heart ached. "That's such a long time. You two must have been very close."

"She said we were like an old married couple. Her husband died about ten years ago, but she always said at least she had me."

I stayed crouched in front of the oven, talking with Iggy for a long time. All about the baking disasters they'd had, the scramble right before a big banquet, the way Nan had claimed every day she wasn't ever going back into those woods for those darned linden branches and how every morning she showed up with a bundle more.

"She could've just used magic of course, or sent someone else for them, but she always went herself. Just for me," Iggy finished quietly, sniffling, but no longer sobbing.

I swallowed against the lump in my throat.

"Until one day." Iggy let out a heavy sigh. "One day, she just didn't come into the kitchen. I waited and waited. They didn't tell me she was gone till the next day. Everybody forgets about the flames."

Sucker punch to the heart. I sniffled and wiped away a puddle of tears from my eyes. "I'm so sorry, I've been so thoughtless. And those things I said to you before...." I shook my head. "I'll never forgive myself."

Iggy coughed out a laugh. "Well. I haven't been a hearth fire to you, myself."

I wiped my hands on my apron, making a decision. "Iggy, I've been unfair to you. Giving you no choice but to bake, when you were heartbroken and not even bothering to get to know you. I'm quitting. I don't want you to have to suffer anymore, and I don't want to fight my friends for a job I've never deserved." I knelt up, ready to stand and go tell Amelia.

"Hold on."

I hesitated. Iggy slid over the logs, closer to me, his voice lower. "I, uh—I don't want you to quit." He didn't meet my eyes.

Shock held me still. "You... don't?"

Iggy shook his head, still looking down. A sly smile pulled his mouth to the side. "You might be clumsy, airheaded, and the least magically talented person I've ever met."

"Warming my heart here." I huffed through my nose.

"But you also remind me of Nan in some ways. You're kind, and you care about people and... and you'd make a great royal baker."

He glanced up at me. Tears welled up in my eyes as I gave him a tight-lipped smile.

"Oh, don't go getting all sappy." He looked away.

"I wish I could hug you." I cocked my head to the side, wondering how I'd never noticed how cute he was.

"Again with the empty head—only hug me if you want third-degree burns."

"All right, so... I guess that means we're a team?"

"Yeah. I guess so." Iggy grinned, then suddenly grew serious. "On one condition."

I gulped. "Now I'm worried again."

Iggy pulled himself even closer, the heat of his flames making my cheeks sting. "I want you to help me catch Nan's killer."

35

A PARTNER

"You want me to help you catch Nan's killer."

"Stay with me," Iggy deadpanned.

"I thought... well, I knew there were rumors, but I thought she died of a heart attack?" I frowned.

Iggy shook his head and lowered his voice. "Nan may have been old, but she was tough. You should have seen some of the crises she handled. Plus she hiked through the forest every day with a bundle of logs in her arms for me. She was healthy."

Iggy gave me a pleading look. "Believe me, she was murdered. I just know it, in my gut. She'd told me she'd had a funny feeling for weeks. She thought someone was following her, and then she wound up dead. And now Glenn's death proves it."

I raised my brows. "You think the same person killed Nan and Glenn?"

"It makes sense, doesn't it? The only person who could've killed Glenn was in the tent yesterday for a baking competition to become the next royal baker, after the royal baker's killed? Someone wants that job."

"Enough to kill for it?"

"It's not the job, Imogen." Iggy huffed. "The royal baker makes food for the most powerful people in all the kingdoms. Someone from the Badlands Army, for instance, in that position could poison the king or put a mind control spell on the queen. They could do a lot of damage."

I pressed my hands to my mouth. "Iggy, this is serious stuff. We should tell the police."

Iggy rolled his eyes. "If the police aren't idiots, they've already considered it. And if they think they're just going to stand around until someone slips up and reveals themselves as the killer, they're even dumber than they look."

"But I'm not an investigator," I hissed.

"No, but you know everyone and can talk to them. Snoop, without it seeming like you're snooping. We might be able to learn something. I'm telling you, Imogen, it's someone in this tent."

I sighed. "The police think so, too. In fact, I'm pretty sure I'm their top suspect. I had the most access to Glenn's dough to add the poison, and I was definitely about to be eliminated that day, giving me the most motive to kill to stay in."

Iggy nodded. "See? All the more reason to figure out who the real killer is, to clear your name."

I tilted my head side to side. He had a good point. "All right. What about the judges or Amelia?" I glanced around, hoping no one had overhead us. With all the clanging pots and trays and the birds chirping like crazy outside, I doubted it.

Iggy shrugged. "Maybe. But it'd have to be in partnership with one of the contestants, otherwise what would they gain?"

I sighed. "I hate to say it, but you might have a point. Glenn might have been an accident, except how did the snake venom get into the tent in the first place? And no one besides the people here could have done it. I hate to think that of anyone though." No one seemed capable of something so awful. "Well, except Pritney." I rolled my eyes, then jumped. "Oh my God, do you think it could have been Pritney?"

"Keep your voice down," Iggy hissed.

Inspector Bon chose that moment to pop his head round the corner. "Everything all right down here? Planning more dastardly deeds?" He chuckled, though his dark eyes focused in on me like a hawk.

Before I could answer, Amelia appeared behind him. "You have one hour left, Imogen. I'd get baking if I were you."

Shoot! One hour? I grimaced at Iggy as Amelia and Bon moved on.

"Go, go," he urged. "We can only solve the murders if you're still in the competition and have access to the other contestants."

"Right." I jumped up. This would be tight. The pie needed at least forty minutes to bake, and I still had to roll out my crusts and fill them.

I rolled and poured and pinched and shaped as quickly as possible, then slid the pie in, turning over my hourglass and ordering, "Forty minutes."

Were magical hourglasses sentient like magical flames?

"Please," I added, just in case.

I glanced up at the big hourglass that marked how much time we had left. Urg, this would be so close. And now, on top of my whole personal future riding on this pie, the capture of a killer apparently rested on it, too. A lot of pressure for a pie. I hoped the little guy could handle it.

I sat in front of the oven, pretending to check the color of my crust when the Inspector or one of the judges passed by. But in reality, Iggy and I talked suspects.

"So, yeah, Pritney definitely seems the most evil of us, doesn't she?"

Glowing away, Iggy nodded. "I suspected her, too, especially with Nan. I never understood why she hired her, wasn't very good at baking and such a wench. But somehow she won Nan's favor and got promoted to Nan's assistant. She was next in line for the job, and with the personality of a male elephant seal"—I raised a brow—"the ones that crush their own babies, she naturally aroused my suspicions." Iggy shook his head. "But she went home to visit family when Nan died. She was gone the whole week, not even in France."

"Hmm." I couldn't quite give up on the idea of it being Pritney. "Maybe she was slowly poisoning her and left after administering the last dose, giving herself an alibi."

Iggy shook his head. "No. Nan was perfectly healthy, up until the end. That's what made it such a shock."

I pulled my lips to the side. Pritney might be a wench, but not necessarily a killer wench.

"Though, I was in the kitchen when Amelia delivered the news that they were holding this competition." Iggy scoffed. "She threw a fit, tossing pans at the wall and screeching like a banshee when she found out she wasn't being automatically promoted."

I lifted my head and peered over the countertops to the back row. I didn't see Pritney at her station. I looked the other way and of course, found her holding out a slender hand while Nate wrapped gauze around a fingertip. She made a show of wincing and pouting.

I rolled my eyes and sank back down. "That could've just

been her wanting the promotion though. And if she was out of town, I don't see how she could have killed her." I frowned. "You're sure she actually left town?"

36

SUSPICION

Iggy nodded. "Randomly, her purse got stolen while in transit, so she filed a police report in Germany, nearly the same hour Nan died. There's no way she could have been here."

"Even with magic? There's not some way to instantly transport yourself?"

Iggy shook his head. "We have ways, but they're highly regulated and you can only travel from a Magic Port. And even if she flew, she couldn't have made it in time."

"Flew?" I did a double take to the pouting blond in the back. "Pritney can fly?"

Iggy grinned. "All witches can. You can too. By broomstick of course."

"Oh, of course." I scoffed. "Wait, that's real?"

"Let's get back to the murders?" Iggy opened his round eyes bigger.

I needed to learn magic pronto if it meant I could fly. "By the way, how's the pie looking?"

"Leave the baking to me, all right?" Iggy looked quite pleased with himself. "I've got this part."

A tightness released in my chest. It felt quite nice to have a partner in baking. "So, who else could it have been?"

"Well, there's Wool."

I frowned. "But Wool didn't know Nan, did he?"

Iggy shook his head. "No, but maybe you could try to find out if he'd been to Bijou Mer before? If he was here when she died and could have had the opportunity?"

"All right, I'll try." I shifted and sat more on my left side. One cheek had gone numb sitting on the grassy ground in front of the oven. "I did see him lose his temper with Glenn. He's been acting regretful."

I peeked over the countertops again. Wool rubbed his arm over and over again, his brows drawn together in a slight frown. His normally beautiful dark golden skin looked pale and gray. "Hmm. Something's definitely up with him."

"What about Sam and Hank. Any suspicions there?" As Iggy glowed away, heating the oven, the filling began to bubble out the slits on the top crust, a warm, sweet smell emanating from the oven.

I shook my head. "Nothing. But I'll keep an eye on them. Oh, actually." I frowned. For some reason I didn't want to share the way I'd seen Hank's face change. But after thinking on it a moment, I decided to. After I'd explained it, Iggy frowned.

"It could definitely be some kind of mask or facade, though he'd have to be a mighty powerful witch to withstand the magical field. But if the field isn't looking specifically for disguises...." Iggy shook his head. "I'm positive that Amelia has personally vetted each of you for security reasons."

"Unless Amelia's in on it too," I hissed.

Iggy cocked a brow. "That's a thought. It'd explain why

she didn't promote Pritney and pushed to have this competition. I thought she just wanted to further her career as an events coordinator, but maybe it's because she wants to place her man on the inside."

I nodded. I hated thinking these things about the people I knew, but it was important to consider every possibility. "Well, that just leaves me, and for some reason you trust me."

Iggy laughed. "You wear your emotions on your face. No way you're hiding anything. Besides, like I said, you're kind."

I warmed a little at the compliment.

"But you're forgetting someone."

"No, I'm not, I—"

I followed Iggy's gaze behind me to Maple. She stood behind her station, tidying up and humming her little baking ditty. I laughed and turned to Iggy.

"Maple? You're not serious."

He held my gaze.

"Iggy, she didn't do it. She's—she's Maple. She's quiet, and gentle and sings silly songs—" I paused, thinking about the first one I'd heard her sing about killing a rat. I shook my head. It was just a song, and about a rat, not a person. "She's my friend."

"How well do you really know her?" Iggy blinked at me. "You've only known her six days."

Had it only been six? In the environment of the competition it felt much longer. We spent practically every minute together.

I shook my head, still refusing to even consider it. "Why then? Answer me, why would she? Even if she were capable of it, which she absolutely is not, she has no reason, didn't even know Nan."

I froze, chills creeping up my spine.

"What is it?" Iggy asked.

My chest tightened. I didn't want to say. "She... she did mention that her dad tried to get her a job under Nan, and was rejected. Her dad and Glenn had a big rivalry, because Glenn claimed the Earth Kingdom's Baking Guild was so superior to Water's. And she's been telling me how much pressure her dad's been putting on her to beat him, and I did see snake eggs in her dad's bakery, which can be a source of venom, but...."

I looked at my rosy-cheeked friend, smiling and humming and scrubbing dishes, and tried to picture her sneaking snake venom into Glenn's cake. I shook my head. "No. Absolutely not. I don't care what it sounds like, I know, in my gut, the way you know Nan was killed, that Maple had nothing to do with it. And you'll just have to trust me on that, the way I'm trusting you."

Iggy gave a noncommittal raise of his brows.

"Iggy?"

He huffed. "Fine." He retreated to the back of the oven. "This is done, by the way. Let it cool though."

With mitts on, I slid the pie out of the oven. The tart, buttery aroma had my mouth watering. The perfectly golden-brown fluted edges bordered a lighter brown center, the four slits on top revealing the juicy, dark red cherry filling.

As we moved into judging, I felt more confident about my bake than ever. Rhonda's eyes rolled back in her head when she took a bite, and Francis commented, "The filling looks like blood." His pupils dilated and his fangs protruded. I took that as a compliment.

But I felt more uneasy in every other way. Was one of my fellow contestants a murderer? After testing everyone's bakes, the judges deemed it time for Wool to leave.

Trembling and with bright pink cheeks, Maple managed to give him a hug and whisper, "I'll miss you."

Wool gave her a long look. "I'll miss you too, Maple." He looked up at the five of us who remained. "Best of luck." He gave Hank a clap on the back. "Take care, man. And all of you, watch your backs." He shook his head. "Be careful till they find the killer."

Though I'd miss Wool, I was happy to have made it through. I dashed back to Iggy to tell him the good news, that the judges had loved our pie, before heading to the big house.

"Hm. Guess it wasn't Wool then."

I shook my head. "What would be the point in murdering for the job, just to get eliminated? He would have done something underhanded to stay in."

I left Iggy with a pile of firewood.

"Imogen?"

I paused on my way out.

"Be careful tonight, okay?"

I grinned and nodded. "Get some rest."

Amelia, Inspector Bon, and his officers escorted us to the house. Our little group had dwindled to just me, Maple, Hank, Pritney, and Sam. Before they left us, Inspector Bon gave us each a hard look. "No one is to leave the house tonight until you're escorted to the tent in the morning. Understood?"

I nodded, though in my head I already knew I'd be breaking the rules. On our way to bed later, I pulled Maple into my room and closed the door, listening for a moment to make sure no one stood outside listening.

Maple gave me a puzzled look. "What's all this about?"

I put a finger to my lips and stood close, whispering, "Where's the forest on the royal grounds?"

37

THE FOREST

Maple pulled back, frowning. "Why?"

I told her about my conversation with Iggy and by the end she had tears running down her cheeks. "How sad."

"I know, right?" I left out the part about Iggy thinking her capable of murder. "So I want to do something special for him and get those linden branches."

Maple nodded. "What a sweet idea." She pulled her lips to the side. "But I think you can only find them on the royal grounds. It might take a few days, but I can help you get a permit to collect some. We can't summon them because of the wards around the palace. A permit might be tough with security right now though, so—"

"Thank you." I squeezed her shoulder. "But I really want to do something for Iggy. And Nan always gathered them herself. If an elderly lady can do it, I can too."

Maple opened her eyes wide. "But... but the inspector forbade it. And you just said yourself that you're his top suspect. How would that look? Breaking rules and sneaking around the grounds at night, if you could even find a way in.

The boundaries are spelled and the gate's the only entry point, and it's guarded."

I nodded. "I probably won't be able to get in, but I'm going to try."

Maple bit her lip and fiddled with the hem of her shirt. "Oh, I don't like this at all."

"Please, Maple." I batted my lashes at her, hands clasped and pleading.

She rolled her eyes. "Fine. I'm coming with."

I shook my head vehemently. "Nope. No way. You'd be in big trouble if you were caught."

Her mouth dropped open and she pointed a finger at me. "That's what I just told you!"

"Yes, but it's *my* stupid idea to go in, and I'm not ruining *your* chances at winning."

After another ten minutes of arguing, Maple finally caved when I told her I'd go with or without her help, and wandering around without any idea where to go would be more dangerous than if she just told me.

"When you enter the gate, you'll head left into the dense thicket of trees. And there you'll be, in the forest. Do you even know what a linden branch looks like?"

When I winced, she huffed and made me get out a blank sheet of paper. She drew a rough map of the circular perimeter of the royal grounds and where the gate sat, along with the palace, the forest, and a quick outline of a tree. She lifted her hands above the paper and sang:

"Map show me the way,

Lead me true,

To linden branches,

I'll follow you."

"Did you just make that up?"

"Shh!" She held her eyes closed and a flash of light

pulsed from her hands, making the lines she'd drawn glow gold. The lines branched and spread and a much more detailed map appeared before me, with a small drawing of a girl labeled, "Imogen."

"Hey, that's me!" I tapped at it.

"Good, you can read."

"Uh!" I punched her shoulder. "I'm usually the sarcastic one. What's gotten into you?"

She flashed her blue eyes at me. "Oh, just concern for my friend's life. Now follow the map, it'll tell you where to go once you get inside the gate. *If* you get inside the gate, which, for the record, I think it's a huge mistake to even attempt."

She folded her arms and stared at the wall.

I couldn't help but grin. I picked up the map, threw my arms around her in a big hug from behind, and leaned my cheek on her shoulder. "Duly noted. Thanks, friend."

As I made my way out the French doors I looked back at her. She stood hugging herself in the middle of my room, looking miserable. "Be careful, Imogen."

"I will." I shut the door quietly and listened for voices or footsteps, but only crickets chirped, and waves crashed just past the bluff's edge.

I snuck along the back of the house and across the field, skirting along the line of cypress trees. I followed the map and found the road to the palace, though I stayed off it, creeping along just inside the tree line to stay hidden. With the house out of sight, I began to question the sanity of my plan.

I rounded a curve in the road and spotted the gate. Made of elaborately twisting gold, it stood at least twenty feet. Two uniformed guards held their long lances across the gate.

That alone should have been enough to stop me, but I froze for another reason.

A figure crept along the tree line about one hundred feet ahead of me. A dark figure, crouched low. I felt almost certain, from the way they moved, that it was the person I'd seen sneaking across the field before.

38

SNEAKING

I glanced down at the dry pine needles and sticks just waiting to snap under my feet, and didn't dare take another step. Instead, I crouched low and watched.

The dark figure straightened, blue-green light flashed, and then they stepped out of the shadows onto the road. I could see that it was a man now, tall, with broad shoulders and a narrow waist, and as he glanced up and down the road, I had to press my hands to my mouth to stifle my gasp. Hank!

Or rather, the Hank I saw sometimes, when his dark eyes turned blue, pointed chin grew square, and crooked nose turned straight. My chest grew tight with anxiety. What did it mean? He walked down the road to the gate, in plain view. He spoke a few words to the guards, who smiled and chuckled and—I blinked and leaned forward—bowed. They bowed, deep and low and long, and opened the gate for him. Then closed it behind him, crossing their lances again.

"What?" I mouthed. "What the what?" I now knew that Hank had access to the royal grounds, which meant the palace, which meant he'd had the opportunity to kill Nan. I now knew he also donned a disguise, though I had no idea which face was the real one. But why would he have killed Glenn?

A memory floated into my head, of Hank shouting at Glenn, practically growling at him. Glenn, rest his soul, had been incredibly annoying, and no one found him more so than Hank. I didn't know if all of that added up to murder, but it certainly shot Hank to the top of my suspects list.

I needed to know where he went once inside the grounds. If I could find some way in. Maybe he'd made a funny joke? Or maybe it'd been his confidence? I thought those highly unlikely, but I had no better ideas, so I decided to do as Hank did.

I took a shaky breath and stepped out from the tree line onto the road. I pictured Hank. I squared my shoulders like he had, I thought tall, I thought confident. I pictured his blue eyes, big straight nose, and square jaw. I stepped forward, imagining his long strides. *Be like Hank, be like Hank*, I chanted in my head, like a mantra.

A strange sort of tingling came over me, head to toe. I looked at my glowing hands and they suddenly appeared bigger, wider, and rougher. I flipped them over and over again. *Be like Hank, be like Hank.*

I approached the gates, the guards watching me with puzzled expressions. They turned to each other, then lowered the sharp ends of their lances at me. *Uh-oh.*

"But... we just let you in," the shorter one barked.

Just let me in? I must look like Hank! I'm doing magic!

My arms still glowed. A strange sort of spell seemed to come over the guards. They rubbed their glassy eyes and seemed unable to focus.

Without another word, they stepped aside and opened the gate.

"Thanks a bunch."

Once inside, I ran to the left and hid behind a stone fountain of a fish. I doubled over to catch my breath. "What is happening?" I whispered. I looked at my normal-looking, not glowing hands. "I just did magic." I murmured the words out loud, then stifled a giddy laugh.

Me? Magic! I grinned wildly. I couldn't wait to tell Maple. Though what would I tell her? I had no idea what I'd done, or how I'd done it. My best guess was that I'd somehow used magic to look like Hank and fool the guards. I didn't have time to ponder it, though, I was on a mission.

I scanned around and found no sign of Hank, just a wide grassy lawn stretching out in front of me. A white gravel driveway divided the lawn in two and led straight to a white palace that glowed in the moonlight.

Though disappointed that I'd lost Hank, I could still get Iggy his branches. If someone didn't spot me first.

I followed the map to the edge of the trees, the little drawing version of me dashing across the royal lawn. I had to duck behind shrubbery when a patrolling guard passed by. Then I ran on. When I reached the tree line, I suddenly wished I'd brought a flashlight, or a cell phone or something.

Oh right, I didn't have a phone anymore. At least the moon shone fairly bright in a cloudless sky.

I picked my way through the forest, the trees crowding closer together. I stumbled over thick roots and ducked under low-hanging branches. An owl hooted to my right, and at one point I bumped into a dead, hollow tree, which sent a cloud of screeching black bats flapping out.

Thank goodness Maple had given me the map. I'd have no idea how to get back out without it.

I found my way to the linden tree marked on the map and plopped down on a stump to catch my breath. I sat still for several moments, lost deep in thought about Iggy and Nan and all the events of the day.

A sharp crack snapped me out of it. Then came another and another. Someone, or something, prowled through the forest. I froze, holding my breath.

This was a stupid, stupid idea to come sneaking into the woods by myself. Why did no one warn me?

I hunkered low on the stump, trying to hide, but the movement attracted the thing. It turned and for just a moment, it stood outlined in the dappled light of the moon shining through the thick trees.

Sam?

Sam, the sweet man with the lisp blinked his milky blue eyes at me, and suddenly disappeared. I blinked rapidly, trying to clear my vision. I'd heard nothing, and in the undergrowth of the forest it was impossible not to make noise. So where'd he gone? Had he even been there in the first place, or had that been some trick of the forest? Or maybe some trick of my weary eyes.

I let out a shaky breath as quietly as I could and stood on trembling legs. I crept over to the spot where I thought I'd seen Sam. Leaves rustled underfoot. I leaned closer for a better look—then screamed!

"Ahhh!" I lurched backward as a four-foot-long snake slithered past, stopping for a moment to look back at me, its forked tongue flicking the air. I scooped up an armful of fallen branches and ran out of the forest.

How in the world did an old lady do this every day? Nan

definitely didn't die of any heart attack if she could manage that.

When I reached the gate, I cleared my throat and the guards let me out, barely glancing my way. Getting out was much easier than getting in.

Once back at the house, I snuck in through the French doors, dropped the logs, and knocked on the shared wall. Maple tapped at my door moments later and threw her arms around me. When she pulled back and saw the pile of logs on the floor, she gaped.

"Tell me everything."

39

A SHIFT

I could barely make it through breakfast, I felt so on edge. Every time Hank, sitting next to me, took a bite of his toast or told me he liked my shoes, I jumped. Could I be sitting next to a murderer?

I knew he donned some kind of magical disguise, and he'd been angry with Glenn. He'd snuck into the royal grounds and would have had the chance to kill Nan. But why? Did he just want the job of royal baker so badly? Could Iggy be right that he was a member of the Badlands Army and had dastardly plans in store for the royal family?

And what about Sam? He sat apart, avoiding my eyes. Had he been in the woods last night, or was it some kind of magical illusion? How'd he disappear, and if it was him, why was he in the forest at night and how? He too could've killed both Nan and Glenn. But I still didn't know how either of them could have smuggled snake venom into the tent.

I'd told Maple everything, and she was playing it even less cool than me. When Hank lifted a hand to summon the salt, she screamed, then turned bright red and stared at her plate.

When Amelia came to collect us, dark bags pooled under her eyes. "Inspector Bon and the police are waiting for us at the tent." She swallowed. "They have a special announcement to make—apparently there's been some break in the case."

Just before she turned to lead the way, she flashed Hank a pursed-lip, wide-eyed look. I glanced at him in time to see him nod, ever so slightly.

Oh no! Maybe Iggy had been right. Amelia had a man on the inside, and it was Hank. She'd know ways around the magic field and could have snuck in the poison herself, or shown Hank how to. And they both had access to Glenn's dough while it sat proving in the pantry, and access to the palace grounds to have killed Nan.

My heart raced in my chest. Under one arm, I carried a few of the linden branches I'd gathered last night. I gripped Maple's hand tight with the other one, so that she turned, panicked, toward me.

I mouthed, "It's Hank and Amelia." Then jerked my head at each of them.

Maple's mouth fell open. "What do we do?" she mouthed.

"Police," I mouthed back.

Hank, who walked slightly in front of me glanced back and raised a brow, a puzzled expression on his face at our silent but animated conversation. Maple and I grinned like madwomen. As soon as his back was turned, we mouthed silent screams at each other.

It wouldn't do any good to expose them now. We had to hope the police had already figured it out and stood ready to make the arrests. As we entered the tent, the familiar tickle of magic played across my skin. The magic field still worked.

We fanned out to our stations. Eight officers stood posted at regular intervals, surrounding us.

Inspector Bon strode forward and stopped in front of Amelia. He came up to her shoulder. "Lovely of you all to join us. I'll take it from here."

Amelia gave him a curt nod and retreated to the perimeter to stand beside Rhonda and Francis. I gave Nate, lounging in his medic's corner, a little wave. He nodded back, a smaller version of his roguish grin playing across his face. I threw a fresh log in the oven for Iggy and while I crouched beside him, whispered, "I think they're making an arrest today."

Iggy didn't answer for several long moments. Then he said quietly, "These are linden."

I peeked into the oven and gave him a tight smile. "Just offering an olive branch."

He frowned. "I just told you they're linden."

"Figure of speech, human thing." I grinned. "I just meant, it's an offering of friendship."

Iggy pulled the log into his mouth with tiny flame arms. "Oh, it's delicious." His eyes rolled back. "But how did you—"

"I snuck past the guards and went into the royal forest like you said Nan did, and while I was in there I saw—"

A man cleared his throat behind me, and I whirled.

Inspector Bon stood over me. "Am I interrupting something?"

I shook my head and stood slowly, to find that everyone watched me. My cheeks flushed hot. Bon slowly strode among our stations, weaving between Sam, Hank, Maple, Pritney, and me.

"Quite a case, this. Quite a case," he said, hands clasped behind his back. "A man is murdered, with a limited number of suspects. An intriguing mode of murder, this poison. How did the killer bring it into the tent, a banned substance?"

Bon paused in front of Maple's station and gave her a long, hard look. "Yes, quite a conundrum, and then last night we received a new piece of information, something that made it all too clear."

Bon fixed me with his dark, piercing gaze, and I swallowed, shifting nervously on my feet. "Yes, it's quite clear now, how the killer brought the poison into the tent. So obvious, yet so strange—brilliant, really. So before I blow this case wide, if anyone has anything they'd like to confess, I guarantee you the law will look more kindly on a confession than an indictment."

Bon gazed furiously around the tent. "Speak now, culprit! And you shall know the clemency and leniency of the law. But hold your tongue, and you'll find yourself plagued."

Should I speak? Should I tell Bon what I'd seen Hank do, what I suspected?

Bon held up a pair of golden handcuffs that pulsed with light at regular intervals. "Guess I'll just have to make the arrest then. Once I do though, I warn you, there's no going back, and you'll find the full force of the law beating down upon you."

Bon stalked toward me. I opened my mouth to accuse Hank and Amelia, and Sam yelled, "Wait!"

40

SAM

He took off his glasses and what little of a chin he had disappeared into his neck as he looked at his feet. Bon paused midway to me, and turned.

"I-I must confessss. I didn't think me being me would be ssssuch a problem." He shook his head, his deep voice warbling. "Oh, I jussst wanted the chanccce to bake. I never meant to hurt anyone. What a ssssillly ssssnake I am."

"Sam, what are you saying?" Rhonda moved toward him, one hand extended.

"Sssstay back." Rhonda stopped advancing, and Sam let out a big, gulping sob. "Ssssilly, sssilly ssssnake." He lifted his head, blinking his milky eyes. "I did it. I brought the poisssson into the tent."

"Stay there, you're under arrest!" Bon spun on his heel and as he and his officers closed in, Sam began to tremble, and in the blink of an eye, he disappeared.

"Where is he?" Bon shouted, red in the face. He jabbed a finger at his officers. "Close the flaps, trap him in here."

His officers obeyed, but Rhonda frowned. "If he's still in here. Maybe he just popped off somewhere."

Bon barked orders as his men dashed here and there, combing the tent for Sam. I pressed myself up against my station to avoid being trampled.

Suddenly, Amelia let out a bloodcurdling scream and clawed at Francis, somehow climbing up his tall body and throwing herself onto the nearest tabletop. She kept screaming too, as she jabbed a slender finger at the grass, babbling through her sobs. "It's there—there... oh great goddess, it could be anywhere—AHHHH!" She scrambled back from the edge.

What had she seen? My heart slammed in my chest. Then one of Bon's officers shouted, and another screeched, and then another and another. I threw myself onto my tabletop and craned my neck to see the danger. A snake slithered, fast as lighting, between the stations. It looked about the same size as the one I'd seen last night... right after Sam disappeared.

"Sam?" I gasped.

Bon saw the snake, blubbered incoherently, and scrambled onto Hank's station. Hank stood beside him and stared Bon down.

From his safe perch, Bon screamed, "Well, catch it! Catch him—ur—catch the snake!" Sam, in snake form, slid under the side of the tent, right past two guards who scrambled and pranced like their feet had caught fire.

"After him! He's outside!" Bon screamed as he stood on the countertop. But his men, on Bon's orders, had already sealed up the tent flaps and now had to waste time casting a spell to unseal it.

Once undone, all eight officers dashed off to find Sam. I watched them for a time. Judging by the lack of screams, no one came across him. Eventually, Bon slid off the tabletop with as much dignity as he could muster and strutted about, nose in the air. "Well then, job well done. Looks like Sam's the killer, and it will only be a matter of time before we apprehend him."

Hank slammed a hand down on his table, which made Bon jump. "Job well done? And what do you mean by, 'looks like he's the killer'? What about this conclusive new evidence you found last night, huh?" He threw an arm my way. "Because it looked to me like you were on the verge of arresting Imogen."

"Don't remind him," I whispered.

Hank cast me a quick glance, then stared back at Bon. Bon cleared his throat and drew himself up as tall as he could. "Police tactics, young man. There was no evidence, we merely were putting the heat on in hopes the culprit would confess. And we did a bang-up job, if I do say so myself. Sam confessed."

"He confessed to bringing in the poison, but how could he have?" Amelia, now on the ground again, brushed off her skirt.

"It appears Sam was a shifter. We all just saw him transform into a snake. He could have done so in the tent and collected some of his own venom, then changed back."

"But the magic field also keeps shifters out," Amelia cried, throwing an arm wide.

"Actually...." Francis floated forward, feet dangling just above the ground. He raised one skinny white finger. "You cast a spell that would reveal the second form of a shifter."

"Exactly." Amelia planted her hands on her hips. "It should have turned him into a snake."

"Unless snake is his original form, and human is his second."

Amelia and the others gaped at Francis.

"B-but, that's unheard of," Amelia spluttered.

Francis sniffed. "Unheard of, but not impossible. If the magical community would stop fearing shifters for a minute, and actually learn about them, we might know of quite a few more like him."

"But that would mean Sam grew up a snake, living in the forest or wherever, and at some point discovered he could shift into a human, learned to speak, and—and how to bake and— It's preposterous." Amelia shook her head.

Francis lightly patted her shoulder. "Think of what courage it must have taken him to enter this competition, knowing his kind was banned, feared, and despised."

Amelia shook her head. "He killed a man, and you want me to have sympathy for him? No." She folded her arms.

Francis lifted his slim shoulders in the slightest of shrugs.

Hank broke the long silence that followed. "So what now?"

Bon cleared his throat. "My officers and I will continue to search for Sam until he's caught, and then justice will be done."

"And what of the competition?" Amelia strode forward.

Bon cleared his throat and stepped back. "Yes, well I should think you can continue, not today, but tomorrow should be all right. We'll want the rest of the day to secure the location. I feel confident that we'll apprehend him quite quickly."

Hank sniffed, arms folded. "You'll excuse me if I don't share your confidence."

Bon scowled but let it go. He called back a couple of his officers to stay in the tent, and then headed out to join the snake hunt. I tried to regain my equilibrium. I'd been a breath away from accusing Hank and Amelia of murdering two people. Had I just been completely wrong? But what of Hank's changing face and sneaking out at night?

And did that mean Sam had killed Nan, also? I had seen him on the royal grounds last night, and I knew that Nan went into the woods each night to gather branches for Iggy. Maybe he'd waited and scared her, or bitten her with just enough venom to cause a heart attack? Why? Maybe he'd applied for a position in the bakery, as Maple had, and also been rejected by Nan. I couldn't picture gentle, soft-spoken Sam hurting a fly. But he'd confessed after all, and had the means, motive, and opportunity to kill both Nan and Glenn.

I crouched down to check on Iggy.

"Looks like they caught Glenn's killer. Probably Nan's, too."

Iggy nodded and blinked. "Yeah. Strange. I thought it'd make me feel better."

I pressed my lips together. "But it doesn't?"

Iggy looked up at me. "No. Thing was, after we talked yesterday, I already felt better. I'm glad they caught him, and I want justice for Nan. But I also want to carry on her legacy, everything she taught me about baking."

I pulled my lips to the side. "I'd like to help if I can, too."

Iggy nodded. "See you tomorrow. Just another linden branch, though, before you go, if you please."

41

FEELING THE HEAT

The next day I could hardly eat breakfast, my stomach felt so tight with nerves. Our once large circle felt tiny now, just Maple, me, Hank, and Pritney.

Heading to the tent and seeing Rhonda and Francis felt reassuring. Though when Nate grinned and waved from his corner I couldn't quite call it calming. More like he'd stirred up some butterflies in my stomach to add to the stress cramps.

"Semifinals!" Amelia grinned, arms lifted. "I won't say we haven't had our trials and tribulations, but we've made it and you should all be very proud of yourselves."

"Here, here!" Rhonda clapped above her head.

I couldn't believe I'd actually made it this far. Granted, a few of my competitors had been chased off by violent utensils, been murdered, and slithered away as snakes. But I wasn't going to let that undermine my sense of accomplishment.

"For today's challenge, we want cupcakes displayed marvelously. You've got three hours... and bake!"

I looked over my shoulder and grinned at Maple. She gave me a nod. I chatted with Iggy, made sure he had more of his favorite linden branches, then got to baking. I chose to make chocolate cupcakes, 'cause hey, chocolate's always a good thing.

As I cast about for inspiration, a thought occurred to me. I'd talked with Bern, the inventor from the Air Kingdom, about his home one night. He'd described hot air balloons and dirigibles of every size, shape, and color. People lived aboard the balloons, connected by rope bridges.

As I stirred the batter, I planned it out in my head, occasionally dictating notes to my magical quill.

I'd top some cupcakes with a swirling mountain of blue frosting, then decorate that with fondant clouds. I'd make others to look like the balloons themselves, with the cupcake as the basket and would use some magical help from Maple to spell cookies shaped like the balloons to hover above. Then I'd use spun sugar to create the rope bridges between, creating what I imagined the Air Kingdom to look like.

I just hoped my idea of the Air Kingdom was closer to reality than my idea of a unicorn. I needed to remember to ask Maple about that. "Ask Maple about unicorns," I said to my quill.

"Focusing, I see," Iggy drawled from the oven below the counter.

I stuck my tongue out at him, but grinned. I should have been nervous. I had been all morning, and the whole night before I'd barely slept. But once at my station, stirring and mixing and baking... I felt right at home again.

You've got this, I told myself. *You've got this.*

Amelia had informed us they hadn't located Sam, but the police still felt confident it was merely a matter of time.

"Better be, with the summer solstice in two days," Amelia had muttered to herself.

But at least without spectators, police or civilian, and without the mystery of Glenn's murder to solve, I could relax and focus on baking. I finished whipping up the batter and poured it into my cupcake tin, using some liners Maple magicked up for me that looked like the sky and others that looked like the basket of a balloon. I relaxed a little when Maple's idea of a balloon basket and mine coincided. That was a good sign.

With the cupcakes in the oven and my timer set, I dashed to the pantry to get marshmallows to make my own fondant.

"Marshmallows, marshmallows...." I patted around the shelves, peeking behind jars and tins.

"Marshmallows?"

I turned, then froze. I stood chest to chest with Hank. Well, maybe chest to ribs. I looked up and he looked down, our faces suddenly quite close. I looked down again, then to the side. Why was finding someplace to look suddenly so difficult?

"Uh, you're looking for these?" He shook a glass jar of the puffy white cylinders.

"Right, yeah." He handed them to me. "Thanks."

We stood in silence for a few moments in the cramped, dimly lit pantry. I glanced up at him, ready to announce that I must get back to baking, when I giggled. One of the dried herbs hanging from the ceiling had gotten tangled in his hair, and a sprig of rosemary now sprouted from the crown of his head.

"What?" Hank blinked at me.

I tried to bite down on a grin. "You've got a little antenna —on your—"

"A what?" He turned left and right.

"Here, I'll...." I reached up, and he ducked. I plucked the rosemary from his dark hair and held it up to him. He smelled of vanilla bean and sugar, and a white streak of flour dusted one cheekbone.

His dark eyes focused intensely on my face.

I should be scared. I'd seen this man change, seen him sneak into the royal grounds. But I only knew that because I also snuck onto the royal grounds. We breathed into the same space, our faces just inches apart. I knew I should be pulling away, getting out of the pantry, but something rooted me to the spot. I reached up, slowly, and brushed away the flour from his cheek with my thumb.

"You're just a mess," I heard myself mumble.

He caught my hand in his before I could drop it. I closed my eyes and leaned in.

A cough from behind Hank made me jump. I stepped back, smashing my back into a shelf. The jars rattled and clinked into each other. *Ow.* A light flared brighter, and I winced, then tried to blink my eyes open. Squinting, I made out Nate's tanned face and Hank's scowling one. Well, they both scowled, actually, at each other.

"Medic." Hank rounded on him.

"Just checking everything was all right in here. No one needs any, uh, medical assistance?" Nate nodded at me. "Imogen." He held a wand aloft like a flashlight.

The tiny pantry could barely fit these two tall, broad-shouldered men. "Nope. All good." My cheeks burned as I edged past them, brushing against Hank's back and Nate's muscled arm. "As they say, three's a crowd, so... back to baking."

I jabbed my thumb at my station and spun, speed

walking away and not daring to look back. Maple gave me a quizzical look as I passed, but I just shook my head and mouthed, "Later."

42

SECRET INGREDIENT

I kept so busy with my bake that I hardly had any time to think about what had happened with Hank. So how come I kept thinking about it? I'd nearly kissed the man I'd almost accused of murder just yesterday. What was wrong with me? I mean, it'd been a while since my last... but was I really that desperate?

I couldn't deny the chemistry between us though. I'd wanted to kiss him. I felt the pull, even now. I fanned myself. Had it gotten hotter in the tent?

I kept trying to put it out of my head as I swirled on frosting, cut out fondant clouds, piped balloon sugar cookies and dripped golden caramel to form spun sugar. But the sweet scent only reminded me of Hank and how much I suddenly wanted to—

"Imogen? Earth to Imogen?"

Iggy's voice startled me.

"Sorry, head in the clouds." The pantry, was more like it. I crouched in front of Iggy and pulled out a tray of sugar cookie balloons.

"If that is meant to be a pun on your bake, I'll burn the next batch," Iggy growled.

In the end, I barely finished on time, though I felt exceedingly proud of our hot air balloon city with its fluffy white clouds, gold-and-purple balloons, and amber bridges of spun sugar.

Pritney had made cupcakes that shone like gold and diamonds, Hank had created a scene of cupcake nests with bird cookies of all shapes and sizes and chocolate eggs, and Maple had baked hers to look like sea anemones and puffer fish.

As usual, she hung her head and wrung her hands next to me. "They're going to taste like rubbish."

I nudged her with my shoulder. "You say that every time and every time the judges love what you've made."

"Not this time, I just know it." She shook her head and sighed.

I bit back a grin. The girl was going on to the finals, I had no doubt of that. From the beginning she'd been the clear winner in my book. Creative, talented, and she knew her stuff. I, on the other hand, could definitely be cut. I waited with bated breath as the judges made their way down the short line. They found Pritney's display impressive.

When they got to Maple she shook her head. "I'm sorry."

Rhonda raised a finger. "If you say that one more time, you will be."

Maple raised her eyes and grinned. They pronounced her cupcakes delightful.

I came next. I told them about my inspiration. They peered at it. "Quite close really, for never having been to the Air Kingdom," Francis said.

"I quite like Imogen's version better," Rhonda chuckled. They picked a cupcake and cut it open for a taste test. I watched carefully for any facial expressions that would give away their feelings as they chewed.

At first they each frowned, then their foreheads smoothed, their eyes grew hooded, and they turned toward each other. Tall, pale, skinny Francis stared for a long moment at short, dark Rhonda—and then they lunged at each other.

My first instinct was that they'd gone mad and were killing each other, but the reality struck me as even crazier. They kissed, deeply, passionately, locked in each other's arms.

"By the great sea mother," Amelia breathed.

Suddenly, with lips still locked, it was if a spell had broken. They opened their eyes wide, stared at each other, and then yanked apart. Francis shuddered and Rhonda screamed and shook her hands like I would if I'd just seen a cockroach. Panting, they came back to themselves, then rounded on me.

"What did you put in that?" Rhonda demanded.

"A lot of sexual tension, is my guess," Francis drawled.

"What? I— Just flour and sugar and—" I stopped. It had never occurred to me before, but maybe I performed a little magic sometimes when I baked, without realizing it. Maybe I had put some of what I'd been feeling into those cupcakes. And I'd certainly been feeling a lot of tension and desire.

I could definitely not admit that right now, with Hank standing beside me and Nate watching from the medic's corner. So instead, I just shrugged. "Maybe you just really liked them?"

Rhonda squinted and Francis raised a slim brow. But they dropped it, thankfully, and moved on to Hank's bake.

"It tastes... confused," Rhonda mused, around a mouthful. "It's partly sweet, but partly sour... I'm not sure the flavors work together."

I glanced at Hank, but he stared straight ahead. I knew he could feel my eyes on him, but he refused to look my way. What was that about? After a short deliberation, the judges returned and spoke a few words to Amelia. Maple took my hand as we waited for the news.

Amelia gave Hank a long, long look, then said, "You have all worked extremely hard and deserve to be proud of yourselves. Unfortunately, we can only have one winner, and the person who is out today is... Hank."

I turned to him. He refused to look at me, but the veins in his neck popped, and his broad chest heaved. He nodded at Amelia and the two judges. "Thank you for your time and consideration. It's been an honor." His words came out clipped.

I reached up and lightly touched his arm with my fingertips. "Hank, I'm sorry, we'll all miss—"

He turned so quickly, I startled. He breathed heavily through his nose. "This was you. You got in my head, and I couldn't keep things straight and—" He stepped toward me, dark eyes focused on my face. He leaned down, his face getting closer and closer to mine.

Suddenly, he seemed to remember where he was and turned it into an awkward bow. He said his goodbyes to everyone else, then tossed his apron on the ground and stalked off across the field.

"Congrats, ladies. I'll see you tomorrow." Amelia waved us good night, then jogged off after Hank.

Rhonda drew Pritney, Maple, Francis, and me into a group hug. "All right, lovelies, rest up. Tomorrow's the big day." Normally, I was a fan of group hugs, but with Pritney cringing away from having to touch me, I couldn't get out of that one fast enough. Rhonda turned to me as I walked off. "And Imogen."

I nodded.

"Don't ever make me kiss Francis again." She lowered her voice and sidled closer. "Now if you want to give me and medic boy some of those cupcakes, I certainly won't complain." She wiggled her brows at Nate, and I turned. He gave me a nod and a thumbs-up as he packed up his bag.

"Finals are tomorrow," Rhonda sang as she skipped off, Francis hovering beside her.

Finals. My stomach turned with nerves.

43

FINALS

The nerves hadn't subsided the night before, as I lay in a cold sweat, tossing and turning and dreaming of being attacked by giant, angry muffins. And they certainly hadn't eased up during breakfast or the first two hours of the contest.

And when Amelia shouted, "Bakers, thirty minutes left. Thirty minutes!" my nerves caused me to dry heave. Luckily no one heard over the roar of the crowd. I glanced up at the hourglass. *Focus, Imogen, it's the final.* My hands trembled as I pulled another tray of cinnamon rolls from the oven.

I set the tray to the side to cool and touched a fingertip to my scones—pleasantly warm. I ducked back down to grab the bowl of butter I'd left near the oven to melt. I stayed for an extra few moments, grateful to hide from the roaring crowd on the other side of my station.

Amelia had practically bounced like a toddler with a new toy when she told us that morning that the police had cleared security for the final and that we'd have a crowd again. They'd cast a new spell to repel all shifters, making a special exception for Francis.

"Taking a nap? It's the final, get to it!" Iggy sent a blast of heat out at me, and I snapped out of it.

Back on my feet, I brushed the tops of the scones with melted butter and placed a purple and yellow pea flower on top, using the butter to glue them down. I worked as fast as my trembling hands would let me. I glanced up at the top row, at the boxes that held the Water Kingdom's royalty. Still no dreamy Prince Harry.

But today, some members of the Fire Kingdom's royal house had joined them. A beautiful young woman and man, who looked like siblings, sat to the left of the king. The Water Kingdom wore blues and greens and silver, while the young man and woman stood out in reds and golds. Watching the royalty would not help my nerves. I kept working through the scones.

"How are the muffins, Iggy?" I brushed butter onto another scone.

"Nearly there. Few more minutes."

I glanced up at the nearly empty hourglass. Three hours had hardly been enough time to complete three different breakfast bakes. I just needed to finish these scones, glaze the cinnamon rolls, and finish baking the blueberry muffins, then plate them all on a three-tiered display. And I had...

Fifteen minutes," Amelia called out. "Fifteen minutes left in the final."

The crowd on the bleachers clapped and cheered. I spotted Maple's family in the lower rows, her father yelling the loudest. "Go Maple!"

I worked away, the next few minutes a total blur. And when Amelia called out, "Time's up," I teetered with my heavy display to the front table. I trembled with a mix of nerves and exhaustion. In any case, I'd done my all.

I eyed my display—muffins golden brown and crumbly on top, cinnamon rolls a good color though I worried about the centers being cooked through, and the scones looked beautiful, though I'd messed up in a rush and torn a couple of the flowers. I'd put those scones in the back—hopefully Francis and Rhonda wouldn't notice. When the two judges stepped out in front of the long judging table, the crowd erupted into applause.

Francis nodded his long face, and Rhonda raised her arms, grinning and shaking her head. "No, no, do go on!" Eventually the crowd settled down, with one last, "Maple's the best!" from her father. Maple's cheeks turned a darker shade of pink, and I took her hand and held it in mine. She sighed and tipped her head to my shoulder.

"I think I might collapse," she whispered.

"In front of your lover?" I batted my eyes in fake surprise, but she immediately straightened, fixing her blond milkmaid's braid. I skimmed the crowd and found Wool and Bern sitting together with their respective families. Lillian and Zeke sat nearby. I didn't see Hank, though. I took a shaky breath as Rhonda and Francis turned to us. My stomach clenched and twisted with nerves.

"You ladies have worked very hard and deserve to be proud of yourselves. You all made it to the finals and you're all winners!"

I smiled at Rhonda. No matter what happened, I *was* proud of myself. The judges and the crowd cheered and clapped, but over the din I could still make out Pritney grumbling, "Yes, but who's the *real* winner?"

Rhonda and Francis started with Pritney. They nibbled at her mini quiche, licked pink frosting off her doughnuts, and wolfed down a cheese Danish each.

"Pritney—umph—you've outdone yourself." Rhonda's eyes rolled back in her head.

"Oh my." Francis smiled like a cat. "And I don't even like doughnuts."

Maple and I gave each other confused looks. Pritney had made it this far based on her precision and perfection. Each day the judges seemed unable to find any fault with her bakes, but they'd never seemed particularly wowed by them either... until now.

Rhonda moved to Maple's. "What have we here?"

"I've made bread and then stuffed it with mascarpone and diced strawberries for french toast served with warm maple syrup."

My mouth watered. Though of course I'd done my best to win, in my heart I knew Maple deserved it and rooted for her.

"I've also made bagels with cream cheese and a homemade blackberry jam, and lace pancakes."

I'd watched Maple drizzle the batter, singing one of her magical songs, to create beautiful, delicate pancakes in the shape of sea shells. I squeezed my friend's hand as the judges picked at her creations, chewing and frowning.

"Sorry, but we just don't taste much of anything. We should be getting the sharpness from the berries and the creamy richness of the cheese, but...."

"Nothing." Francis shook his head, his long dark hair plastered down so much it didn't move.

"Nothing?" Maple's voice quavered.

Nothing? That couldn't be right.

"And the pancakes are just... rather bland. Bake and texture looks good, just lacking flavor."

My heart felt like it'd dropped into my stomach. How could that be? I tried to catch Maple's eye, but she kept her gaze down at her shoes. The judges moved to me. I blinked at them, my feelings a jumbled mess of nerves for myself and indignation for my friend.

They peeled off pieces of my cinnamon rolls, took bites out of the blueberry muffins and tried the scones. Rhonda shook her head. "Same here. Very bland flavors."

Bland? They'd never critiqued me for that before. I ran through all the ingredients in my head again. Had I forgotten to add something?

"We're in consensus." Rhonda rose on her toes to whisper in Amelia's ear.

Already? I turned to Maple, but she kept her eyes down. I blinked at the crowd. This was moving too fast; something didn't feel right. Amelia nodded and turned to the crowd, then to us. "We have a winner picked."

The crowd erupted into applause. I squeezed Maple's hand. It didn't look good for either of us, but there was still a chance… a very small chance.

"And the winner is…"

44

THE WINNER

The crowd hushed to hear Amelia's next words.

"Pritney Pricehouse!"

The crowd erupted and Maple and I dropped hands to clap. How could it be over? And like this? I felt like someone else took the bouquet of flowers Rhonda handed me as she said, "You did amazing. I'm so proud of you—you should be proud too."

I nodded, numb. Pritney squealed and hopped and snatched the blue apron with the Water Kingdom's crest embroidered in silver on it from Francis. She threw it over her neck and tied the strings behind her.

"I did it!" She grinned and waved at the crowd. "I did it. I'm the winner."

She sneered at us. Luckily, the look was lost on Maple, who continued to stare at her shoes.

"Bland," she muttered. "And on the final. Dad's going to be so disappointed."

"If your dad's disappointed, he's daft," I said, taking her by the shoulders and turning her to face me. "Because *you* have been incredible. You made it to the finals."

Amelia put a hand on Pritney's shoulder and gathered us together. The crowd had already begun climbing down off the bleachers. I hoped Wool and Zeke and the others would wait around so we could say hello.

"You may recall that the winner can choose to bring the two runners-up on board with them to work in the royal kitchens."

Amelia smiled back and forth between us and Pritney's scowling face. "So Pritney, how about it? You going to bring these two hardworking ladies on as your staff?"

Pritney squinted, and pursed her lips in a bad imitation of regret. "No. I've worked in the kitchens, if you remember, and I know what quality of people are necessary."

Amelia's face fell. "Oh, uh, well, I suppose that is your prerogative." She turned to us. "Sorry about that, girls. But I hope you come to the Summer Solstice Festival tomorrow. You're both welcome to continue your stay at the house, we have it for one more night."

Amelia dashed off to deal with some logistical issue. The crowd now milled its way up to the tent, eyeing our bakes and taking nibbles of them. I stood, too stunned to be annoyed with Pritney or nervous about tons of strangers trying my bakes. I just couldn't make sense of it.

"This isn't bland at all, it's delicious!" Maple's dad growled. "Delicious, I say. Where are those judges, this was rigged!"

Maple blushed bright red, and I grabbed her hand and pulled her out of sight of her dad. We wound our way through the crowd, people recognizing us and clapping us on the shoulders or saying, "Well done!" I didn't feel like being praised at that moment, though. I felt like crawling into bed and sleeping for three days. We wound our way to the only people who would understand that. I gave Lillian a big hug, and then Zeke. We filled them and Bern in on Glenn's death and Sam's escape. Maple continued to sulk.

But then Wool turned to her directly. "I just tried your bakes, as well as Pritney's. The judges are damn fools. You're the clear winner." The twin fires on his shoulders blazed brighter.

Maple blinked at him. "Really?"

He nodded, his face deadly serious. "Best French toast I've ever had."

Her cheeks flushed and she perked up a little.

I found a moment while the others talked to ask Wool in a low voice, "Have you heard from Hank?"

Wool shook his head. Worry twisted my gut. I didn't like how we'd left things. And I wanted some answers on his changing appearance and sneaking around. As I milled about, another familiar face caught my eye. Nate flashed me that bright white smile, though something hard hung in his eyes.

"I'm sorry you didn't win."

I shrugged. "Gave it my best and all that."

"Yeah, but...." His face hardened. "Pritney didn't deserve it. You remember that, okay? You deserved it and you deserve good things."

I gave him a little smile. "Thanks... for everything. I can't believe it's already over."

His dark eyes sparkled. "I regret that I didn't get to know you better."

My stomach tingled. "Are you going to the festival tomorrow? Maybe I'll see you there?"

Nate's Adam's apple bobbed, and he stepped closer. "I—yes, but I'll-I'll be working."

"Oh. Yeah, of course." I gestured at his uniform. "Big event, medics needed on hand."

Nate pulled me into a tight hug. I hesitated a moment, and then wrapped my arms around his hard back. "I'm sorry it had to end this way."

I smiled against him. "You sound so grave. It is just a baking competition, after all."

I pulled back. Nate slid his hands down my arms and finished by holding my hands. "Take care, Imogen. It's been a pleasure."

I didn't think myself capable of giving an intelligible reply, so I nodded, and Nate disappeared into the crowd. I gave Francis and Rhonda hugs. As I headed with Maple back to the house, Rhonda threw her head back and froze, a hand thrown across her eyes. When she slumped, coming out of her vision, she turned to me.

"Ooh, girl. I sense a doozy of a dilemma coming your way."

Goody. "Any advice?"

"Go with your gut."

"I always go with my teeth," Francis murmured.

"How'd it go with your dad?" We sat in our pajamas, Maple behind me, braiding my hair. We had the house to ourselves, as Pritney had insisted on moving into the royal baker's quarters immediately. Well, us and Iggy. Maple had helped me magically transfer him to the fireplace in the library, with a big pile of linden logs.

Maple sighed. "It went all right. He said the judges had big piles of whale dung for brains if they thought my food tasted bland. But he's my dad, so he's biased."

"I tried yours, too. Everything was amazing, but especially that French toast." My mouth watered just thinking about it.

"You're biased too." I could hear the smile in her voice.

"So what are you going to do now?" My head bobbed as she pulled my hair into a French braid that twisted around my head.

"Go back to working for my dad." Maple sighed. "But I've decided to test into the baking guild in two months. And then I can work toward running my own bakery."

I smiled. "I'll be your first customer."

"Psht! Are you crazy? You'll be my partner... I mean, if you want to?"

A little tingle of excitement rose in my belly. "You mean it?"

"Of course! You're an amazing baker and... and we're friends, aren't we?"

I laughed. "Of course we're friends! Oh Maple, that sounds amazing. I wish I could just speed up time and be working with you in our own little bakery already." I picked at the white blanket over my lap.

"What are you going to do?" She ran her fingers across my scalp, gathering up a bit of hair.

"I'll stay for the Summer Solstice tomorrow. But after that, I'll have to take all the money I have left and get a plane ticket home." I sighed. "Which means home, home, to my family in St. Louis. I'd prefer Seattle, but my apartment is burned to bits, and I don't have a job." I shook my head. "But I'll get a new job, and I'll keep baking and I'll get back here again as soon as I can get a visa for it."

"It's a lot easier to get one if you have a job here, right?"

I nodded, forgetting Maple held my hair. "Ow. Yeah, that's what Amelia said."

"Well, then, I'll just have to work really hard and open that bakery as soon as possible so you can come back."

"Maple, I have a big favor to ask you." My stomach knotted. This was important to me. "Will you look after Iggy? I can't take him with me, but I know he doesn't want to work for Pritney in the royal kitchens."

She finished the braid and hugged me from behind. "Of course, I will."

I scooted around and looked her in the face. "And you'll keep him baking? He said he wants to keep Nan's legacy alive."

She grinned. "He'll be baking as much as he wants to. We could use another flame, especially one as talented as Iggy." She frowned a little. "Though I do hope he'll be nicer to me than he was to you."

We talked and laughed, and by the time Maple snored lightly next to me, I felt certain that her spirits were back up and that she'd be fine. But try as I may, I couldn't sleep myself. I felt haunted by the knowledge that I'd be leaving the magical world the day after next, with no idea when, or *if*, I'd be able to return.

45

THE SUMMER SOLSTICE

Maple smoothed her skirt and fussed with her hair.

I grinned at her. "You look beautiful. Who you trying to impress anyway?" I bumped my shoulder into hers. "A certain tall, dark, and handsome baker perhaps."

Her cheeks glowed with a blush.

"Magic doesn't cut down on the bureaucracy, huh?" I rose on the toes of my gold wedges to see better. "Almost there. Just a billion more people first." We shuffled as the long line of guests trying to enter the royal grounds inched forward.

"It's not usually like this." Maple shrugged, her shoulders covered by pretty peach cap sleeves that flowed into a pleated bodice and skirt. The perfect dress for lots of twirling. "Guess they've tightened security."

"I can't imagine why." I blinked, and widened my eyes. "What with a maniac killer slithering around and threats from the Badlands Army."

Maple shook her head, pressing her lips together. "Can't

imagine." She grinned. "You look amazing. Your hair's the best part, if I do say so myself."

I fluffed my curls and raised my brows. "Grew it myself."

Maple and I had gotten ready for the festival together. I'd found the perfect dress amongst my magical wardrobe. The bodice was made of skin-colored netting and covered in gold sequins that glittered and glowed. The dark navy blue of the high-waisted skirt made my hair seem redder, and breezed around my ankles. The dress felt beachy and fancy at the same time.

Maple used magic to curl my hair in loose waves, and swirl half of it up into a chignon. I'd helped Maple with her makeup, keeping it sweet and simple, and with her flowy pink dress, peaches-and-cream complexion, and halo of gold curls, she looked like a doll. It took us another twenty minutes to reach the front gate. I handed over my visa and they looked me up and down.

"Miss Banks, this gate is spelled to reveal any hidden magical items and to detain you if you are a shifter. Do you have anything you'd like to admit to now, before passing through the gate?" The guard sounded stern, but his words came out mechanically. I supposed this was probably the billionth time that day he'd asked.

"Nope."

He handed back my passport and waved me inside, about the same time Maple's guard waved her on. We stepped through together, the magical field tingling cold on my skin. I gasped. The royal grounds looked so different from the other night. People filled the entire broad lawn leading up to the palace, which glowed blue, green, and gold.

White lights bobbed among the tree branches, and trays of hors d'oeuvres and champagne flutes floated on their own through the crowd. Had Pritney and her team made all those hors d'oeuvres?

I shook my head. I'd promised myself that tonight would just be for enjoyment. Yes, I had to take a bus to Paris tomorrow and board a flight to New York, then on to St. Louis. But tonight, I got to attend a beautiful, magical festival, and I planned to enjoy every minute of it. Which meant no thinking about Pritney.

"This is incredible," I breathed, taking it all in.

Maple smiled. "You haven't even seen half of it."

We walked on together, weaving between the many clusters of guests, all dressed in glittering gems and luxurious-looking fabrics. I smiled as I spotted Ben's grandpa and his date from the wedding. How strange to see someone I'd met in Seattle, here.

The woman who'd given me the contest flyer spotted me and smiled, scrunching up her nose and twiddling her fingers at me in a wave. I waved back and considered going over, but she and the retired ambassador stood surrounded by a circle of important-looking men and women. I'd catch up with her later. I plucked a couple of champagne flutes off a passing tray and handed one to Maple.

"To magic and new friends."

"Cheers!"

We clinked glasses and I sipped the sweet, bubbly liquid that wasn't champagne, but was delicious. A loud boom sounded overhead, and I crouched down. Maple laughed and pulled me up.

"Just fireworks, see?"

I followed her finger and gazed up into the dark night sky. Among the stars, fireworks exploded in the shapes of swimming schools of fish, then a starfish, and then a mermaid kicked across the sky.

"Okay, magical fireworks are way better than regular ones. And they're already pretty great." I tipped my head back to watch, grinning. Boom, crackle, boom! They drowned out the music from the mermaid band we passed.

Three beautiful women with their long hair draped over their chests sat atop an enormous clam shell, singing an alluring song. Human, or rather witch, women played the guitar, harp, bassoon, and xylophone behind them, clad in navy-blue velvet suits with deep V-necks.

Behind the band, more mermaids swam, dove, and twirled inside a giant glass fishbowl. I was too busy gawking at everything to pay attention to where I walked, and a moment later I bumped into someone. I turned from watching the mermaid band and apologized.

"I'm sorry. I was just—"

Strong hands gripped my shoulders, and I looked up eagerly. I didn't realize I'd been hoping it was Hank, until it turned out to be Nate and my smile fell a fraction. That was silly, I was kind of into Nate, wasn't I? I supposed my feelings had changed a bit after the pantry incident.

"Nate? So good to see you."

"Imogen?" He said my name like a question. He pulled back and dropped his hands, his lips twitching toward a smile, but not quite making it. "Good to see you, too." He scanned out across the crowd, his hands balled into fists at his side.

I nodded. "You're working, I see—on the lookout for someone? More scorched fingers in need of bandaging?" I held up mine and turned it. "Mine's good as new, thanks to you."

"Uh, yeah, I mean not really. Just on the lookout in general." He nodded, glanced at me, and then looked past me. "Well, gotta get going. Have a good time."

"You too," I said to his back, as he'd already pushed past me into the crowd.

I turned to find Maple waiting with a big grin on her face, but when she saw my puzzled expression her smile dropped. "Everything okay?"

I nodded and caught up with her. "Yeah, fine. Just... Nate seemed a little off. Distracted, I guess."

"Ah well, maybe when he gets off duty you two can have a dance or something." She waggled her brows, and I chuckled.

"I'm not too worried about it."

Maple looked hard at my face. "Yeah. You're not, are you? I thought you and him kinda had a thing. You over it?"

I shrugged. "I still think he's cute, and I wouldn't be opposed to a dance." I quirked my lips to the side, then shrugged. "I don't know, maybe it's just that I know I'm leaving, can't think too seriously about anyone."

"Hm." Maple mulled this over as we walked on, toward the palace. We passed a fountain that poured both water and fire, in honor, I supposed, of the Water and Fire Kingdoms coming together for the solstice. A deep temple bell sounded and Maple pulled me left, toward a big crowd.

"Come on, it's almost time."

46

MAKING A SCENE

We slid past people up to a waist-high stone railing and looked out over a sharp drop to the water below. The tide had risen and the moon and stars reflected brightly off the water. But as I looked, I realized it was more than that.

Hundreds of fishing boats dotted the sea, and the people inside them held lanterns in gold and red. The temple bells continued to toll and when they'd finished, the people in the boats threw their lanterns into the air. Thousands of them floated up, gold and red and beautiful. My throat grew tight, just from the beauty of it.

"Now the mermaids go," Maple whispered.

I followed her gaze, squinting to make out little heads and fins popping up amongst the boats below. The water glowed, brighter and brighter, until I could make out the silhouettes of thousands of merpeople below the boats. A torrent of water geysered up and suddenly, little droplets of water hovered amongst the lanterns, floating and drifting with them. The water droplets caught the gold light. I felt silly tearing up, but I couldn't help it.

"This is the most beautiful thing I've ever seen."

Maple bit her lip. "It's always amazing, but they do seem to be going all out this year." We watched the lanterns and water droplets float up and up into the night sky. Behind us, a man called out over the crowd.

"Cherished guests, please enter the palace and take your seats. Dinner will be served shortly." He retreated into the palace, and Maple and I turned to follow.

Rows and rows of long tables covered in blue and gold and red tablecloths lined the great hall. The noise of so many people, there had to be thousands of them, bounced off the stucco walls and mosaic tiled floors. Laughter, singing, and chatter surrounded me. We found a couple of seats at a table in the center of the hall and sat.

Ornate floral centerpieces burst with lace-like coral, starfish, driftwood, anemones, and flowers. Further down the table, an ice sculpture of a mermaid swam around a twisting flame. I leaned forward and looked down the line to the raised table at the head of the room. The glass wall behind it rose stories high and presented a perfect view of the sea beyond and the sky lit up with the floating lanterns and water droplets. *Not a bad view.*

After some announcements, the royal family entered the hall and I stood along with everyone else and curtsied, eyes on the ground. Once the royal family were seated, we sat as well. Food magically appeared on our plates and on the table.

"Dig in!" The king cried from the high table. Laughter echoed around the room, and dig in we did. I ate three plates worth and leaned back, in slight agony over my overstuffed stomach.

"You're not done yet," Maple said, rubbing her belly. "There's still dessert."

I groaned.

Our plates magically disappeared, along with the crumbs and remains of the main platters. Champagne flutes of the bubbly pink liquid I'd had earlier appeared before each setting.

The king stood, dark haired with a white streak. He raised a golden goblet and waited for the hall to quiet.

"Honored and esteemed guests, citizens of my kingdom and of all the kingdoms, I welcome you here tonight. Thank you for joining in this Summer Solstice Festival. They are always special nights, honoring the peace and cooperation between the Water and Fire Kingdoms. But tonight is even more special."

The hush over the room deepened and I leaned forward to get a better view of the table. The queen sat beside the king, looking up at her spouse, and to the left of her sat the four couples I'd seen at the baking competition.

To the right of the king sat a young man I hadn't seen among the royalty before. And beside him sat the royalty from the Fire Kingdom. Something tugged at the back of my mind. Something about that young man beside the king seemed familiar. Where had I seen him before?

"Tonight," the king continued, "we honor a very special joining of our kingdoms. A joining in marriage."

A gasp resounded throughout the dining hall.

"Oh, it's got to be Prince Harry," Maple whispered, edging closer. "He's the only single one."

"Prince Harry." I frowned. "The one who never came to watch the competition?"

"Yep." Maple nodded and arched a brow. "He's the one to the right of the king." She sighed. "So handsome."

"That's Prince Harry?" I narrowed my eyes as he stood. Where did I recognize him from? It's not like I knew many people here, and if he hadn't attended the competition, where would I have seen him?

The king put an arm around his son. "Tonight we celebrate not just the solstice, but the engagement of my youngest son, Prince Harry, to the beautiful, fierce Princess Shaday of the Fire Kingdom. To a happy and peaceful union between these two young people, and between our kingdoms."

The Fire King stood and raised his glass to the Water King, and they drank from their goblets, then everyone else followed suit. I didn't even sip from mine though. I simply couldn't peel my eyes away from Prince Harry. And not just because he was handsome. Though he did have a square jaw, bright blue eyes, and a straight nose, that while large, suited him.

Oh my God!

I pushed back from the table and leapt to my feet.

Maple tugged my hand. "Are you all right? Imogen? What are you doing?"

My chest heaved as I stared at Prince Harry, the king's arm around his shoulders, the impossibly gorgeous Princess Shaday standing at his side.

"And to commemorate this special evening, our new royal baker, Pritney Pricehouse, winner of the recent competition, has prepared a fitting dessert."

I walked toward the high table like a woman possessed. I knew where I'd seen Prince Harry before. It was Hank, or at least what Hank looked like when his face changed.

I couldn't make sense of all the pieces, but something was wrong. Hank and Amelia seemed tight. Maybe they'd kidnapped the real Prince Harry a week ago and Hank had been putting on a magical disguise, posing as the prince at night when he snuck into the palace. It would explain why

Prince Harry didn't attend the competition—Hank couldn't be in two places at once, could he?

I neared the table, no plan in my mind, I just knew I had to stop this. A three-tiered white cake, dripping with gold and red frosting sat on the high table. The king continued to speak and Harry, or really Hank, cut a slice of the cake with a silver spatula and lay it on a glass plate. His large hands trembled slightly.

As I advanced, he cut another couple of slices and handed them to the kings and queens of the Fire and Water Kingdoms. Then, using a little golden dessert fork, he cut a bite off and handed the fork to Princess Shaday. I heard the murmurs behind me.

"Who is that?"

"What's she doing?"

"Stop her!"

"Guard!"

Prince Harry looked up then as Princess Shaday froze, fork midway to her mouth.

"Hank." I said it quietly, watching his face for a reaction.

His brows shot up and he swallowed, his throat bobbing. "I-Imogen," he stammered.

47

HANK

"Imogen. What are you doing?" Hank pretending to be Prince Harry looked down at me from the raised platform. Gasps and murmurs echoed around the great dining hall behind me. Though my cheeks burned hot with embarrassment, I kept my feet planted firmly in front of the royal table.

"You know what I'm doing. I have to stop you."

Next to Hank, Princess Shaday had a pretty good poker face. Just one impeccable brow lifted.

Hank's expression darkened. He leaned forward and growled, "I can explain everything. Later."

"Later?" I lifted my chin and my voice. "After you've poisoned the royal family?" My voice carried, and more gasps sounded behind me.

"Apprehend this young woman!" The king scowled at me and guards rushed forward, their boots scuffing across the tile. I tensed, my shoulders bracing.

"No!" Hank huffed and put a hand on his father's arm. "I know her. It's all right."

The king gave me a sharp look, then lifted a palm. The

four guards who'd rushed forward stopped short, but kept their golden lances pointed at me. My heart pumped in my chest.

Hank's throat bobbed and he licked his lips. He lowered his voice. "What do you mean, poison?"

"Drop the act, Hank." My voice, though it trembled, came out louder than I thought myself capable of in that moment. "I know you're not who you claim to be. And my bet is, that cake is poisoned."

I looked at the princess. Shaday watched me with her intelligent, dark almond-shaped eyes that turned up at the outer corners. Her smooth caramel-brown skin glittered with freckles. With her unflappable expression and poise she looked every bit royalty. "Princess, I know I seem like a crazy woman. But don't eat that cake!"

She looked down at the gold fork in her hand, the chocolate cake resting on the end of it, then at me. She held her face so still, I couldn't tell what she was thinking.

Hank slammed a fist down on the table, startling me. "Stop this," he hissed. "I know—I know you have questions, and I will answer them all, but now is not the time." His blue eyes blazed.

"Test it! I beg you, test it for poison. He killed Glenn!" I pointed at Hank, shouting to be heard over the gasps and murmurs from the guests behind me.

"Enough of this," the king spat. He pointed a bejeweled finger down at me. "Arrest her! And eat your cake," he added testily, glancing at his wife and son, and the Fire Kingdom royalty to his left.

The guards lunged forward and something in me, some instinct, reacted. I don't know how I did it, but I felt it, a pull. I pulled from each of the four guards simultaneously, a thick stream of golden light from each, and drew it into my center, right above my belly button.

I took a long, deep inhale, feeling stronger, taller, and more alive. At the same time the guards crumpled to the ground, unconscious, screams rising up behind me.

As Shaday's parents and the king and queen froze, their forks almost to their mouths, I pulled again. I had to stop them. All I could think was, *I have to get the poison out of that cake.* I threw my arms out, fingers spread wide, and pulled, pulled with every ounce of magic I had inside me.

Dark green bubbling streams flowed into me this time, oozing out of the bites on the forks. The queen saw it. Her eyes grew wide and she screeched and dropped her fork. Shaday paled and dropped hers as well, dark eyes blazing. I pulled not just from the bites on the forks, but from the actual cake itself, the green murky sludge shooting straight into my core.

The impact knocked my head back and as the green sludge flowed through me, as the poison flowed through me, I grew weaker and weaker. I dropped hard on my knees, but even that pain didn't compare to the burning in my stomach, the ache in every inch of my body. I couldn't even manage a scream; the pain choked it out of me.

I collapsed to the ground, curled in on myself. I gasped for breath, but the relentless cramping in my stomach made even breathing difficult. I closed my aching eyes, my whole body now trembling and twitching.

"Guards!" the king shouted. "Guards!"

"Father, she doesn't need to be arrested. She needs a medic! Look at her!" Hank shouted, his voice rough. "She was right, don't you see? The cake was poisoned, and she swallowed it. Medic! Medic!"

I seemed cocooned in a bubble of pain. The screams and pounding footsteps all around me barely registered. But I found the voice to scream when strong arms slid under me and lifted me up. I gagged and felt foamy liquid trickle over my chin. I blinked my aching eyes open and looked up into a familiar face. Nate! Nate had lifted me into his arms. I dipped my head and pressed into him, my body tensing with another round of cramps. I moaned through gritted teeth.

"Nate. Take her to the infirmary, I'll meet you there." Hank's voice again.

No. I tried to mentally communicate with Nate. *No, don't take me there, he'll kill me. Maybe you, too.* But all I could manage was to scrunch my eyes tight against the pain and groan. I bumped along in Nate's arms, and the din quieted.

I peeled an eye open. He ran with me down a corridor, waiters and maids pressing themselves against the walls to make way for us. Good, we'd left the chaos of the dining hall. My stomach twisted and my head lurched forward. I vomited up another round of white-green foam. That couldn't be healthy.

Nate ran and ran, and though normally a trip in his arms would have been lovely, I wanted badly to be on the ground again, puking my guts up in peace, instead of being bumped and jostled with every step. Through blurry, half-closed eyes I watched our progress.

He ran, twisting and turning through hallways, until we stopped at a heavy metal door full of rivets. Nate fumbled with some keys, cursing when he dropped them, and stooped awkwardly with me to retrieve them. He opened the door and jogged down a tightly winding stone staircase. I relaxed a little. The air here felt cooler on my burning skin and the darkness was a relief to my sensitive eyes.

Nate's footsteps echoed around the stone space, the only

other sound a persistent drip, drip, dripping. Nate deposited me on a hard surface. I blinked and patted around with my trembling hands. I lay on a table, a stone table, in a stone room with no windows. We must be far underground.

"Where?" I gasped. At another stomach cramp, I rolled to my side and tucked my knees up to my chest, the soft blue fabric of my dress pooling around my legs.

Nate closed a heavy metal door and turned. He swallowed, his chest heaving, and fixed me with his dark eyes. "We're in the dungeons, Imogen."

48

NATE

Dungeons? That's not how I pronounced infirmary. Another cramp sent me into a fit of agony.

"Do you know how much poison was in that cake?" Nate's voice sounded closer. Through the fog of my pain I became aware that something wasn't quite right.

Uh, if I had, pretty sure I wouldn't have magically sucked it up.

I peeled an eye open. Nate paced back and forth in front of the stone table. He pulled at his thick, black hair. *Is this what his emergency medical training taught him to do?* He deserved a refund.

"Enough to kill the entire royal families from both kingdoms. You just ingested enough poison to kill fifteen people, Imogen. Why?" His face hovered inches from mine. "Sea snakes, you're fading. You're fading. I've got to do something." He resumed stalking back and forth.

How did he know how much poison had been in that cake?

"You tried to kill them." My voice sounded foreign to me, a hoarse, quavering whisper. My teeth chattered.

Nate gritted his teeth. "Stop looking at me like that. Stop it!"

I flinched. "You killed Glenn? And Nan?" I retched up some more white foam. "And now you're going to kill me."

He jabbed a finger at me. "*You* swallowed that poison. I liked you. I still do."

"You tried to frame me!" I groaned, clutching my stomach. My feet and toes cramped and my throat burned.

"No, Imogen. No. That was Pritney."

He pulled at his hair.

"She's a mediocre baker at best. I had to sneak her potions that would make the judges like her bakes—the last one, the day of the final, was spelled to make them dislike yours and Maple's. She came to see me for them, or I'd hide them in the garden. Glenn caught her digging up a potion in the garden that day. She tried to bribe him to keep quiet, but he was going to tell the judges. It would have ruined months of undercover work. I didn't want to kill him, but it was the only way. Pritney spelled her dragon cake to burn him and when he went to see me, I administered the snake venom."

Something I'd read flashed into my head, about snake venom being used for medicine. "And since you're a medic, you were allowed to bring it into the tent. They didn't make you pass through the magical security field," I panted.

"Exactly. Exactly, see you understand? But framing you, that was all Pritney. I was so furious with her for that. When Glenn collapsed, and I rushed to his side, she pulled the vial of poison off me and dumped it into his bake, so it looked like it was the bite he took that had killed him. And since you'd accidentally taken his dough, you looked guilty."

He shook his head.

"I kept telling her that you weren't the enemy. It's those

smug, elitist princes and princesses out there. They're who we're fighting. Let's throw a great party, while the citizens outside our golden walls are ripped apart by monsters." Nate shook his head. "If you knew what I had gone through, you'd understand and you'd want to help, I know you would, Imogen. So I'm going to save you."

"Yes," I croaked. I would never want to join him, but I could tell him that *after* he healed me.

He shook his head. "I only have basic training. It was an act, a way to get me inside." He pulled out a wand and held it above me, his other palm hovering over my stomach. "I'll do my best." Light flashed from his wand, and I felt a momentary relief from the pain. I opened my eyes, only to squeeze them shut again as the pain returned.

"Aahhh!"

Nate tried another spell, and another and another.

"Take me to a healer," I ground out, writhing on the stone table.

"I can't. I can't, they'll arrest me."

"You'd rather let me die?" How had I ever liked this guy?

"I'll get it right. Pritney would tell me to let you die. But I don't care if she's Horace's latest fling, he and I have been friends since we were children. I know he'd want a swallow for the army."

A swallow? What did he mean? And Horace! The man wanted for being leader of the Badlands Army? This was Nate's cause?

I groaned. I didn't know what he was talking about. I just wanted the pain to stop. The cold stone below me made my hip and shoulder ache, and the musty smell of the damp room made me even more nauseous.

A loud crash sent my eyes flying open. The metal door

to the room exploded open and swung hard against the stone wall behind it. Hank ducked his tall frame into the room, wand pointed at Nate, who spun on him, his own wand drawn.

49

POISONED

Hank growled. "I knew you were trouble. Even back in the tent, I knew."

Nate spat at him. "You don't know me at all, Prince."

"Let me take her to a real healer."

Nate shook his head and crouched, his back to me. Hank advanced on him. "She's with us now."

Hank's face darkened and a muscle in his jaw jumped. "She'll be no good to you dead."

Nate lunged, and a ball of fire shot from his wand. Hank dove out of the way. Nate fired again and again at him, as Hank dodged in the small room. The heat of the fire made my head swim.

Suddenly, Hank threw a hand out, catching the fire in his palm. Nate cried out as Hank continued to stretch his palm toward Nate. A thick thread of golden light flew from the medic into Hank's hand. Hank blinked and shook his head to clear it as Nate dropped limp and unconscious to the floor.

"That's what I did with the guards, isn't it?" I muttered as

Hank rushed to my side and scooped an arm under my head as a pillow.

He knelt beside me. "Yes. I'm a swallow. And I think we just discovered that you are as well."

"Why does everyone keep calling me that? And why does it sound so naughty?"

Hank coughed out a laugh. "I'll explain later. Did he tell you anything about the poison they used?"

I shook my head the tiniest fraction, but even that much movement had me retching again, though nothing came up. "You really are a prince?" I gasped.

Hank pressed his lips together and nodded. Ever so gently, he brushed my damp bangs out of my eyes, his eyes dancing over my face.

My eyelids fluttered and the world went dark. Shooting pain woke me back up.

"Stay with me, Imogen." Hank shook me until I opened my eyes. "Swallows can pull from others, that's how we summon our magic, you and me. I'm going to siphon the poison out of you." His chest heaved. "I think you're only alive because you pulled strength from those four guards before ingesting it. Otherwise you'd be...." He shook his head. "It's had time to work its way deep into your system—it's easiest to siphon with direct contact, is that all right?"

"Yes," I croaked. If getting the poison out involved walking over hot coals, I'd do it at this point. Well, if I could stand, which I seriously doubted.

Hank leaned over me and held my hand in both of his. His palms felt wonderfully cool against my burning skin. He closed his eyes, and I felt the slightest tug, the tiniest easing of pain in my fingertips.

His eyes flew open. "Not enough." Hank leaned closer and pressed his forehead to mine, cupping my face in both his palms. I closed my eyes in relief, the cool of him like heaven against my hot, clammy forehead. My headache eased slightly, along with the cramp in my jaw.

My eyes opened, no longer aching. His face hovered an inch above mine, his eyes squeezed shut in concentration. I found the strength to lift my chin and press my lips against his. He froze for just a moment, and then pressed his mouth hungrily against mine.

With the arm under me, he pulled me closer, our kiss deepening. With his free hand, he ran a thumb down my jaw. All my pain slipped away as I savored this kiss. A kiss unlike any I had ever experienced. Then, it changed.

Hank tensed, and I felt the pull as he siphoned the poison from my veins. I could feel it drag out of my toes and joints and bones, out of my stomach and neck. As he pulled more, he stumbled back, letting me go. A floating green rope of poison connected us, flowing from me to him. And then the connection broke and Hank fell back against one of the stone walls, slumping to the floor.

He sat, his long legs splayed out in front of him, his head lolling to the side. I panted on the table. I felt better, slightly, but my stomach still cramped. The arm I'd lifted for Hank dropped onto the stone table.

"You—" I paused to catch my breath. "—don't look so good."

Hank gave a dry chuckle. "You're one to talk." His chest heaved as he stared at me, his blue eyes troubled. "I got some, but not enough." He shook his head. "I should have thought of this earlier." He leaned his head back against the hard wall, tilting his chin in the air. "Francis!" His voice echoed all around the room.

Like, Francis, Francis? The vampire baking judge? He

would not have been my first choice of backup in this situation.

With a pop of smoke, the vampire materialized in the room. He turned to Hank in the corner.

"Hey. I thought no one could do that."

Francis and Hank turned to me in surprise. Hank smiled. "Francis is an exception to a lot of rules." He turned his gaze to the vampire. "She's poisoned. I took as much as I could but it's strong. I'm afraid she doesn't have much time left."

"Say no more." Francis floated over to me, kicking Nate's unconscious body out of the way. He placed all ten bony, pale fingertips along my collarbones. I recoiled, pressing into the table beneath me. "Don't worry, Imogen. This won't hurt, or so I've been told. My fangs secrete a numbing agent."

I let out a high-pitched whine as Francis dipped his head. I felt two small pricks on my neck and then the whole left side of it went numb.

I closed my eyes.

"She tastes of death," Francis called to Hank. "Yummy."

My world went dark.

50

THE INFIRMARY

I woke up screaming and thrashing. It took me several moments to realize I had a fluffy white pillow in a headlock. I blinked rapidly, and my blurry eyes slowly focused.

Iron-framed beds stretched out in two long rows down a high-ceilinged room with big open windows. Birds chirped just outside the window over my head, and a lazy breeze played with the billowing white curtains. Hank, or rather, Prince Harry, lay on his side in the bed to my right, watching me.

"I think you won."

I followed his gaze to the pillow crushed in the crook of my elbow.

"Poor defenseless pillow." Hank shook his head.

My lips twitched toward a smile, but I willed them to stay in a straight line. I didn't want Hank thinking he'd charmed his way out of all his lies. "You owe me an explanation."

Hank took a long breath. He looked up and down the long room, empty except for the two of us and a few nurses who bustled about in the office at one end. He propped himself up on an elbow and slowly rubbed his wrist. "I woke up before you, obviously, so Francis and Amelia have filled me in on some of it."

I settled in on my side, facing him. "That too. But I meant—who are you, really?"

Hank stared at the narrow strip of white tile between us. "I'm sorry. I really am." He took a deep breath and spoke as he let it out. "I'm Prince Harry."

My stomach tightened. I guess part of me had been hoping he'd tell me he was the prince's body double or something. That he was an ordinary guy. An ordinary guy who'd take a regular girl on a regular date.

He lifted his eyes. "But Hank's my nickname." He looked down again. "I wouldn't have used it if I'd known my whole family was going to show up at the competition."

I watched him. "Why were you in the competition?"

He played with the edge of a white blanket. "I've always loved baking. While my brothers were out practicing their sword fighting and jumping into mud pits, I'd sneak into the kitchens and the bakers would teach me."

He tipped his head to the side. "Not that I didn't have my fair share of fights and mud puddles, too. My father tolerated my interest in baking while I was young, but as I got older he felt it was 'unprincely,' so I had to visit the kitchens in secret."

He paused and licked his lips. "As the youngest prince, I'll never be the ruler of this kingdom, but it's expected that I'll—that I'll play a role in diplomatic liaisons, that I'll help form alliances by—"

"Marrying Princess Shaday," I said, my throat dry. At least it didn't burn, like it had in the dungeon. In fact, my body felt remarkably free of pain. Tired, but better than I'd thought possible. Still, my heart felt heavy.

He nodded, his eyes flicking to my face, then back to the floor. "It's a political alliance. I'd only met her a couple times before yesterday. 'Normal people have love, people like us have power,' my father always says. My mother says there are many different kinds of love, and respect and affection come with time and knowledge of each other and—"

He waved his hand as if pushing the thoughts away. "And anyway, a few months ago my father informed me I'd be marrying Shaday. My whole life is planned. When you're a prince, you're born into your job, there's no choosing, no option to be a baker if I wanted to, or date or...." He shook his head. "So when Nan passed—" He stopped and swallowed. "No. When Nan was murdered, but we didn't know that at the time, I wanted to do something to make the Water Kingdom known for its bakers, like the Earth and Fire Kingdoms are. So I had the idea to hold a contest to generate interest. Amelia, she's coordinated our royal events for forever, put it on with my secret backing. And...."

He ran his long fingers through his hair. "And, it was stupid, I know, but I thought, just once, I wanted to be like a normal person. So I submitted a bake, anonymously of course, and Rhonda chose it. I got in."

He looked up at me, his thick brows lifted, pleading. "Please understand, as the prince no one tells me anything straight. They treat me differently, whether they mean to or not. I wanted an unbiased opinion, to know if I was any good, and when I got in, I was thrilled. I knew I had to turn it down, but it felt so good just to be chosen, and the more I thought about it, the more I convinced myself I could make it work in disguise. Amelia refused, obviously, she thought I was mad, but I convinced her. We had to keep it a secret from my family, especially my father—he'd have been furious to know I was still baking after all these years."

That explained those knowing looks between him and Amelia that had made me suspect them of conspiring together. I let out a heavy breath as I thought over the rest of his words. "I know how hiding it feels. I kept it a secret from my adopted family, too."

He looked up and our eyes locked. Hank's blue eyes shone in his paler than normal face. He'd ingested a lot of poison, too.

He licked his lips, and I realized I'd been staring at them a little too long. "Right. You were saying?"

We'd leaned toward each other, across the narrow space between the beds. Hank shook his head. "Right. Well, Amelia only allowed me to enter if I could guarantee my safety. So we brought Francis in. He's an old family friend. Like, he knew my great-great-grandfather old—and he's a vampire. He can materialize anywhere, is immortal, and has ancient magic. He makes a good bodyguard."

I arched a brow. "How is having your bodyguard as a judge fair?"

Hank grinned. "Rhonda was the only real judge. I mean, Francis has a pretty good palate, but only Rhonda's thoughts and reactions factored into who won and who was eliminated. Even she didn't know Francis was a fake judge." He rolled his eyes. "Though of course, the seer's now claiming she knew all along."

I thought about the competition. "I guess she did vote you out. If Francis was biased toward you, you would have won, right?"

Hank nodded. "Yeah, you beat me fair and square. I was not happy about that, and I said some stupid things. I'm sorry." He looked at the floor again. "I knew going into the contest that I needed to keep my distance from all the other competitors. It'd be too easy to slip up, and I also just felt it wasn't fair to lie about who I was when forming friendships."

He sighed. "Plus I had to sneak back into the palace each night to be the prince again and come up with excuses for why I'd been away all day."

"I saw you sneaking! So that's why."

He nodded. "But it happened anyway—I came to care about people. Wool became like a brother to me, and despite trying to convince myself I disliked you... I just couldn't. And those feelings of confusion—I channeled them into that last bake without meaning to, then blamed it on you."

"You tried to dislike me?" I shook my head, smiling all the same.

He sighed. "Ugh. I thought, since I'd worked so hard to give myself a fair and unbiased competition, I wanted to compete against only the best, to really test my mettle. And I thought you, who had just discovered she was a witch and had no knowledge of magic, couldn't possibly give me a true challenge."

He laughed. "I'm an idiot. You challenged me more than anyone else in that tent. And not just in the baking—I couldn't understand how you saw through my facade."

51

A CONNECTION

"How *did* I see through your disguise?"

"You're a swallow, Imogen."

I wrinkled my nose. "Yeah... sounds a bit... er, you know."

He chuckled. "Oh, I know. I'm one, as well. You can imagine the teasing I got from four older brothers on that."

He leaned toward me and gestured with his big hands. "See, most witches and magical folk draw their energy from within themselves. So if they're tired or hungry, for instance, they won't be as powerful. But they just need to rest or eat to generate more power. Swallows, like you and me, are different and quite rare. I've only ever met one other. We pull our energy from things around us—living things, like trees or other people, or from the ocean or music, and take that energy into ourselves and use it for magic or baking, for example."

Ah. That explained those sexual-tension-filled cupcakes.

"Does it—does it hurt the other things?" I fiddled with the edge of a sheet, thinking of the guards I must've pulled energy from at the festival. They'd collapsed.

Hank nodded his head to the side. "It can."

My face must've fallen because he reached out and rested his warm hand on my forearm.

"It doesn't usually. Once you know how to use your magic, you'll make sure you don't hurt anyone."

"But I haven't been able to control it, at all." I looked him square in the face, and chewed my lip. "I hurt those guards, didn't I? Oh God, did I kill them?"

Hank shook his head and squeezed my arm. "Imogen, no. You defended yourself out of instinct, and they're all fine. It was like you just took all their energy and they crashed. But they slept it off, I promise. And you didn't know how to use your magic before because the advice everyone gave you doesn't work for a swallow."

I blinked back tears, still feeling awful about the four guards.

"I'll help you learn. I promise. Once we're both better, we'll do lessons."

I looked back up at him. "But you're the prince and you have to do princely things and that doesn't involve associating with commoners in unicorn tees—" My eyes opened wide, a sudden thought occurring to me. "You sent the clothes, didn't you?"

Hank blushed—actually blushed! He looked away, then grinned up at me, shyly. "I-I just wanted to do something nice for you."

I bit my lip and smiled. Why, oh why did he have to be a prince? With his face so close to mine, I couldn't think those things. "So, tell me about Pritney and Nate. Ugh." I shook my head. "I can't believe I actually kinda liked the guy."

Hank swallowed, his eyes bright. "What? With those biceps, I kinda liked the guy, too."

I grinned. His hand still rested on my forearm, and I wasn't about to tell him to remove it.

"He and Pritney infiltrated the palace months ago, Pritney as a baker and Nate as a medic. Pritney used spells to ingratiate herself with Nan. She knew her routine and how she went into the woods each night. She waited till she was next in line for the royal baker's job, then she and Nate coordinated. She went out of town and filed a false police report at the exact time of the murder a country away, to give her a solid alibi. Meanwhile, she told Nate where to find Nan in the woods, and he gave her a potion that induced a heart attack. Pritney thought she'd positioned herself to be promoted, and she would have been, had I not had the idea for the competition."

Hank shook his head. "Their goal all along was to have Pritney in place as head baker so she could poison the cake at the Summer Solstice festival and kill me and my family, as well as the Fire Kingdom's royalty. She and Nate are part of the Badlands Army. Francis took Nate into custody from the dungeon, and the police managed to nab Pritney as she tried to hijack a hot air balloon and escape. Nate's clammed up, but the police actually got Pritney to talk. Apparently she's enamored with Horace, the leader of the Badlands Army, but she and Nate have clashed. I think they're jealous of each other, and she was all too happy to blame their failed plan on his interest in you."

"Me?" My heart quickened in surprise.

"Says you distracted him." Hank's eyes flicked to my face. "Guess I'm not the only one."

My throat grew tight. "What now?"

"They'll be tried in court."

I shook my head. "So, using my magic, I pulled energy

out of the guards to knock them out, and then pulled the poison from the cake?"

He nodded. "If you hadn't pulled from the guards first, you wouldn't have had the strength to withstand that much poison."

I remembered Nate running with me through the halls. "Why did Nate take me to the dungeon?"

"I think he wanted a secluded place to try and heal you."

I nodded. "He said I'd sympathize with the Badlands Army, and that Horace would want me for my powers."

Hank cocked a brow. "I dare say he would, but there's no way you'd be one of them, Imogen. They're violent and don't care who they hurt to get more power. You could never be like that, you're too kind."

My throat grew tight again. "And then you...?"

"I watched him take you out of the hall. I knew something was wrong when he went right, instead of left toward the infirmary. The dining hall dissolved into pandemonium, slowing me down. I followed the trail of confused staffers who pointed me in your direction, and when I got to the old dungeons—we don't use them anymore—the door stood ajar. I think he must've lifted the keys sometime during his months in the palace posing as a medic. Anyway, I'm not sure how much you saw or remember, you were pretty out of it. But Nate and I fought, and I disarmed him."

"You pulled from him."

Hank nodded.

"And then you pulled the poison from me."

He sighed. "I got some, but it'd worked its way through your whole system. So I called on Francis. He materialized and drank more of your blood."

"Oh my God, am I a vampire now?" I gripped the sheet with both hands.

Hank's eyes widened, and his mouth pulled into a grin. He squeezed my arm and happy tingles shot through my body. "No. Ha, no. You're not a vampire. Francis filtered a lot of the poison out of your blood. Then he brought us here, and the healers did the rest."

I looked at Hank till he met my eyes. "Thank you for saving me."

His face lit up and he laughed. "I *tried* to save you. Tried, being the key word."

I grinned. "All right then. Thank you for *trying* to save me."

He bit his lip. "And thank you for *actually* saving *me*. If you hadn't barged up to the high table and made the biggest stink I've ever seen, my whole family and I would be dead."

"Stink, huh?"

He chuckled. "You're going to be the talk of Bijou Mer for years."

"Well, if you'd just listened to me...."

"And admitted in front of my father that I'd secretly entered a baking competition and had fallen for the—" His eyes grew wide, and he stopped, looking away.

My heart felt so large I thought my chest might explode. With him so close I could lean a few inches and our lips— I had to stop thinking like that. I grasped for the thread of our conversation. Me accusing him, right. "I'm sorry I thought you capable of, you know, of killing Glenn and Nan."

It took Hank a couple of breaths to answer. "You knew something was off, and you trusted your gut. You don't have to apologize for that."

"So, earlier when I asked how I could see through your disguise. That was because I'm a swallow, you think? I was pulling your facade down?"

He nodded and met my eyes again, then his gaze dipped

to my lips. "Could be." He blinked slowly. "But like I said, I've never met anyone like you before. Maybe when two swallows meet—"

"There's some kind of reaction? Like we're both pulling from each other?" I definitely felt a pull. I leaned closer to him, past the edge of my bed.

He nodded and his lips parted, his eyes focused on my mouth. "Maybe that explains what I felt when—when I pulled the poison from you, and in the pantry when...."

My mouth slid to the side in a grin. Our faces were so close. He smelled like almond extract. "Maybe in the interest of magical knowledge, we should test this theory."

He grinned. I wanted those lips. The room seemed brighter, and I realized that golden threads swirled between us, sparking and popping like live wires. Hank followed my gaze and saw them, too. When he looked back up at me, I saw the same hunger and desire I felt spelled out across his face.

He leaned forward, and just as his nose brushed my cheek and his breath brushed across my lips, wood doors slammed and we jerked apart. The golden threads snapped and fizzled out.

52

A NEW ADVENTURE

Guilt and disappointment broiled in my stomach as the king and queen strode down the long room, followed by Hank's four brothers and their wives and Princess Shaday and her family. His fiancée, I reminded myself.

Their heels clipped down the white tile floors, echoing through the large, open space. The nurses rushed out of their office and bowed low. As the royal families reached Hank's bedside, I looked away, embarrassed.

I noticed I had a side table. Atop it sat an enormous bouquet of flowers, with an aqua-colored card sticking out. I plucked the card and tried to drown out the tears of the queen and the teasing of Hank's brothers as they crowded around him.

"Oh, my baby," the queen moaned.

"Mom, you're smothering him."

I focused on the card. *To Imogen, for when you wake up. None of the flowers are poisonous, I promise, but I wouldn't try eating them. Aw, probably a terrible joke, sorry. I hope that either these flowers or my dimwitted note make you smile. Hank.*

His letters had started out large, then the writing had gotten smaller and smaller as he ran out of room, until I had to lift the note to my face to read the signature. I chuckled, my chest flushing warm.

No. I set the note on the table. *I must not feel giddy over an engaged man's dorky note.* Then how come I did? I shook my head to clear it, my nerves on edge from blocking out the royal family as they talked over each other and laughed and cried behind me.

My feelings softened when I noticed the plate of cranberry scones. A note tucked beneath the plate read, *In case I'm not here when you come to. I'm sure they're not as good as yours, but hope you like them all the same. Love, Maple.*

My heart swelled with gratitude, and also an ache to see my friend. I had so much to tell her. I opened another note in a sealed envelope with well wishes from Wool, Rhonda, Bern, Lillian, and Zeke. I hugged the note to me, grateful to have met so many kind and caring people.

In an instant, my heart fell and tears welled in my eyes. As soon as I felt better, I'd have to leave and head back to St. Louis. Maybe I could (cough, cough) pretend to be ill for another month or two or forever, so I could stay.

I gasped with gratitude when Maple burst through the wooden doors. "You're awake!" She sprinted down the long room, slowing when she spotted the royal family, her fair skin turning bright pink. She walked stiff legged up beside my bed, her eyes widening further when she spotted Hank in the bed beside me, and dropped into a low curtsy.

When she rose, the queen smiled at her, and she turned a deeper shade of red. Hank and his family resumed their talk, and Maple plopped down onto the bed next to me.

"Oh no, I shouldn't bounce you." Her hands flew to her mouth.

"It's all right. I actually feel surprisingly good."

"So I can hug you? It won't hurt?"

"Please." I opened my arms wide and she threw hers around me. We hugged and rocked for a while.

"I'm so glad you're all right," Maple said into my shoulder. "I've been so worried."

I squeezed her tighter. "I'm sorry I scared you."

"Are you feeling well enough to tell me what happened?"

I nodded and filled her in on everything, from thinking Hank was disguised as the prince, to being kidnapped by Nate and saved by Francis. I left out the part about kissing Hank until we could be together in private.

Maple scowled. "I can't believe that Nate would do that. He's a killer!" We sat in silence for a moment. "Oh!" She clapped her hands. "I have such good news though, I can't believe I didn't tell you right away!" Maple's blue eyes glowed and she took my hands in hers.

I couldn't help but smile back. "I could use some good news."

"Well, with Pritney arrested, I was the runner up, and... I'm the new royal baker!"

"Ahhh!" Our screams startled the royalty beside us into looking over, but I was too happy to care. I threw my arms around Maple again and we hugged and laughed. "You're amazing, you know that?" I told her. "You deserved it from the beginning. I knew you'd win, I knew it!"

"And the best news is...."

"It gets better?" I raised my brows.

"I get to bring on staff, remember? So how about it, want to work in the royal bakery?"

A rush of happiness filled my chest. I nodded through

the tears that streamed down my face. "Yes," I managed to gulp out. "A thousand times, yes!"

We hugged again and rocked. My future looked much rosier. I was going to get to do what I loved most in the world, bake for a living, in the most magical, beautiful place I'd ever been. I cried big happy tears on Maple's shoulder. A thought occurred to me. "You get to hire one more person from the competition, right?"

Maple pulled back and nodded.

I gave her a sly look. "So... Wool then?" I waggled my eyebrows.

Maple tilted her head to the side. "I did think about it, but I know he's been offered a job in the Fire Kingdom's royal bakery. And... well, I don't know if you talked to Sam much? But he had the station next to mine and he was always so kind and gentle."

"Sam, the shifter?"

She nodded. "They found him last night during the festival and arrested him. I guess he thought he'd accidentally got venom into Glenn's bread, though it's impossible, and that's why he confessed. He's not in trouble anymore, once all the stuff with Pritney and Nate came out. Shifters are really discriminated against in the kingdoms, and he's quite a good baker really, and I just thought—"

"Maple, I think hiring Sam is a wonderful idea. He's all those things you said, and you are so wonderful to do that for him. It's going to change his whole life."

Maple smiled. "It's going to change all of ours, isn't it? You won't mind working with him then?"

I shook my head. "It'll be a pleasure to. Now, how about we bust into those scones."

Maple turned to grab the plate, and as she did I glanced over toward Hank, just as he looked my way. With his family distracted with some story one of his brothers was telling, we shared a long look. I gave him a tight-lipped smile and his brows drew together, his face falling.

I sighed and turned away again, accepting the scone Maple handed me. I'd have to find a way to keep my distance from Hank, which wouldn't be easy working in the palace. But I'd find a way to make it work.

Maple lifted her scone and bumped it against mine in salute. "To new adventures!"

I nodded. "To new adventures!"

THE END

KEEP READING FOR A SNEAK PEEK AT BOOK 2...

A NOTE FROM THE AUTHOR

I've always dreamed of being a published author, and to realize that dream, and have people like you actually read my book—I can't tell you how much it means to me. So, truly, thank you.

If you enjoyed the story, and you'd like to help me as an author, please leave me a review on Amazon. It doesn't matter how long or short, a review is the very best way you can help me stay in business and keep writing. Plus, you'll help other readers discover Imogen and her adventures.

Thanks so much,
Erin

P.S. Keep reading for a sneak peek at book 2...

Sign up for the Erin Johnson Writes newsletter
at www.ErinJohnsonWrites.com

That way, you'll always know when the next book's coming out, and I'll send you a fun weekly newsletter. I'll also let you know about giveaways and exclusive deals.
Plus, I'll send you *Imogen's Spellbook*, a custom illustrated collection of recipes featured in the story.

READ ON FOR A SNEAK PEEK AT BOOK TWO...

A carnival bakery booth. A deadly magic show. Is it the perfect recipe for murder or a clever sleight of hand?

Palace pastry chef Imogen is struggling to control her newfound magic and her potent feelings for the prince. So when the carnival rolls into the kingdom, she jumps at the chance to run the royal bakery booth. But her plan to escape her problems backfires when murder rocks the magician's table... and her dear friend is found holding the bloody saw.

Determined to cook up a way to keep Rhonda out of witch's prison, she sifts through the clues and the long list of suspects. Between devious dark magicians, cagey stage assistants, and a strongman with more to offer than just muscles, everyone at the fairgrounds seems to be hiding secrets—even Rhonda.

With the final night of the carnival approaching, will

Imogen's shaky powers be enough to flush out the murderer before her good friend ends up on the chopping block?

Black Arts, Tarts & Gypsy Carts is the second book in the Spells & Caramels paranormal cozy mystery series. If you like feisty heroines, enchanted carnivals, and dueling magicians, then you'll love Erin Johnson's whimsical whodunit.

Buy Black Arts, Tarts & Gypsy Carts to fall under the spell of a festive mystery today!

∽

Keep reading for an excerpt from Black Arts, Tarts & Gypsy Carts

THE ROYAL BAKERY

I leaned my hip against the butcher block counter, one arm folded across my apron, the other holding my latest borrow from the royal library. I skimmed my finger along the text.

"To mix the ingredients thoroughly, one must simply draw on the unity within you and transfer that to the ingredients."

I'd gone through hundreds of books in the last week since starting work in the royal bakery. Not that I'd read them cover to cover. That'd be nuts. Maple helped me cast a spell that located any books mentioning swallows and the pages to read, so I'd skimmed them. Most were about as helpful as the one I held in my hands.

"Of course, swallows will do things differently." I skimmed the rest of the page and flipped it over, finding no more mentions of swallows.

Seriously? That's it? Swallows will do things differently? I growled and flipped the book over, glaring at its embossed gold lettering.

"Thanks for nothing, *Magical Makings*." I huffed. I had

stacks more back in my room to comb through that evening, though I didn't have much hope. I'd been trying to learn to harness my powers on my own. Apparently, just about all other witches and wizards pulled their powers from within. But I was different.

As a swallow, I pulled power from other people, living things, and even nature and emotions to create magic. So no one's advice helped me learn to use my powers, and the only other person I knew who was a swallow and could help, was not an option. *Sigh*.

I glanced at the enchanted hourglass on the flour-covered worktable. A couple more minutes on my cinnamon rolls and then I'd check the oven. They smelled heavenly, of cinnamon and sugar. Plus, I knew Iggy, my magical flame and baking partner, would let me know when they were done.

Without any expectations, I'd opened the book to the next marked page to see if I could glean any more information that might help me learn about using magic, when a shriek startled me and I dropped the book onto the table.

"Oh no, oh no, oh no!" Maple rushed to one of the arched brick ovens that dotted the walls all around the royal bakery. Black smoke billowed from around the wooden cover we always left partially open to keep the fires burning. Smoke drifted up to the white stuccoed ceiling three stories above.

"I'll get the windowsss!" Sam dashed forward, his heels clipping the white marble floors. He pulled a wooden rolling ladder in front of the teal shelves that held the copper pots and pans. He scurried up and used a long stick with a hook on the end to pull the windows, tall as doors, open.

I grabbed my red oven mitts and sprinted over to Maple

who'd already tossed the cover off. I slid one of the burning pans from the oven. We shoved them onto the nearest long work station. I backed away, burying my nose in the crook of my elbow, and coughed, my lungs burning.

Annie, the plump older baker from the Earth Kingdom, adjusted her headband, pulling her gray hair back from her face. She grabbed another metal tray and fanned it across the table, dispersing the smoke and cooling the two trays of charred cherry-crisp coffee cakes.

"Wiley, these are yours." Annie turned her head to cough and kept fanning. Yann dropped his pestle into the bowl of lavender he'd been crushing, and stomped over.

"Oh." Yann's face fell and the giant bear of a man shook his head slowly. "Oh, and dey are da queen's favorite."

"They may turn out yet." Annie raised her thin brows at Yann, who plucked up a nearby tray and waved it back and forth over the cherry coffee cake. With arms as thick as my torso, Yann moved quite a bit more air than Annie. I winced as a gust blew my bangs back from my face and my apron nearly over my head.

I smoothed it down in time to see Maple eyeing Wiley like she might take one of the trays to his head. Bright red streaks glowed on her fair cheeks, and she held her arms stiff at her sides. Wiley ignored her, popped a piece of the dough he was rolling into his mouth, and talked through it to K'ree.

"Yeah, it gets pretty wild on Main Street. I found this great little club off the canal, you should come out this weekend." The guy was probably in his late twenties like me, but acted like a frat boy. He towered over K'ree, whose dark eyes darted between him and Maple as she played with the edges of the black-and-gold scarf she wore wrapped round her head.

Since Maple, Sam, and I had started at the royal bakery a week ago, Wiley had given Maple nothing but trouble, from bigmouthed retorts to purposely ruining bakes. I'd talked to her about showing more authority—she was the new head baker after all, and deserved respect. Though as the youngest, sweetest, and most soft-spoken person on the staff, that wasn't proving easy for her. I guessed those power poses we'd practiced were paying off, though. I half expected lasers to shoot out of Maple's bright blue eyes and explode Wiley on the spot. That would mean a lot of cleanup for the rest of us, though. I waved a hand and tried to catch her eye as she advanced on him.

"Maple? Uh, royal baker head boss? A word?"

She ignored me and stalked over to the tall oaf. A voice behind me made me jump.

"This is going to be good," Iggy drawled in his deep English voice.

I glanced over my shoulder and gave the little flame in the brick oven behind me a leveling look. Rows of the small ovens lined two of the walls of the bakery, stacked two high. My flame's heat warmed my back as he warmed the oven.

He grinned back. "My bet's on Maple."

FANNING THE FLAMES

I followed his gaze. *Oh geez*. Maple's face glowed bright red and she stood directly in front of Wiley, who completely ignored her.

"Wiley." My friend could be a ventriloquist. She'd somehow ground the word out without unclenching her jaw.

K'ree whimpered and scampered down the long table that spanned most of the huge room. Wiley set down his rolling pin, wiped his hands on his apron, found something interesting on his nails to pick at, and then finally turned to Maple. The guy had to be at least six foot five, and looked down at the top of her head. He gave Maple a lazy blink, and raised his brows. "Yes?"

Maple's arm shot out, a trembling finger pointing at the charred cherry coffee cake that Yann and Annie still fanned. "Care to explain that?"

Wiley lifted his brows and leaned to the side, as if glancing around Maple, despite the fact that he could clearly see over her head. He turned back to Maple. "Looks like a burned coffee cake to me." He winced, scrunching up his nose. "Queen's favorite, she's not going to like having to eat something else for breakfast. Maybe we could see if the kitchen will whip her up some porridge?" He shook his head and leaned in, pretending to lower his voice. "You should really manage your employees better."

All the color drained from Maple's face, and her eyes blazed. I tried to jump in before she unloaded on him. I leapt forward, ducking under the pans Annie and Yann waved over the cake.

"Hey, this isn't so bad. Mostly just burnt around the edges." I plucked up a knife and began slicing the black crumbly bits off. "See, we can drizzle with some frosting, give the queen the middle pieces, she'll never know. And hey, you guys can probably do something with magic, right?" I inhaled deeply, wafting the curling plumes of smoke toward me. "Hmm, the smoke actually adds kind of a nice dimension to the coffee."

At the mention of smoke, Maple, who'd looked like she was softening slightly, shrieked and whirled back on Wiley. She had to stretch up onto her toes to poke him in the chest.

"You did that on purpose!"

"Wish I could say I did, but I had no idea the smoke would actually complement the flavor." Wiley widened his stance and crossed his arms over the apron at his chest. His lips pulled to the side in a bratty grin.

"You've been sabotaging bakes since I started. If you don't stop, I'll—"

Wiley raised his brows and widened his blue eyes. "You'll what?"

Maple drew herself up to full height, which still had her eye level with his ribs. She sucked in a deep breath through her nose, held the breath as they glared at each other, and then let it all out in a rush. "I'll fire you and hire someone who'll actually do their job."

Oh shoot! I darted a wide-eyed look at Iggy, who'd frozen with his little flame mouth agape. About the harshest words I'd ever heard out of Maple's mouth up to this point had been the time she gently chided a seagull for pooping on her shoulder.

Wiley paled. Then he licked his lips and scoffed. "Good luck. You're not going to find anyone else to work here with *him*." He lifted his chin toward Sam, and my stomach dropped. "You already lost half the staff when you brought the shifter in."

I still couldn't understand the magic community's discriminating attitude toward shifters. It hadn't just been kindness that'd prompted Maple into hiring Sam. He was a good baker. I glanced at the gentle guy. He stood by the ladder with his head hanging, his arms limp at his sides. As a snake that had the ability to shift into human form, Sam often didn't quite know what to do with his arms when he wasn't using them. My heart went out to him.

I lifted my chin. "We're lucky to have Sam."

Sam lifted his head, and his lips twitched toward a sad smile. I nodded at him.

Wiley turned to me and pressed his hands to his chest. "Listen, Red, you don't have to tell me. I stayed, didn't I? I'm down with shifters." He tilted his head toward Maple. "But boss lady here's trying to tell me how easily replaceable I am, and I'm simply reminding her of her current staffing shortage."

Five experienced bakers had quit because of Sam.

"You may not like it, but I am the new royal baker." Maple jutted her chin in the air.

"Yeah, 'cause Nan was murdered and you won a contest

in a tent—sorry, my bad. You came in *second*, and by default got the position." Wiley slow clapped. "Very impressive."

"Look, we—" Maple took a deep breath and nodded. "We all just need to show each other some respect." She looked at Sam, Annie, Yann, me, K'ree, and Wiley towering above her. "Especially, *you* need to show *me* some respect." She gestured between Wiley and herself. "I don't know if this is how you—"

She stopped short when Wiley suddenly dropped into a low bow, his eyes on the marble floor. I frowned and looked behind Maple. Prince Harry stood in the arched doorway at the top of the eight steps that led down into the bakery. I dropped into a curtsy, as did all the others.

With her back to the prince, Maple shoved her hands onto her hips, her elbows jutting out wide. "Very funny, Wiley, very funny. A normal amount of respect will do, thank you very—"

"Maple!"

She stopped midsentence and glanced my way, a question on her face. I widened my eyes and jerked my head toward the prince. She frowned and turned, then let out a little squeak and dropped into a curtsy herself.

"Oh come on, how many times do I have to tell you." Prince Harry, or Hank, as I knew him, bounded down the steps in two long strides. I rose as the others did.

"Annie, did you ever curtsy when Nan was royal baker?" Hank drew the older woman into a one-armed hug at his side. She wrapped her arms around his middle. My stomach clenched a little, and I frowned at myself. Did I really just get jealous of Annie? More evidence to support my current plan of action. I started inching along the wall toward the storeroom in the back.

"Hiding again?" Iggy laughed at me.

I gave him a look and hissed, "Quiet."

"I've been coming down here since I was old enough to walk." Hank released Annie and clapped Yann on the back. The big guy flushed and grinned.

I sidestepped closer to the storeroom, willing myself to be invisible. Hank tried for a light, teasing tone, but I could hear the strain underneath. He'd told me that he'd secretly entered the baking competition to test his mettle as a baker, since as a prince everyone treated him differently. The bakery was the one place he could be a normal guy. He'd been sneaking down here since he was a kid, though his father, the king, had no idea he still did. And that hadn't stopped since Nan, the last royal baker, was killed and Maple, Sam, and I joined the bakery.

In fact, Annie had hinted to me that his visits had gotten more frequent. She seemed to think that had something to do with me. Though, as I made sure to either hide in the storeroom or run to the market for ingredients or basically be anywhere but the bakery whenever he came by, I didn't see how that could be.

"Don't let me interrupt, but Maple, can I have a word?"

I paused my retreat and glanced over my shoulder. Maybe Hank hadn't come by to see me.

COMPLICATED

Annie and Yann worked on saving the cherry coffee cake, and K'ree, Sam, and Wiley busied themselves with other pastries. I eavesdropped as Maple and Hank moved into one of the shelf-lined alcoves tucked into the wall.

"What can I do for you, Prince Harry?" Maple nodded and curtsied. Then bowed for good measure.

I grinned. So awkward.

"Again, you can call me Hank." He cleared his throat and ran a hand through his dark, wavy hair. "You know the Summer Sea Carnival is in town? Starting tomorrow?"

Maple nodded. "Of course, Prince Harry."

Hank pressed his lips together and then let out an exhale. I felt for the guy. But as an outsider, I'd only ever known him as Hank. Maple, on the other hand, had grown up in Bijou Mer, always thinking of him as the prince. It'd be a hard habit to change.

"What do you think about setting up a baking booth?"

"A booth?" Maple blinked at him.

"I know, I know." Hank lifted his large hands. "I'm sure

you're incredibly busy, just getting settled in, learning the ropes, bonding with your team."

Right. Lots of bonding.

"It might not be convenient to be away from the bakery right now, but I thought it'd be such a great opportunity to promote baking in the Water Kingdom. The Earth and Fire Kingdoms are renowned for it, but I want to raise awareness of all the talent we have right here in Bijou Mer. I have a special project in mind, and thought you could sell pastries to raise money for it."

Special project?

Maple glanced at Wiley, then back at Hank. "I'll do it. Absolutely. How long do you need me at the booth for? A few weeks? Months?"

Hank chuckled. "The carnival only lasts a week, and if that's too long to be out of the bakery, you can always rotate shifts with the others."

"Nope." Maple shook her head vehemently. "No, this is a special project for the prince, and as royal baker, I should definitely oversee it. Definitely. At the carnival, far away from the bakery." She glanced at Wiley again.

I groaned. This was not the time for her to be out. She needed to establish her presence as our leader, let everyone get to know her and see how wonderful she was. I walked over and joined them in the alcove. Hank straightened and blinked at me.

"Sorry, couldn't help but overhear." *'Cause I was lurking.* "Maple, remember what we talked about?" I referred to our nightly pep talks where I encouraged her to speak up more and show the others how knowledgeable and experienced she was, despite her age. "You should probably be here, don't you think?"

She bit her lip, her blue eyes bright and wide. She gave

me a broad grin, then smiled up at Hank. "Nope. I like Hank's plan. I'll be at the booth."

I clicked my tongue at her.

Hank looked down at me with his intelligent blue eyes. "With Maple out, you'll be even more needed, Imogen, and I'm sure knowing some magic would be a big help."

Here it came. I cringed inwardly.

"Why don't we pick a time and we can work on it together?"

He looked at me with such earnestness I could hardly meet his eyes. I looked all around for any escape. My eyes landed on Maple. I slid up to her and threw an arm over her shoulders.

"Oh darn." I tried to grimace and look disappointed. "But Maple was just saying how much help she'll need, getting the booth ready, selling the pastries, running the pie-eating contest—"

"The what?" Maple frowned at me.

"Maybe that's a human thing, I'll explain it. But all the more reason she needs me working the booth with her, right?" I flashed my eyes at her.

"Oh, yeah. Right."

"So, I'm sorry. Bummer. But I won't be able to study with you." I pulled Maple to me like she was my conjoined twin, and kept my smile plastered on as I stared up at Hank. His head brushed the ceiling of the dark, small space. His flat eyes held none of their usual sparkle.

"Maple, will you excuse us a moment? I need a private word with Imogen."

My arm tightened around her shoulders. She turned to me, her expression apologetic. I shook my head tightly, willing my thoughts telepathically into her head. *Maple. Don't leave me alone with him. Maple!*

She inched away, and I knew I'd have to save myself. "I have to check on my cinnamon rolls!"

Maple peeled my arm from her shoulders. "I'll check for you." She gave my hand a little squeeze before slipping out of the dim alcove into the bright bakery. She cast an apologetic glance over her shoulder, then moved off to the ovens.

I folded my arms across my chest and stared at my feet, trying hard to ignore my closeness to Hank, the darkness of the space, and how he smelled like cloves. He took a step closer, and I backed into a shelf that dug into my lower back. *Ow.*

He reached an arm out, but stopped short of touching my elbow. "Imogen. You're avoiding me."

"What? No, I'm not. I'm...." I looked around for an escape.

He sighed. "I get it. I do. It's a... complicated situation."

Not that complicated. *We almost kissed in a pantry, much like the alcove we're currently in, then you did kiss me to save my life, then it was so nice we almost kissed again, but your fiancée showed up and reminded me that, oh yeah, you're engaged. To a princess.*

"But you've got to learn to use your magic."

I finally looked up at him, standing so close, and I froze. His dark, thick brows pulled together, and he pressed his lips tight, and pulled them to the side. *Stop.* I willed myself to look away from his lips. "Look, I made it through the baking contest without magic, didn't I? I'm doing fine."

He scoffed. "Hardly."

I frowned at him. "Hey."

He sighed. "What I mean is, you hardly made it through without magic. You use magic all the time, you just don't know how to control it. Besides, I'm not concerned about your baking, which is better than fine."

My stomach fluttered at the compliment.

"It's your safety. Nate almost...." He looked away and swallowed, his throat bobbing. He turned back to me, his eyes intense. "You need to be able to defend yourself."

"I am learning, all right?" I lifted my brows and tried for confidence. "I've been reading books and studying on my own and—"

"And how's that going?" He shook his head. "You're talking to another swallow, you don't think I tried that as a kid? It wasn't until my mother realized what I was and found another swallow to teach me, that I was able to control my magic."

He stepped closer and his warm hand slid gently around my elbow. "If something happened to you—"

"Princess!"

We both turned. Outside the alcove, the bakers all bowed and curtsied to the beautiful Princess Shaday and her handsome brother, Prince Roo. Decked out in the red and gold silks of the Fire Kingdom, they stood at the top of the stairs, glowing. Well, the beam of sunshine streaming in through the open second-story window onto their heads helped, but they shone on their own, too.

Hank dropped his arms to his sides and gave me a downcast look, before composing himself and striding out of the alcove to join his fiancée. I sighed as I watched him go.

"I was told I might find you here." Princess Shaday had a deep, melodic voice, though her tone with Hank was the same as her tone with any of us. She was a tough cookie to read. "We are wanted for the meeting with the trade council."

Hank and Shaday bowed stiffly to each other. I leaned my head against the white stucco wall and watched them leave. It didn't matter that Hank's dad, the king, had arranged his marriage to Shaday and that he barely knew her. It didn't matter that he and I had a deep and magical connection that went beyond the sparks of two swallows gravitating toward each other. Shaday and Hank had about as much chemistry as a cake with too much baking soda. *Ba-dum tshh! Thanks folks, I'll be here all week.* Bad baking joke—it makes a cake flat, just like the interactions between Hank and Shaday—but they'd be married.

And even if he didn't marry *her*, Hank was a prince, and I was definitely not a princess. Which made him off-limits, and made the two of us working magic together a bad idea.

At least the carnival would get me out of the palace for a week.

THE TENT

"Sam, that's amazing!" I clasped my hands together and bounced on my toes.

Sam continued to wave one hand through the air as if he were conducting a symphony, while he paused with the other to push his glasses up his nose. He smiled at me, his milky blue eyes bright. As he swept his hands through the air, our baking booth came together.

Long branches floated into place, twisting themselves into the grassy ground to stand upright like poles. Then the thick white canvas fluttered in overhead and dropped into place, creating a peaked tent with an open front. The sides flapped in the salty sea breeze.

Sam hummed in his surprisingly low voice as pastel-colored bunting strung itself across the top of the open side, and a long wooden table appeared, topped with three-tiered cake stands and vintage leather suitcases lined with pink cloth to use as displays.

A banner floated into place, announcing in blue and gold lettering, "The Royal Bakery Booth" and a chalkboard with a list of items for sale and prices swung into place, hanging from one of the poles.

Sam let his arms drop, and shrugged. "Well, it'sss not perfect, but hopefully—"

"It's beautiful!" I pulled Maple and Sam into a hug.

Maple peeked around me. "Sam, you have such a good eye for design."

Sam ducked his head to hide his blush, what little of a chin he had completely disappearing.

"What is it with you lot and baking in tents?" Iggy guttered in a glass-enclosed lantern at my feet. "Shall we see if the oven is up to standard?"

"Is anything up to your standards?" I ducked to lift the lantern and a couple of my library books I'd brought along to study during the slow times. The four of us stepped under the colorful bunting into the tent. Right behind the long wooden table stood a tall stone wood-fire oven. As I opened the glass door on the lantern and coaxed Iggy out, I noticed the logs already in the oven and piled at its base. I turned to Sam, a wide grin on my face.

"Sam! You even remembered that Iggy loves linden branches." I turned from Sam to my flame. "Iggy, wasn't that thoughtful?"

Sam ducked his head and rubbed the back of his beet-red neck. "It wasss nothing. I wasss out ssslithering in the foressst and sssaw sssome."

Iggy nestled into the oven, munching on one of the branches, which crackled and glowed. "Well, I don't know how he carried a pile of logs back without arms, but I'll take it."

I tilted my head to the side and gave him a *be polite* look.

He shrugged, but peeked around the side of the oven, a

log still hanging out of his mouth. "Thanks, Sam—logs are delicious."

While Sam busied himself in the back of the tent arranging the pantry, Maple and I worked up front, spreading out a linen tablecloth and arranging another table to be our workstation for baking.

"Have you heard from Wool?" We pulled the ends of the tablecloth taut.

Maple stared at her hands as she smoothed the cloth. "No." She pulled her lips to the side and sighed. "I'm sure he's busy."

I made a sympathetic noise. "I'm sure." Maple kept her eyes down. "Hey, why don't you write him?"

She glanced up, her eyes wide, then looked back at her hands as she arranged the various display trays. "I couldn't."

I unpacked some boxes of rolling pins, measuring cups, and other utensils. "Why not? You're a strong, independent woman."

She sniffed. "Ha."

"What? You are!" I opened my mouth wide in mock surprise. "Unless... it's because you can't read and write?"

She narrowed her eyes at me. "Hilarious."

I grinned. "Well, think about it. I'm sure he'd love to hear from you."

She didn't say anything, but that wasn't a hard no. We worked for a few moments in silence, and my thoughts wandered back to the palace.

"What do you think the chances are that Wiley hasn't burned down the royal bakery at this point?" I set out a glass jar containing wooden spoons and whisks.

Maple grinned. "He has to actually be in the bakery to burn it down. He's probably still sleeping, and will be late as usual." Maple kept her eyes on her work, folding and refolding striped towels. She let out a heavy sigh and tossed a towel in a crumpled heap. "You know, would it kill him to be on time and bake? Am I asking so much?" She shook her head and pressed her hands to her cheeks. "Did I do something to make him hate me?"

"Nope. He was like that with Nan at first, too. She just didn't put up with any guff." Iggy peeked out of the oven, gnawing a linden log.

"How did she handle him?" I rested a hand on my hip.

Iggy grinned. "She said if he was going to act like a child, she'd treat him like one." He chuckled. "When he was late, she docked his pay, and when he mouthed off, she'd put a binding spell on him and make him sit in 'time-out' in the hallway for ages. Oh, oh!"

Maple and I exchanged a look as Iggy burst into a fit of giggles. My flame was not prone to giggling.

"And one time, during the love festival week, she told him he was to be the centerpiece for the dessert buffet, with all the cakes and cookies served off his lounging body. He was looking forward to it, boasting about all the women he'd get once they saw his 'bod.' But what he didn't realize was, it was for the Aged Witches and Wizards early bird social."

Iggy cackled and wiped tears from his eyes, the little droplets sizzling. "He lay there on that table for three hours, in broad daylight, in nothing but his boxers, as little old ladies and old guys with hairy ears picked pastries off his chest." Iggy shook his head, devolving into laughter.

I chuckled with him until he let out a wistful sigh. "I miss that woman."

"Aw." I tilted my head to the side. "I'm sorry, Iggy. Hey, we're still going to do that Night of the Dead ceremony, right?"

He looked up and nodded. "Don't forget to get that list of things I gave you."

I nodded. In a few days, people would visit the graveyard to honor their loved ones. The ground in the graveyard had a special enchantment over it. Any loved ones buried there who had passed in the last year would return as spirits at midnight, giving the ones they left behind a chance to say goodbye. He'd asked me to go with him to visit Nan.

"I look forward to meeting her."

"I'm just not as good as her," Maple muttered.

"What?" I turned to my friend and put a hand on her shoulder. "Where'd that come from?"

Maple huffed and threw her hands in the air. "Come on. I have no idea what I'm doing. I can bake, yeah, but I've never been in charge of anything. Wiley might be the most vocal about it, but none of the others listen to me either. And why would they? They've probably been baking longer than I've been alive." She sunk down onto a wooden stool.

I pulled one up beside her. "You started a week ago." I put an arm around her shoulders. "Everything takes time to learn, right? By the time you're Nan's age you'll be crusty and tough, too."

"Just like old bread," Iggy added.

"Exactly. There goes Maple, the crusty old bread woman, people will say. And her even crustier friend."

Maple chuckled, and I gave her shoulders a little shake. "Honestly, Maple, you're amazing. I knew from the start of that competition you'd win—or at least deserved to. I didn't account for all the murdering and cheating."

Maple's lips tugged to the side, though she kept her eyes on the ground.

"You're smart and you just have to show them your personality—how much you know, how sweet and caring you are. You don't have to do it like Nan did. You'll find your own style."

Maple nodded.

"But you're only going to find your style and give them the chance to love you if you're actually, you know, in the bakery."

She glanced my way. "Prince Harry said he wanted me to—"

"You know Prince Harry would be fine with you delegating out the actual running of the booth." I gestured at the organized chaos all around us. Though our tent was pretty much done, scores of booths and tents were being erected.

The sounds of hammers and saws, many of which worked away magically on their own, filled the air. Men and women called directions to each other, and poles and wooden planks flew through the air to become part of booths, a Ferris wheel, and stages. "You're the royal baker. You should be in the bakery, not out here avoiding your problems."

Maple gasped, and Iggy barked out a laugh. The two of them exchanged looks.

"What?" I shoved my hands to my hips. "What?"

Iggy smirked. "Something about the kettle calling the cauldron black."

I frowned.

Maple chuckled. "Oh, come on. You're just out here to avoid Prince Harry."

My mouth dropped open, and I searched for the words. "No. No." I shook my head harder. Maybe that would convince them. "I'm out here to... support you, my friend." I swept a hand toward Maple before crossing my arms tightly across my chest.

Maple swallowed, then looked at Iggy and they both burst into laughter.

I glared at them. "Yeah, super funny, laugh it up."

A loud crack made us all jump and look up. A long shadow stood out against the bright sunlight filtering in through the tent fabric. Another loud crack sounded, followed by shouting, a woman's scream, and the shadow—what looked like a tent pole, thick as a tree—fell toward us, growing larger.

THE STRONGMAN

I had only enough time to scream and raise my arms above my head before the pole crashed into our tent. I fell forward off my stool under the heavy tent canvas.

I lay there, stunned and breathing heavily. Finally, I sat up and raised my arms over my head, creating a pocket of air.

"Maple? Iggy? Sam?" Frantically I crawled under the canvas. It felt as if I were lost in a cloud, nothing but white fabric all around me, and too heavy to stand under. "Maple?"

I found her trembling hands and pulled her into a hug.

"What happened?" Her blond hair lay over her face like a mop.

"Something fell on our tent. Let's find Iggy and Sam."

As we crawled on, calling for our friends, the fabric suddenly lifted from us, revealing a stranger in our tent. He stood with his massively muscled arms overhead, bracing up the enormous tent pole. He grunted under the strain, the veins in his neck popping. Sweat beaded on his red forehead and dripped onto his enormous curled handlebar mustache. "Any time now, fellas," he shouted.

"Ready!" came a yell from outside. "Heave! Heave!"

The treelike tent pole lifted and the shadow retreated, leaving the man with his arms overhead supporting the heavy tent fabric. He looked my way and we stared at each other for a long moment. "Your hair, it's red. You look just like—"

I lifted a hand to my lopsided bun. I was sure my hair looked wild, but it seemed an odd thing to notice at a time like this.

He shook himself, sweat dripping into his eyes. "Just like you were almost crushed by a tent."

I gave a slow nod, not sure what to make of that. Then I noticed the stone oven, still intact, and rushed to the arched opening.

"Iggy? Iggy! Are you okay?"

"Well, aside from almost being smothered by some reckless carnies, yes. I suppose I'm okay." He frowned at me.

I tilted my head to the side and pressed a hand to my racing heart. "I wish I could hug you, grouchy little flame."

"If you're going to talk cutesy to me, I'm putting myself out."

I grinned at him, but turned at a cry from Maple. I pushed my way through the fabric toward the sound of her voice. She knelt next to Sam, who lay prone on the ground. "He's unconscious!"

I dashed to her side and helped her roll him onto his back. Cracks spiderwebbed one of his glasses lenses. My heart stopped. I held a hand over his nose. "He's breathing."

Maple's blue eyes grew larger. "We need a medic."

"Call a medic!" the stranger holding our tent up

bellowed. "And bring the barnacle-loving tools in here, for great ocean's sake!"

Moments later the tent fabric lifted all around us and I stood, taking a deep breath of the fresher, cooler air. A shorter man rushed in, his round straw hat with a red ribbon band sitting askew on his head. He looked wildly about, hammers, rope and a saw hovering magically around his head. "Get to it, tools," he commanded, and the things flew off and began repairing our crushed tent poles.

"Our friend's hurt." I pointed to Sam, still on the ground with Maple beside him.

"Already called the medic, little lady."

With the tent fabric magically supported and the tent being repaired, the muscled man let his tattooed arms drop, and moved to Sam. He put two fingers to his throat and looked his head over. "Your friend will be all right." He stood and moved to me. "My guess is the canvas caught him."

I looked between the two men. "What just happened?"

The tall guy with the mustache folded his arms across his broad chest and glared at his companion in the hat and striped vest. "Mick and I were helping erect the tent next door. I told them, *many times*, to check the guy line."

The shorter guy, Mick, pulled his hat off his head and turned it in his hands. "We did. Honestly, I swear. I don't know what happened."

The buff guy frowned at his friend, then turned to me. "My apologies, miss."

I raised my brows. "Apologies? You saved us from being crushed. Thank you." I swallowed. "And also, how is that physically possible?"

The buff guy smiled, his mustache quirking to the side. He extended an arm as thick as my leg and wrapped in tattoos of red, yellow, and orange flames. "I'm Edward, the strong man."

"Ah, that explains it. I'm Imogen." I shook his huge, warm hand. Seriously, he could have thumb wrestled a bear. *Do bears have thumbs?*

"Most people call me Edward the Strong."

I grinned. "That does save a lot of syllables."

His dark eyes focused on mine for a long breath, and then he burst into a hearty laugh, clapping Mick on the back, which sent him flying. "I like you, Imogen. Really glad I kept that pole from crushing you."

I nodded, grinning. "Me too."

The next face to come rushing into the tent was a familiar one.

"Amelia!" I sighed with relief. Right behind her a team of medics with a magically floating stretcher entered. They carefully loaded up Sam, and Maple moved to my side.

I put an arm around her and was comforted when she hugged me back. The medics' blue uniforms with the royal crest reminded me of someone I'd rather not think about. They carried Sam out of the tent, Amelia lingering behind.

"They're taking Sam to the infirmary. Give them a few hours, and then you can go visit. They said he should be fine, but they want to run some tests."

We nodded.

Amelia smoothed her white pencil skirt, which matched her tight-to-her-head hair, and adjusted her lavender blouse. "I heard someone needed a medic and came to make sure everything was being handled. I didn't expect to see you lot here. Though maybe I should have expected it— trouble follows you around."

I smiled. "Good to see you too, Amelia. You're coordinating the carnival?"

She smiled back. "Yes, sorry. A million fires to put out today. Don't need word getting out of people being nearly crushed by tents. Everyone's freaked out enough with the recent BA attack."

Ah. The Badlands Army. I was all too familiar with their recent attack—I'd stopped it by throwing myself in the line of fire (accidentally), and barely survived. We'd passed many wanted posters of their leader, Horace, on the way through town to the carnival. They still startled me, life-sized and realistic. I felt like his hooded blue eyes watched me when I walked by. At least there'd been extra security posted at the entrance to the carnival.

"Also, Prince Harry gave me a heads-up you lot would be working the carnival." She swept her arm toward the pier. "Past the pier is a field where the workers are camping out. I've arranged a tent with a couple of beds for you. It's nothing fancy, but it's a place to crash for the night if you don't feel like hiking up the mountain back to the palace."

Maple and I smiled at each other. Knowing Amelia, it was going to be fancy.

Amelia pressed a dark, slim finger to her glowing earpiece that looked like a gumball-sized pearl. "Yes, Liam, the human cannonball was approved. Weeks ago." She rolled her eyes and gave us an exasperated look. Her eyes shot wide open. "No, it's not a ride, it's for an act. Get those kids out of it. Now!" She dashed out of the tent.

"I hope Sam's okay." Maple's lips quavered and her eyes shone with unshed tears.

"Me too." I gave her shoulder a squeeze. "We'll go check on him soon."

The hammers and various tools finished their work and flew to Mick's side again. Edward the Strong cleared his throat. "Nice to meet you, ladies, though I wish it were under better circumstances."

Mick spread his arms wide. "To make it up to you, I run the canal ride—unlimited lifetime rides for you both." Edward elbowed his friend hard. Mick rubbed his arm. "Ow."

I cleared my throat to hide a laugh. I supposed that would compensate for nearly killing us. "Thank you both."

Edward the Strong gave me a long look as he bowed his head to duck out of the tent. "Hope to see you around, Imogen."

Buy Black Arts, Tarts & Gypsy Carts now to keep reading!

ABOUT THE AUTHOR

A native of Tempe, Arizona, Erin spends her time crafting mysterious, magical, romance-filled stories that'll hopefully make you laugh. In between, she's traveling, napping with her dogs, eating with her friends and family, and teaching Pilates (so she can eat more).

Erin loves to hear from readers! You can find her here:
www.erinjohnsonwrites.com
erin@erinjohnsonwrites.com

Copyright © 2017 by Erin Johnson

All rights reserved.

No part of this book may be reproduced in any form or by any electronic or mechanical means, including information storage and retrieval systems, without written permission from the author, except for the use of brief quotations in a book review.

❀ Created with Vellum

Made in the USA
Coppell, TX
20 March 2022